Desperate to sto[...] tech hole at full thruster power. As he came around the curve he saw the guards he had passed moments earlier, drifting with the air-currents. He wanted to decelerate to a stop and peer cautiously into the tunnel before entering it—but was traveling so fast he'd have had to overshoot it and beat back, and he didn't have time. Instead he threw himself into a power turn and rocketed right into it at max acceleration.

That probably saved his life. The assassin was still in the tunnel, waiting to scrag Jay the moment his head showed. But Jay arrived like a right hook, smashing solidly into him before he could fire.

The assassin was a very good shot. But Jay was a very good dancer—and fortunately the gun was a pulse job rather than a continuous-beam laser.

He twisted, arched, feinted, leaped, con-tracted, and bolts of shining death missed him by centimeters. But Jay could not hope to close; it was all he could do to stay alive. And any second his luck must run out.

He had time to realize that he was going to die protecting people he did not like or even respect, and then the tunnel had a blowout. A jagged hole appeared in its wall with a *phuff*, the shriek of escaping air tore at their ears, and pressure began to drop...

STARMIND

SPIDER & JEANNE ROBINSON

Copyright © 1994 by Spider & Jeanne Robinson

A Baen Books Original

Baen Publishing Enterprises
P.O. Box 1403
Riverdale, NY 10471

ISBN: 0-671-31989-2

Cover art by Patrick Turner

First Baen paperback printing, May 2001

Distributed by Simon & Schuster
1230 Avenue of the Americas
New York, NY 10020

Production by Windhaven Press, Auburn, NH
Printed in the United States of America

This one's for Tia Marguerite Vasques,
Nana (Agnes Meade),
Tenshin Zenki, and all bodhisattvas,

with gratitude, respect
and love

Acknowledgments

We would like to thank master roboticist Guy Immega (again!), ace physicist Douglas Beder, and Renaissance man Bob Atkinson for technical assistance in matters both scientific and speculative; K. Eric Drexler, Chris Peterson and Gayle Pergamit for explaining the nearly infinite potential of nanotechnology with their historic and indispensable book, *Unbounding the Future* [Quill/William Morrow], a follow-up to Drexler's classic *The Engines of Creation* (almost none of what we read there made it into this volume, but we couldn't have written the first word without all of it); Peter Mathiessen for hipping us to the Kingdom of Lo and the Festival of Impermanence in the quarterly journal *Tricycle*; Murray Louis for continuing to help us believe that meaningful words can be written about dance; Barbara Bourget and Jay Hirabayashi for the inspirational *butoh*-influenced dance of Kokoro, and Lafcadio Hearn for preserving and translating the eerily appropriate *hauta* found in Chapter 20.

We also thank Tenshin Zenki (Reb Anderson), Zoketsu Norman Fischer, Herb Varley, Robert and Virginia Heinlein, Theodore Sturgeon, Jon Singer, Jordin and Mary Kay Kare, Greg McKinnon, David

Myers, Dr. Thomas O'Regan, Marie Guthrie and all the members of Jeanne's women's group for an assortment of things too numerous, blessed, shady, trivial, profound, personal or otherwise unmentionable to mention.

Ongoing thanks go to our beloved agent Eleanor Wood and our editor Susan Allison, without whom all of this would not have been necessary. And we would like to take this opportunity to thank all of you who voted the original "Stardance" story the Best Novella Hugo in 1977; without you this book would not exist. We might not either.

In addition to all the sources cited in *Starmind*'s two prequels, *Stardance* and *Starseed*, and the ones cited above, we drew upon *The Book of Serenity—One Hundred Zen Dialogues*; *The Tibetan Book of Living and Dying*, by Sogyal Rinpoche; and Thich Nhat Hanh's *Touching Peace*. Musical influences this time around included Charles Brown, Stan Getz, Holly Cole, Kenny Loggins, Paul McCartney ("Off the Ground" was a favorite track), Dianne Reeves, the Oscar Peterson Trio, Wynton Marsalis, Jake Thackray and virtually the entire blues and R&B catalogues of Holger Peterson's Stony Plain Records and Tapes.

Finally, we thank our daughter, Terri Luanna—for this whole saga was begun when she was an infant, for the sole purpose of getting her back home to Canada after we'd gone broke while showing her off to our families back in the Old Country. She is now a twenty-year-old college junior—fully grown and out of the nest . . . and so at last, more than a quarter of a million words later, is the story she inspired. We two have already agreed between us to collaborate on other books in the future. But *this* tale is now complete.

—Spider & Jeanne Robinson
Vancouver, British Columbia
24 October 1993

PART ONE

1

Provincetown, Massachusetts
1 December 2064

Rhea Paixao was considered odd even by other writers. But some things are universal. Like most of her colleagues, Rhea got some of her best writing done in the bathroom.

And this was her favorite bathroom. She stopped in the doorway and examined it before entering. She had known it since earliest childhood, and the passage of time and changing fashions had altered it very little.

True, it now contained a modern toilet and bath; there was such a thing as carrying quaintness too far. But the wall opposite her was simply that, a wall, not programmable in any way: it displayed nothing, could not even become a mirror. An actual silvered-glass mirror hung on the wall, over the sink, its image speckled and distorted by surface impurities. Between mirror and sink, offset to the left, was a widget that had once been used to hold toothbrushes and a plastic cup of germ culture. Farther to the left was an antique cast-iron radiator, unused in decades. The sink itself had mechanical taps, two of them, completely uncalibrated; one had to adjust the flow-rate and temperature by hand with each use. There was a depression behind the rim meant to hold a decomposing lump of phosphate soap. And slung beneath the sink was an antique seldom seen anymore in 2064: a spring-loaded roller intended to hold a roll of toilet paper. (There was no roll there now, of course—but there had been for years after people stopped using the horrid stuff. Nana Fish had insisted on it. Even after she had broken down and accepted modern plumbing, Nana had insisted on keeping a roll of the Stone Age tissue handy, "just in case." She went back to the days when machinery used to fail all the time.) Every time Rhea saw that roller, she wanted to giggle.

The room was, in fact, almost a microcosm of the town around it. From its earliest days, Provincetown had always conceded as little as possible to the passing of years, changing only with the greatest reluctance and even then pretending not to. That had been the town's—most of Cape Cod's—stock in trade for centuries now . . . and a good living there was in it, too. Even in these days, when "progress" was no longer quite as dirty a word as it had once been, there were still people who would pay handsomely for the illusion of an allegedly simpler time. P-Town, as the natives called it, was tailor-made for the role.

She stepped into the bathroom and let the door

close behind her. No terminal in here, no phone, rotten ventilation—it was possible to make the mirror steam up—and nothing in the room accepted voice commands. In here, all three avatars of the house's AI were blind, deaf, mute and impotent. The wind outside was clearly audible through the walls. Rhea loved this bathroom more than even she suspected. She had plotted out at least three books here, and worked on a thousand poems, songs, articles and stories. At age fifteen, she had renounced Catholicism forever in this very room . . . sitting on that same oaken toilet seat over there!

Just like that, a perfectly good story idea popped into her head—

She gave it a lidded glance, not wanting to seem too interested, and sauntered to the toilet. It followed her, and her pulse quickened. Studiously ignoring the idea, she urinated, let the commode cleanse and dry her, and went to the sink. Again it was at her shoulder. She used her dental mouthwash, making a rude production of it, and spat noisily into the porcelain sink. The idea did not take offense.

She continued to ignore it, studied herself in the mirror. Still a couple of years to go before her fortieth birthday. Black hair, black eyes that others called "flashing," coffee-with-cream complexion. Exotic high-cheeked Portuguese features that always reminded Rhea of old 2-D pictures of Nana Fish as a girl, back in the twentieth century, an impression reinforced by the old-fashioned nightgown and robe she wore now. She ran water and splashed some on her face, rubbing especially at her eyes and cheeks and lips as though her makeup could be washed off, a childhood habit so trivial it wasn't worth unlearning. Colly was asleep, and Rand was not expecting her back in the bedroom any time soon so far as she knew; there was time to dally at least briefly with the idea. She studied it out of the corner of her eye: a short-story idea probably, really no more than a situation—but one she knew she could do something good with.

For Rhea's kind of writer, plot and theme and even character were always secondary, mere craftsmanship, constructed as needed to flesh out the story. For her, the heart of a story, the first flash that impelled and enabled her to dream up all the rest, was always that special suffering called "antinomy." "Conflict between two propositions which seem equally urgent and necessary," as a professor of hers had once defined it. The juncture between a rock and some hard place. The place right out at the very tip of the sharpest point on the horns of a dilemma. Give someone an impossible choice, and *then* you had a story. Once the Muse revealed to you a deliciously impossible choice, you could begin deciding what sort of person would squirm most revealingly when confronted with it, and from that you could infer your theme, which gave you your plot.

This idea, for instance . . .

It had been born in that brief flash of recollection she'd had as she first walked into the bathroom, of the long-ago night when fifteen-year-old Rhea had made up her mind in the privacy of this very room that she *wasn't* scared, dammit, Catholicism was *bullshit*, there *was* no God. As the adult Rhea had remembered that night, and thought of the Catholic

Church for the first time in years, she'd been reminded of an artistically beautiful tragedy she knew about and had never exploited dramatically before.

Donny—Mr. Hansen—and Patty. She could no longer recall Patty's last name. Mr. Hansen had been Rhea's Sunday School teacher, twenty-three and gorgeous and devout in his faith, and every girl in the class had had a crush on him, but they all knew it was hopeless. Donny Handsome (as they called him, giggling, among themselves) was blatantly and terminally in love with Patty, who was also twenty-three, and just as gorgeous and devout, and just as clearly daffy about him. Together they were so beautiful—their love was so beautiful to see—that the girls in Mr. Hansen's class actually forgave her for existing.

Then, a single week before they were to be married, Patty had announced that God had called her to be a nun.

Teenage Rhea had been transfixed by Mr. Hansen's dilemma. He was a good Catholic to the soles of his feet. According to the rules he lived by, *he was not even allowed to be sad.* Not only could he not argue with Patty, try to change her mind . . . he was not allowed to *want* to. It was his spiritual duty to rejoice for his beloved, and the special grace she had been granted. He had, in the metaphorical terms of his church, been jilted for Christ, and was expected to smile as he gave away the bride.

That had been the beginning of the end of Rhea's faith: seeing Donny Handsome stumble around P-Town like a zombie, smiling aimlessly. She had refused to believe that the universe and butterflies could have been made by so sadistic a God. Now, why hadn't she ever thought to convert such a splendidly awful antinomy into a story before?

Her craft-mind went to work on the idea now. Just put it down, as it had happened? No, it was always best to change it in the telling, she found: the way it changed told you what was most important to keep. Besides, that made it art and not journalism. Did she need the Catholicism angle, for instance? Or could she change it to some other, equally inflexible faith? With celibate clergy . . . hmmmm, weren't a lot of those left anymore these days. Weren't a lot of Catholics left, for that matter. Maybe it didn't even need to have religion in it at all. But if not, what else had that same implacable weight?

She tried an old trick. Refine it all down to a single sentence: the sentence that the suffering protagonist screams (even if only inside) at the moment that the point enters the belly. Then throw out everything that doesn't lead inexorably to that scream. Okay, what was Donny Handsome's scream?

My beloved, how can you want to go where I cannot follow?

In the instant of that crystallization, Rhea knew what the story was really about . . . and knew that she could not write it. No matter how she disguised it dramatically. Not yet. And maybe never.

She told the story idea to get lost. Until she knew what its ending was.

She went to the window—missing the sudden chill that used to come from December windows when she was a little girl—and pulled aside the ancient curtain to look out at the night. And was rewarded. In the distance, above the shadowy housetops of P-Town, the silhouette of the Pilgrim Monument showed clearly against the night sky, an eighty-five-meter tower of grey granite—and poised beside it, midway up its length, seeming to be only meters from its crenulated stone windows, was a brilliant crescent moon. The juxtaposition was weirdly beautiful, quintessential Provincetown magic. Rhea became conscious of her breath. It swept her mind clear—of the captive story idea and her ongoing concerns and the day's cares and her self. She watched without thought for a timeless time, long enough for the moon to climb perceptibly higher up the Monument.

She became aware of herself then, and let the curtain fall closed. She felt a sudden close connection with the child she had once been in this room, in this house, in this town. More than that, deeper than that—a connection with the family that had raised her here, and with their forebears, fishermen and fishermen's wives, back seven or eight generations to old Frank Henrique Paixao, who had gone over the side of a Portuguese whaler in a two-man dory off Newfoundland one cold day in 1904. He and his partner Louis Tomaz had successfully gotten themselves lost in the fog, miraculously survived to reach Glace Bay in Cape Breton, landed there without formalities or paperwork, and somehow made their way overland across the border and down the coast to Massachusetts, eventually fetching up in P-Town. The cod fishing there was as good as they had heard. After five years or so, both men had sent for their families back in Portugal, and settled down to founding dynasties in the New World—just as the Pilgrim Monument was being raised.

Rhea felt that Frank's wife Marion must have seen the Monument and moon looking just like this more than once, and could not help listening for the echo of her ancestor's thoughts. She heard only the sighing of night winds outside.

She sighed in accompaniment, went to the mirror and ran a brush through her hair. She was ready to join Rand in bed. A month he'd been home already, and she was just getting used to having him around again. Every home should have a husband. She shut off the light with a wall switch and left the bathroom, walked down the short hallway to the bedroom. In her mind's eye she was still seeing the slow dance of Monument and moon in the crisp cold starlight as she opened the bedroom door and stepped into the New Mexico desert at high noon.

Rhea was so startled she closed the door by backing into it. The sudden sense of *distance*, of vast expanse, was as staggering as the sudden brightness. The horizon was unimaginably far away; she saw a distant dark smudge, bleeding purple from beneath onto the ground below, and realized it was a thunderstorm large enough to drench a county. Between her and the horizon were endless miles of painted desert, broken occasionally by foothills and jagged rock outcroppings; close at hand were scrub hills and cacti and a dry wash. Right before her was an oasis, a natural watering hole. Beside it was an old-fashioned wooden bedframe with a curved solid oak

headboard and a thick mattress. On the bed reclined
one of Rhea's favorite holostars, dressed only in black
silk briefs. He was nearly two meters tall, as dark
as her, and glistening with perspiration or oil. He was
holding out a canteen toward her, smiling invitingly.

She discovered she was thirsty. Hot in this desert.
She stepped forward and accepted the canteen. The
hand that offered it was warm. He was real, then.
Icy cold water, sweet and pure. He looked even
better up close. She handed back the canteen. He
moved over to make room. She let the robe fall from
her shoulders and drop to the sand. His eyes went
up and down her slowly, as she took off the nightgown and dropped that too. She stepped out of her
slippers; the sand felt strangely furry. She spun
around once, taking in the vast silent desert that
receded into infinity in all directions, and leaped into
the bed. That started it bouncing, and it did not stop
for some time.

She nearly drifted into sleep afterward, the desert
sun warm on her back and buttocks and legs. But
an inner voice caused her to rouse herself and nudge
her celebrity companion. Might as well get it over
with. "That was really wonderful, darling," she said
sleepily. "All of it. But really—purple rain?"

His famous features melted and ran, becoming the
familiar face of her husband. His hair lightened to
red and his complexion to fair. "No, honest—I've
seen it, outside of Santa Fe. Near the pueblos. Just
that color. I've wanted to show it to you." Rand
reached out a lazy arm, did something complicated
to nothing at all in mid-air, and the desert sun dimin-
ished sharply in brightness without leaving the center

of the sky. The effect was of a partial eclipse: twilight with the shadows in the wrong places. Power of suggestion made the temperature seem to drop, or perhaps he had dialed that, too; they slid under the covers together.

"I'm glad you did," she said, snuggling. "It's lovely." She looked around at the dusky desert, noting small excellences of detail. An eagle to the east, gliding majestically. Intricate cactus flowers, no two quite alike. Ripples on the surface of the water in the oasis, seeming to be wind-driven. Microfilaments of lightning, convincingly random, flickering in that distant purple rain. "This is the best one yet. Is the music this far along too?"

He shook his head. "Just some ideas, so far. But having the basic visual will help."

"I'm sure it will. It was a beautiful gift, really. The set *and* the sex. Thank you."

He grinned. "You're welcome. I'm glad you liked it."

"*Very* much. So . . . what's the catch?"

"Catch?" he asked innocently.

The reason she knew there was a catch was because it was not possible for her husband to conceal something important from her, not while making love. But she could not let him know that, so she made up a logic-chain. "It's not our anniversary. It's not my birthday. I don't keep score, but I don't *think* I've been unusually nice to you lately. You're not having an affair; you haven't had *time*. It was a wonderful present and I thank you for it, and"—she grinned and poked him in the ribs—"what is it going to cost me?"

He opened his mouth as if to say something, changed his mind, and reached out into the empty air beside the bed again, typing new commands onto his invisible keyboard. The desert went away. So did everything, except the bed and themselves. All at once they were in space, surrounded by blackness and blazing stars, tumbling slowly end over end. High Orbit: the Earth swam into their field of view, huge and blue and frosted with clouds. The illusion was so powerful that Rhea felt herself clutching at the bed to keep from drifting away from it, even though she knew better. All at once the rotating universe burst into song. Rand's fourth symphony, of course, as familiar to her as her name. He muted the sound with a gesture after a few bars, left the visual running.

It was her heart plummeting; that was what made the illusion of free-fall seem so real. "But—but you're not going up again for another eight months—"

"Things have changed, love," he said. "I mean, really changed. Sit down."

"Sit down? I'm *lying* down, what the hell do you mean?"

"You know what I mean."

She lay back. "Okay, I'm 'sitting down.' Go on."

"My brother called. While I was down at the shore a while ago."

"Oh? How is Jay? Cancel that, I don't give a damn how he is: what did he say?"

"Pribhara bombed. Big-time. She hates space, the customers hate her—even the company hates her new work. But most important of all, she says she just can't adapt. She's a born perpendicular. So she's thrown in the towel . . . a few seconds before they would have yanked it out of her hand."

Rhea was confused. She knew there was a booby-trap in this somewhere, but couldn't find one big enough to justify all this buildup yet. "So that's good news, right? Now there are only three of you competing—"

"It goes beyond that," he said, looking uncomfortable. He dithered with his invisible controls until their shared rotation in space slowed and stopped. The starry universe stabilized around them.

She took a deep breath. "Tell me."

"The competition is over," he said. "I won."

"What?" she cried in dismay. "*You* won?"

It was only that: a misplaced emphasis. Had she said, "You *won*?" there might not have been a quarrel at all. That night, at least.

Rand had been one of four competitors for a plum position: Co-Artistic Director and Resident Shaper/ Composer at the legendary Shimizu Hotel, the first hotel in High Earth Orbit and still by far the grandest. The creator and first holder of that position had held it with great distinction for fifty years—then a year ago, both he and his heir apparent had been killed in the same freak blowout while vacationing off Luna. Replacing an artist of Willem Ngani's stature overnight had been a daunting task: the management of the hotel had narrowed the field to four candidates, and then found itself unable to reach a final decision. It had elected instead to postpone the question for a three-year trial period. The first year of that period was nearly over: each of the four candidates in turn had gone to space for a three-month residency at the Shimizu. Rand had drawn the third shift, and had only returned from his own highly successful season a month earlier; the fourth and final composer, Chandra Pribhara, was supposed to be just now entering the second month of her own first residency.

But Pribhara had turned out to be a "perpendicular"—one of those rare unfortunates who simply cannot adapt to space, who cannot make the mental readjustment that allows a human being to retain her sanity in a sustained zero-gravity environment. She had abruptly canceled her contract after only a single month in free-fall, accepting the huge penalties and creative disgrace, and returned to Earth early.

This left the Shimizu's management with a quick decision to make. A hotel must have entertainment. The show must go on. The Resident Choreographer—Rand's half-brother Jay Sasaki—needed a Shaper to collaborate with. *Someone* had to replace Pribhara, fast. They might have simply advanced the rotation schedule, summoned Wolfgar Mazurski back to orbit two months earlier than he was expecting, and continued from there on a three-shift rotation while they pondered their final decision. But Mazurski had other commitments, and so did Choy Mu Sandra, the other contender.

Which left Rhea's husband.

But Rand was only just back from orbit. Returning to space for another three-month shift this soon would raise his total free-fall time to six months in one calendar year: very likely enough time for his body to begin adapting—completely and permanently—to zero gravity. It would take fourteen months for the transition to be finished . . . but deleterious metabolic changes often began much sooner. If they asked him to replace Pribhara now, the competition was over: they would have to give him the permanent position to forestall a costly lawsuit.

The Shimizu management had little choice. And Rand's first season *had* been the most well-received of the four so far. So they had sent word, through his half brother, Jay. The job was his if he wanted it—along with a scandalous salary, outrageous perks, immense cachet and luxury accommodations in-house for himself and his wife and daughter. For life— which was how long they would need them.

Rhea hated the very thought of moving.

And if she *were* going to move, space was the very last place she'd pick. The only one-way ticket there was. Fourteen months or more in space, and you had to stay there forever. You couldn't even *hope* to go back home again someday. . . .

Worse, Rand knew all this. Or at least, he should have known. A decade ago, he had solemnly promised Rhea—as a condition of marriage—that he would never ask her to move away from her beloved P-Town, from her home and family and roots.

When he had first mentioned the possibility of this job, she had been shocked and hurt. But she had not reminded him of his promise . . . partly because she loved her husband and knew how badly he wanted the job, and mostly because she *knew* in her heart that there was no way Rand would ever actually be offered it. That had been clear to her from the start. For one thing, his blood relationship with Jay would work against him—allowing disgruntled losers to cry nepotism. For another, he was the most talented of the four—traditionally a handicap. To nail it down, he was by far the least political—traditionally the kiss of death.

Ironically, it was that which had clinched the deal. Mazurski and Choy *each* had a powerful and influential clique of friends, skilled at vicious infighting: they canceled each other out. Rand was the only choice everybody could (barely) live with. And so it was the very same aspect of her husband's character which had in fact won him the job that caused Rhea to say to him now so injudiciously, "*You* won?"

The ensuing quarrel was so satisfactory a diversion that it was a full hour before they got around to the actual argument they had been avoiding for over a year now.

"God dammit, Rhea, just tell me: what's so awful about space?"

"What's so fucking good about it?"

"Are you kidding? Sterile environment, pure air, pure water, perfect weather all day every day, no crime, no dirt, longer lifespan—and weightlessness! You don't *know,* honey, you haven't been there long enough to get a feeling for it; everything is so easy and convenient and restful in space. Nothing is too heavy to lift, nobody's a weakling, your back never hurts. And the freedom! Freedom from the boredom and tyranny of up and down, freedom to live in three dimensions for a change! To use *all* of a room instead of just the bottom half—to see things from different angles all the time—to let go of something and not be afraid gravity's going to smash it against the wall by your feet. Put that all together, throw in a better class of neighbors and the best view God ever made, and it doesn't sound half bad to me."

"It sounds horrible to me! The same weather, *every day?* The first thing you said: 'a sterile environment,' that's exactly what it sounds like. Living in a little sterile tin can surrounded by cold vacuum, breathing canned air and peeing into a vacuum cleaner. What about Colly? Where's an eight-year-old going to find playmates in space? Think about never again going out for a walk, never getting rained on or snowed on or going to watch the sun rise—"

"—the sun rises fourteen times a day at the Shimizu—"

"—it's not the same and you know it—"

"—no, it's not the same, it's better—"

"—bullshit—"

"—how the hell would you know? You were up there for three whole days! I'm telling you, I've been there for three months and it's better—"

"*—maybe it is, but it's* different, *God dammit—*"

He flinched at her vehemence. After a few seconds of silence, he slapped at his control panel, and set the universe spinning around them again. "What's so bad about different?"

She reached irritably past him and felt for the keyboard, found it and quit the holo program abruptly. Blink: they were in their quaint comfortable moonlit bedroom in their magnificent old home in picturesque P-Town. "What's so bad about what we have?" she cried, gesturing around her at hardwood floor and lace curtains and quilted comforter and scrimshaw and Frank Paixao's barometer and fading photographs of Nana Fish and Nana Spaghetti on the walls.

He looked round, at the familiar trappings of their marriage, of their shared life. When he spoke, his voice was softer. "It's good. You know I love it here too. But it's not all there is."

"It is for me!" she said. *Oh my beloved, how can you want to go where I cannot follow?*

He closed his eyes and took a deep breath, and played his hole card. "It isn't for me."

She clutched his shoulder and played her own. "You promised, Rand! Back when you first asked me to marry you, you promised . . ."

There was nothing he could say to that, because it was true. She had him dead to rights. The argument was effectively over, now. She had won . . .

. . . and cost her beloved husband the professional and personal opportunity of a lifetime, the crowning achievement of his career. . . .

He nodded, and rolled over on his right side, back to her. "When you're right, you're right," he said very quietly, and mimed preparing to sleep. But his shoulder blades were eloquent.

She savored her triumph for as long as she could stand it, staring at the ceiling. Then, keeping her voice as neutral as possible, she said, "Anyway . . . how would we deal with Colly's education?"

His shoulder blades shut up in midsentence.

"Well—" he said finally, and rolled over to face her.

2

Rand Porter had been waiting for that question, of course. Their eight-year-old would get a *better* education if he took the job; Rhea had known that when she asked the question. On his new salary, they could afford to enroll Colly in any school on or off Earth, with full bandwidth and as much individual attention as she wanted. Hell, they could afford to have teachers physically brought up to her if they wanted, in corporation shuttles. And Rhea could have Unlimited Net Access herself too.

And all these things, he added, would be merely perks—over and above a salary so immense that they could easily have afforded to pay for them. Full Medical would be another such perk. Rhea's literary reputation could only benefit from all the publicity that would accrue. Rand stressed all these points, without ever quite saying aloud a point that mattered to him almost as much as the honor or the creative challenge or the prestige or the money *per se*.

If he took this job, he would be earning more money than Rhea, and would be more famous than her. For the first time in their relationship.

He *couldn't* mention that aloud. They had agreed back at the start that they would never mention it; that was how little it meant to them; therefore he couldn't bring it up now.

"Worse comes to worst, why couldn't we compromise?" he suggested desperately. "Have one of those commuter marriages? I'd take the job, and you could come up for three months out of every six. Lots of people do that, when only one half of the team wants to be a spacer."

"Sure," she said. "That worked out just great for your brother, didn't it?" Jay had maintained such a relationship with a dancer in one of his two rotating companies for over five years—then about six months ago, Ethan had sent him a Dear-Jay/resignation fax from Fire Island. The scabs were just beginning to turn into scar tissue.

"We're more committed than Jay and Ethan were," Rand protested. But privately he was not sure that was true—and the stats on groundhog/spacer marriages *were* discouraging.

When they were exhausted enough, they agreed to sleep on it.

At five in the morning he slipped from the bed without waking her and went down the hall to his Pit. Strains of melody were chasing each other in his head, but when he booted up his synth, he could not isolate any of the strands in his headphones. Sounded aloud, they were an inseparable jangle of discord—like his feelings.

So he went to the kitchen, and found he was not hungry. He went to the bathroom and discovered he didn't have to pee. He put the headphones back on and learned that he didn't want to hear anything in his collection. He went up to Colly's room and found that she didn't need to be covered. As he bent to kiss her, he startled himself by dropping a tear on the pillow next to her strawberry blonde hair. He went quickly back downstairs to the living room and wept, as silently as he could. When he was done, he dried his eyes and blew his nose.

What *did* he need?

That was easy. He needed someone to tell him he wasn't a selfish bastard.

He had promised her. Worse, he had thought about it first. He had not specifically envisioned this situation, no—but he had made his promise without reservations. *No matter what, love*—

But this offer was beyond any dreams he'd had a decade ago. How could he have known? The carrot was irresistible. . . .

Or was it? What was so irresistible? The money would be great—but while they had been middle-class for their whole marriage, they had never been poor, never missed a meal. There were other jobs. Indeed, this was about the only job he could possibly take that would require them to move from P-Town, that he couldn't basically phone in. It was certainly the only job that would have required *permanent* exile. What was so great about the damn job?

Two things. It was the most prestigious job in his field, one of the most prestigious there was. And it would make him the principal breadwinner in his family, for the first time.

Not very proud reasons to break a solemn promise to your wife . . .

No, dammit, there was more to it than that. The job was the richest creative opportunity he had ever had. His three-month stint just past had been the hardest work he'd ever done . . . and had drawn some of his very best music and shaping out of him. Collaborating with his half-brother Jay had been exhilarating; although Jay was thirteen years older than Rand's thirty-five, their minds had meshed.

I see: your wife will be a little sadder, but your chops will improve . . .

It wasn't just that. Part of what had made his work better in the Shimizu had been the heart-stopping grandeur of space itself, the bliss of zero gee. Space was as magical as Provincetown, in a different way; maybe more so—surely Rhea would see and respond to that, just as he had.

You hope . . .

Anyway, what was so great about P-Town? Okay, it was beautiful; sure, it was timeless; granted, it was magical. This chair he was rocking in, for instance: beautiful and timeless and magical. But it made noises like rifle fire, and leaned ever so slightly out of true, and wasn't especially comfortable without the pillows that always slipped out of adjustment. So what if it had belonged to Rhea's great-grandmother? So what if it had been the chair in which the infant Rhea had been breast-fed . . . and Colly too?

The answer was all around him—hanging from every wall, perched on nearly every flat surface. Pictures of eight generations of Paixaos, as far back as imaging technology allowed, ranging from faded black and white daguerrotypes of Cap'n Frank and Marion to paused holoblocks of Rhea, Colly and himself. Hundreds of Paixaos and their kin, in dozens of settings . . . and every single image had Provincetown somewhere in the background. Beautiful. Timeless. Magical . . .

On the mantle, amid the more recent Paixaos, was a holo of Rand's parents, Agnes and Tom, taken just before their divorce. The background was Newark, New Jersey.

There was no point to this: he already knew he wanted the job badly enough to take it; whether he *should* want it that badly or not seemed irrelevant. Nonetheless he flogged himself, as his penance, endlessly replaying the argument until it became a loop that annihilated time.

I want to be great. Is that so terrible?

Just as he felt that his brain might explode, thirty-five kilos of eight-year-old reality landed on his lap like a tonne of bricks, shouting, "Boo!" and his heart nearly exploded instead. Daylight and his daughter had crept up on him.

"I scared you, Daddy!" she reported with glee. "I did, didn't I?"

For an instant he was tempted to use Colly as a new club to beat himself—*how can you ask a child to go pioneering?*—but he shifted gears instead, grabbed her in his arms and stood up. "That you did, baby," he said, clutching her close. "That you did."

"Did you catch it, Daddy?"

"Huh?"

"Whatever made you stay up all night. Did you get it?"

"Oh. Uh . . . not yet, sweetheart. I got a look at it, but it got away."

"Don't matter about it," she advised him. "You'll get it next time."

Her optimism—and the boundless, unquestioning faith that underlay it—floored him. *I can't be a bastard,* he thought. *I'd never have fooled her.* He hugged her even closer, making her squeal. "That I will," he agreed. "Right now, let's you and me get us some grub."

"I cook," she said quickly. Her faith in him had practical limits. That was why he could trust it.

"Deal," he agreed.

And she did cook a better breakfast than he could have—albeit somewhat more messily. Rhea came in while she was doing it, and stood in the doorway in her bathrobe watching and trying not to smile. Colly refused to let either of them help, or even coach. By the time they were all sitting down eating together, it seemed to have been decided that today was a happy day. Rhea's eyes were unguarded when they met his. The Issue was still there between them, but it was on hold for the moment.

After the meal, it was Rhea who said, "Colly, sit back down. You can be a little late for playgroup today. Your father and I need to talk about something with you."

"Aw, Mom—do you have to? Sarah's gonna bring her cat in today, and she swears it has thumbs!"

"Yes, honey, it's important."

"Four of 'em! Oh, okay, go ahead." She sat back and adjusted her nervous system to fidget mode.

Rhea handed the ball to him. "Rand?"

He cleared his throat. "Colly . . . have you ever thought about . . . living somewhere else?"

"You mean I'm going to grandma's house again? How long this time?"

"No, honey, that's not what I meant. I mean . . . all three of us moving away from here, to a new home."

"And not coming back?"

"That's right. Not ever."

The notion did not seem to shock Colly. "Where?" she asked practically.

"Well, remember that time we went to visit Uncle Jay?"

She got excited. "Go to space, you mean? And stay there? In that cool hotel? Oh, wow!"

"You really liked it that much?" Rhea asked, surprised.

"Da! Si! Ja! Oui!" Colly said. *"I'm not little in space!"*

Both parents were startled into laughter.

"It's true," she insisted. "I can reach everything there, and look grown-ups in the eye, and I'm as strong as anybody and not clumsy like everybody else. Besides, it's *fun!* When do we go?"

Even Rand was taken aback by support this enthusiastic. "But baby . . . you know if we stay in free-fall for long, we have to stay forever?"

"Sure."

"Well . . . won't you miss your friends?"

She thought about it. "I could still call them up,

right? We could holo-play. And they could come visit me realies, sometimes. And I'd make lots of new friends. I'm good at that."

Rand squelched a grin. "Well . . . yes, you are. But won't you miss . . . this house, and P-Town . . . and everything?"

"And the beach?" Rhea prompted. "And the ocean?"

Colly looked around her. "I guess. But if I do, you can just make it for me, Daddy. Anyway, you can't play six-wall here. I tried."

He didn't have to look at his wife to know that she was looking faintly stricken. Her only potential ally had defected. He wanted to put an arm around her, but was not sure whether that would make it worse.

Colly had gone from fidget to bounce mode. "Can I go tell everybody now, Daddy? How soon are we going, Mommy? I gotta go get dressed! Oooh, Kelly's gonna be *so* jealous—"

"Hold your horses, young lady. Nothing's been decided yet. Your mother and I are still discussing the idea—"

Colly wasn't listening. Her eyes had gone wide. "Wait a minute—this means you got the job, didn't you, Daddy? You get to work with Uncle Jay now! They picked you! Oh, I knew they would! I *told* you they would!"

Rhea winced.

"We are going, we are! Can I go tell Kelly now? And Sigrid? And Bobby?"

The choices were let her go or strap her down. "Maybe you better get dressed first," Rhea said.

Colly looked down at her rumpled pajamas, and giggled. "Oh, okay, if you insist," she said, and ran for the stairs. She was naked before she reached the top.

Rand and Rhea looked at each other. Each waited for the other to speak, with voice or expression.

"We have to laugh," he said finally.

"Oh yeah? Why?"

"Because if we strangle each other, who's going to take Colly to playgroup?"

And so they laughed.

"Come on, somebody," Colly called from upstairs. "Get dressed! I'm almost ready already!"

They laughed harder, and then got up together and sprinted up the stairs, shouting, "Yes, ma'am! Right away, Your Highness!"

"I still don't see why you have to *live* there," Rhea said thirty minutes later. They had dropped Colly off at playgroup in the West End, and now were sitting in the car at the edge of the sea at Herring Cove, half watching a group of eight or ten Trancers in sleek thermal clothing dancing on the shore, spinning and jumping in the December breeze, falling and recovering but always springing back up at once. They made Rand think, as always, of birds trying to batter their way through an invisible ceiling. Provincetown had been a magnet for Trancers since the strange fad had begun and spread around the planet with the speed of a catchphrase. P-Town had always been a Mecca for all kinds of odd behavior.

"It's stupid," Rhea went on. "It's just stupid elitist thinking. There's no sensible reason why you can't phone it in, like any other job. They only *have* the best holo gear in human space."

"That's what the Shimizu is all about," Rand said patiently. "That's what they're buying. The most conspicuous consumption there is. Nothing canned, nothing piped-in—"

"I know, I know—the celebrity artists are all on-site for the customers to press flesh with, and half the robot-work is done by human beings, just to prove they can afford to waste money. Snob logic."

"You can't make art for a place without going there," he said. "Holo isn't enough. I can't explain why, but it isn't. I always go to the site if there is one, at least at first. You know all this."

"So you've *been* there for three months! Isn't that enough?"

It was a fair question. He tried to find the words to answer it. All he could come up with was, "Space is different."

"Different how?"

"Look: you were there."

"For three days."

"Long enough to get a taste. Now, tell me: can you remember what it was like?"

She started to answer, then stopped. "No," she said finally. "I can remember what I told people about it. I can remember what I wrote about it. But no, you're right. I can't remember what it was like. Not really. I have a lingering feeling about it—"

"If you had to write a poem about it, right now, could you? Or a story set there?"

Her shoulders slumped. "I'd have to go back. For

longer than a few days. And either write it there, or right after I got back down."

"That's why Ngani bullied the Board into putting in writing a provision that his successors would have to live in-house. And that's why Jay bullied them into honoring the agreement when Ngani died."

This was all old ground. They had had this conversation over a year ago, when he had first become a candidate for the position. He saw her momentarily as a trapped animal, doubling back on its tracks in search of a way out overlooked earlier, and felt a pang of guilt.

She gestured at the ocean and half a world of clouds, at the crazy Trancers moving in harmony—then turned and gestured in the other direction, at P-Town. "And all of this, we're supposed to give up, forever, so that Willem Ngani's artistic vision isn't violated?"

The question was so unfair that he returned fire with some irritation. "Only if we want me to have the job."

She left the car and walked a short way along the beach, past the gyrating dancers. By the time she returned, he had cooled down and she looked chilly despite her thermally smart clothing. The Trancers too had finally run out of manic energy, and were dispersing, looking blissed-out.

"How about this?" Rand said, as the car heater switched on to normalize the temperature in the vehicle. "We give it a couple of months. I'll complete Pribhara's season. Then if you absolutely hate it, I'll quit."

"You couldn't break your contract!"

"Hell, Pribhara did. I'll reserve the right. If they want me bad enough, they'll negotiate. It's perfectly reasonable—considering they're wrecking my whole schedule on no notice at all. By rights they ought to be paying me a whopping bonus. If they don't like it, let 'em give Mazursky and Choy socks full of dung, and let *them* fight it out."

She thought about it. "Huh. Two more months wouldn't be long enough to change you into a spacer. And it's long enough for me to form an opinion . . ."

"I promise if you want to come back, there won't be an argument."

The device didn't fool either of them; he could see that in her eyes. But it brought the situation a little closer to tolerable. It would buy some time.

"How soon would we have to leave?"

"I'll call Jay."

3

Yawara
Queensland, Australia
2 December 2064

At about that moment, not too far from the opposite point on the planet's surface, an old—no,
ancient—woman switched off her ancient compact
disc player, brushed the headphones out of her hair
with a palsied hand, and decided it was time for
sleep. Or at least for bed. Slowly and carefully she
got up from her rocking chair, then used it to steady
herself while she removed the denim shorts which
were her only clothing. She walked with halting steps
through the darkness to her bed, but when she
reached it, she dropped easily and comfortably into
a squat beside it. Reaching beneath it, she drew out
her chamber pot and removed the lid. When she
maneuvered it beneath her, its weight and a small
sloshing sound reminded her that she had forgotten

to empty it that morning. As she was about to put
it to its accustomed use, she suddenly stopped,
clamping her sphincter and flaring her nostrils. Her
head turned from side to side, twice. Then she
looked down between her legs, bent her head lower
and sniffed. She took the chamber pot from beneath
her and brought it to her nose and sniffed again.

She *knew*, then, but nonetheless she reached up
and got matches from the bed table. In the sudden
flaring light, her eyes confirmed what her nose had
told her. Her chamber pot contained wine.

It delighted her. It had been a long time since
anything had surprised her. This was a good one. She
thought about it, savoring the puzzle. No one had
approached her home closer than a hundred yards
all day. She had not left it for a moment. She had
not emptied the utensil after using it that morning,
she was sure of that. She might be old—no,
ancient—but her memory was still sharp as the long
edge of a war boomerang. There was no logical
explanation . . . so she went inside herself, to her
special place.

And at once, contradictory things happened on her
face. Her eyes brightened, and bitter tears spurted
from them, and years—no, decades—melted from
her visage, and her mouth smiled while her brows
knotted in a fierce frown. She glanced across the
room at her CD player, and ran a hand across her
head to confirm that she had taken its headphones
off. *"Badunjari . . .?"* she whispered, and cocked her
head as if listening.

Whatever she heard caused her to smile even
wider and weep even harder—but the frown relaxed.

She sat back on her heels and began to rock slowly from side to side. After a time, she lifted the chamber pot to her lips and drank from it. The wine was excellent, delicious and immediately powerful. She took a deeper draught.

"Really?" she said in Yirlandji. "What is?"

If there was an answer, no microphone could have recorded it.

Her tears ceased; the smile remained, and became the mischievous grin of a little girl. "Okay," she agreed, and drank again. "I will wait and see."

She had not been this happy in forty-four years. Magic, real Dreamtime magic, was loose in the world again. . . .

PART TWO

4

The Shimizu Hotel, High Orbit
2 December 2064

Jay Sasaki was in the studio when his AI spoke up. "Phone, Jay: your brother, Rand, flatscreen only." It waited patiently while he finished a movement phrase for the camera and toweled off sweat.

"Thanks, Diaghilev," he said then. "Monochrome head-shot, minimum audio, accept." It was the cheapest possible earth-to-orbit call, small black-and-white image and rotten sound, probably relayed on a satellite circuit so old its expiry date began with "19." Rand would have been offended if Jay had tried to reverse the charges—and it was not yet settled whether his kid half-brother could afford to make fullscreen color calls to High Earth Orbit on his own dollar. Jay spoke before the AI finished producing an image, to let Rand know the circuit was completed. "Well, how did she take it?"

"She's right here," Rand said. "Ask her yourself." He swiveled the carphone so that Rhea came into frame. She was smiling wryly.

"'Oops,' he said gracefully," Jay said. "Hi, Rhea. Well, how did you take it?"

"Rectally," she said sourly.

The joke cued him—first, that Rand would indeed be coming back up to work in the Barn . . . and second, that it would not be a good idea to sound too delighted just yet. Was Rhea coming up with him right away? Was Colly? "You'll really like it up here, I promise you," he said experimentally.

"I'd better."

Good. Rand would arrive still married. "And Colly will love it. Space was made for kids."

"It must be," she said. "You like it." But she was smiling.

He relaxed, trying not to let the extent of his relief show. The worst that could happen now was that his half-brother's wife would make Rand's life miserable to the end of his days. *But he'll be able to work with me again!* It would take a lot of the sting out of Ethan not being around anymore. . . .

"We're going to give it a trial period," Rand said. He swiveled the phone again so that he was back in frame. "Two months, so Rhea and Colly can check it out before they commit themselves."

Jay managed to hold his poker face. Fortunately, in zero gravity one's face does not pale as blood pressure drops. If Rhea left in two months, Rand would go with her. With the example of Jay's own disaster with Ethan before him, Rand would not risk losing her in a long-distance marriage. Kate was going to have a blowout when she heard this. "That'll be hard to sell to the Board. They want this settled. Face, you know."

"I've got face too," Rand said. "I require notice before uprooting my family. If the Board doesn't like it, they can start running want ads in the trades."

Briefly, Jay fantasized telling his brother the whole truth. The primary reason the Board had abandoned the audition process and chosen Rand as their shaper was that Jay—feeling reckless in the aftermath of his breakup with Ethan—had privately sent word through the hotel manager that he would quit if they did otherwise. He had just enough clout to pull that off . . . and no margin at all: if the hotel came out of this looking bad, he was out of a job. He was the most famous living human choreographer of free-fall dance—but if he left the Shimizu, where could he go? There were only two other dance companies in space, and neither was hiring. Jay had been a spacer, permanently adapted to zero gravity, for over a decade now: if he could not work in space, he could not work—even if he could have learned to think and choreograph in up-and-down terms all over again.

No—he couldn't tell Rand any of this. If he did, Rand would think—would suspect in his heart forever, no matter what Jay said—that Jay had put his job on the line purely and simply because they shared a mother. Rand would never believe the truth: that he was truly the only one of the four candidates who was any damn good, the only one Jay could stand the idea of being locked into working with for the next umpty years. The hole in his self-confidence would founder him. And the realization that Jay's job *was* on the line would make his problem with his wife even worse.

Well, it was up to Jay to see that Rhea didn't opt out. His other choice was to slit his throat. "You're absolutely right. I'll make them see it that way. Shall I call you back with their answer?"

Rand shook his head. "We both know they're going to say yes. I can afford to call *you* now. Full-band color."

Jay let the grin escape at last. His brother was right. Kate would hate this—but she was committed. As committed as he was. "Damn right. Call me back at . . . what the hell time is it down there?"

"About ten in the morning." The Shimizu was on Greenwich Time; it was nearly 3 PM for Jay.

" . . . at about suppertime. Listen, I don't want to crowd you, but . . . how soon can you come up? The sooner you can make it, the less trouble I'll have selling this trial period."

Rand acquired the harried look of someone who is trying to solve a tricky problem while long-distance charges are ticking away. He glanced sideways. "What do you think, hon?"

After a time, Rhea's voice came from out of frame. "Three days, minimum. I'd like a month. I'd like a year, dammit."

"I think I can get three days, no sweat," Jay said cheerfully.

Rand tried for a diversion. "Anything we can bring up for you?"

"If I think of anything, I'll tell you when you call back." He gave the phone his best grin. "Listen, this is really great news. Really, Rhea—you'll see! Kiss

Blondie for me. Phone off." As Rand's smiling image dissolved, he went on, "Diaghilev, where's Kate?"

"In her office, Jay. Do you wish an appointment to see her? She has an opening in her calendar tomorrow at—"

"No, I want her now. She'll see me. ETA fifteen minutes."

"Yes, Jay. You're right: Ms. Boswell has accepted for her. Fifteen minutes from . . . mark."

"Shower please, Diaghilev."

"Yes, Jay."

The studio shower accepted and cleansed him; ten minutes later he was dry, shaved, groomed and jaunting along the corridors of the Inner Sphere, heading inboard toward Katherine Tokugawa's executive office in the Core.

Heads turned as he floated past, but only one of the hotel guests had the nerve to call out to him. "Hello, Jay. You look happy—good news?"

Jay made a long arm and grabbed a jaunt-loop, braked himself to a halt. His boss would have a fit if she ever heard that a mere guest had learned news of this importance before she did—but Eva Hoffman was more than just a guest: she had been a resident fixture in the Shimizu for sixteen years now. He glanced around mock-conspiratorially. "Are you *sure* those are your original eyes?"

Eva grinned. She was one hundred sixteen years old, and showed most of them—having, most unusually, given up controlling her appearance on her hundredth birthday. She drew stares everywhere she went in the Shimizu these days . . . the most horrified of them coming from those guests whose own odometers had rolled past zero. "Thirty years ago I'd have known exactly why you were looking happy, at twice the distance. So your brother's coming back up to stay, eh? Congratulations."

"Thanks. I'm excited."

"Me too. You two do good work together. Pribhara was a waste of air."

"She . . . had her own way of doing things."

"Yeah. Wrong. Would you like me to take charge of his wife and daughter? What's her name, Spaniel?" Eva, of course, knew perfectly well what Colly's name was. "Help them get reoriented to free-fall, their first day, show 'em around the Mausoleum, and all that, so that you and Rand can get right down to work?"

He was touched by the offer. Eva was a Shimizu institution, and she did not offer her time lightly or often. She was one of very few guests who knew her way around the place as well as Jay, who did not need to follow some AI's trail of blinking lights to get where she was going. "I think I've got that covered," he said. "But if they do need more help, I'll know where to come. Thanks, Eva."

She looked dubious. "Who have you got in mind?" Eva had a low opinion of most of the Shimizu's staff Orientators—which Jay shared.

"The new kid. Iowa."

"Seen him a couple of times; don't know him."

"He's a natural. Spaceborn."

That interested her. "Is that good? Will he know what it is they don't know?"

Jay nodded. "He's been dealing with mudfeet all his life, one way or another. The ones here are just richer, that's all. I think he and Colly are really going to hit it off."

"I'll have to meet him. I always wanted to get to know a spaceborn."

Diaghilev cleared his virtual throat. "One minute, Jay."

Jay was still in Deluxe country—the cheapest of the Shimizu's accommodations, the inner-sphere suites with no windows onto space. It was time to jaunt. "I've got to go. Uh . . . look, keep this absolutely top secret for, oh, at least another fifteen minutes, okay?"

"Twelve, my final offer."

"Okay, I'll talk fast." He kissed her wrinkled cheek and pushed off.

"Drop by for a chat before dinner, all right?" she called after him. "Something I want to ask you."

He waved agreement without looking back.

He passed quickly through the rest of the Deluxe Tier to the inmost core, jaunted past his own suite without stopping, and reached the executive offices on time. Warned of his arrival by Diaghilev, Tokugawa's own AI had materialized its Personal Executive Assistant persona for him, rather than the Front-Desk Clerk avatar it would have shown to a guest. "Good afternoon, Mr. Sasaki," she said. Her voice was oddly flat and nasal, perhaps in an attempt to make her seem real.

"Good afternoon, Ms. Boswell."

"Ms. Tokugawa will see you now." The door to the inner sanctum dilated.

Jay jaunted through it, brushing the doorway

with his fingertips to decelerate himself to a stop inside.

Katherine Tokugawa was sitting *kukanzen* in the center of her spherical office, dressed in black ceremonial robes, her back to him. At the sound of the door hissing shut behind him, she unlaced her fingers, unfolded her legs from lotus, and flexed at the waist, rotating until she faced him. He politely spun until their local verticals matched, and they exchanged a bow. Then they each "took a seat," in the free-fall sense of the term, giving a short puff with their thrusters so that they backed away from each other and velcroed their backs and buttocks to opposing surfaces, Jay maneuvering to avoid sitting on the door he had just come through; they sat more or less simultaneously.

"Well?" she said then, in the slow exhalation of one emerging from profound meditation.

It was all bullshit, of course, and Jay knew it. If she had really been meditating, she'd have velcroed herself to a wall or some other support. A person who sits *kukanzen* in the center of a room in zero gee, unsecured, sooner or later ends up bumping against the air-exhaust . . . and shutting down the airflow only causes a ball of exhaled carbon dioxide to accumulate and smother the meditator. The Manager of the Shimizu was—as the job called for—one of those people who prize appearance over content, style over substance, and Rinzai Buddhism was merely part of her admittedly impressive act. To have actually practiced it would have been an inefficient use of time.

But Jay was not about to let his boss know he saw through her. Not when he was about to piss her off.

He slowed his breathing, adjusting to her rhythm. "My brother said yes," he told her.

She smiled wearily.

Tokugawa—he dared not let himself think of her as "Kate" while in her presence—was a hundred and sixty centimeters long, and massed forty-six kilos. In free-fall her small size had the effect of making her seem to be a little farther away than she actually was. Which made her seem just a little more crisply in focus than other people. She had stabilized her apparent age at forty standard years, with silver streaks in her hair that were in different places each time you met her. Jay had no idea what her real age might be. She was the granddaughter of Yoji Tokugawa, who had succeeded Bryce Carrington as Chairman of the Board of the original Skyfac consortium back before the turn of the millennium, and her family still controlled a large share of space industry today. She had their "look of eagles," backed by a competence that few Tokugawas actually possessed anymore: she *looked* so much like the Manager of the finest hotel in human space that her genuine fitness for the job was almost a happy accident. Neither attribute particularly impressed Jay, but then, he had to work for her.

"Good," she said quietly. "It was about time for something to go right."

"Troubles, Ms. Tokugawa?" Jay asked, testing the waters to see just how bad a time this was to bring up the matter of the two-month escape clause Rand wanted.

She made a flicking-away gesture. "Not really. Just an infinity of minor nuisances."

"How minor? Is the house still pressurized?"

"For the moment," she replied drily. "No, nothing serious. I've got a major economic summit coming up next month, with so much weight I'm going to have to double security, and—"

"Excuse me, I could have sworn you just said you were going to double security."

"I did."

Jay stared. "There is no such quantity. You can't double infinity. *God* isn't as secure as a Shimizu guest."

She grimaced. "If He had security like those five are going to have, Satan would never have gotten off a speech, much less a coup attempt. Their combined resources are . . ." She paused, and Jay waited, curious to hear what word she would choose. " . . . impressive," she finished, and he repressed an impulse to lift his eyebrows. Any personal fortune that impressed Katherine Tokugawa staggered Jay. "If they ask me to, I'll have to taste-test their food myself—or anything else they want."

"That does sound like a lot of pressure."

"Special diets, special requirements, protocol headaches—the Muslim needs to know where Mecca is at all times, precisely, and the Chinese wants me to have that Soto Zen roshi flown in from Top Step to do dokusan with him, and as for the American—well, never mind what *she'll* want—and of course each and every one of them must be honored and coddled and pampered *precisely* as much as the other four, to the tenth decimal, never mind that it's apples and—" She caught herself, glanced down at her meditation robes, and took a long cleansing breath. "Never mind any of it. It's par for the course these days. And not your pidgin. About your brother—any problems I should be aware of?"

Jay's turn to take a deep breath. "One potential glitch . . . but I'll make sure it doesn't express. Don't even give it a thought."

"Fine. What am I not thinking of?"

"He says he wants a two-month trial period. He'll finish out Pribhara's season—but if his wife and daughter don't like it up here, he'll quit then."

Her eyes closed momentarily, and the ghost of a frown chased across her brow; those were the only external signs she gave. Those who choose style over substance are compelled to stay with style no matter how tough it gets. But Jay knew she was furious. And here he was, a convenient and fully qualified target . . .

"Why couldn't his family have come up with him the last time?" she asked quietly.

"His wife was on deadline and couldn't leave her desk for more than a few days," Jay reminded her. "She's a writer. Remember, they thought he had at least two more seasons—two more years—before the Board would make a final choice . . . and only a twenty-five percent chance it'd turn out to be him."

Tokugawa had her hands clasped in the *kukanzen mudra*—but now she was unconsciously twiddling her thumbs. The effect was so ludicrous that he knew she would be even angrier if she became aware of it; he concentrated his gaze on her eyes. "True," she admitted grudgingly. "We are rushing him. His demand is reasonable. But if his wife decides she's a groundhog, the house loses face. Damn Pribhara—this is her fault."

Privately he disagreed. Pribhara could not help being a perpendicular. None of those poor unfortunates could. If anything, the situation was the fault of the Shimizu's Board of Directors, for not simply picking a shaper. The three-year rotating audition scheme had always seemed crackbrained to Jay; something like this had been bound to happen. But his advice had been ignored, and now was not the time to mention it. The blame looked better on Pribhara than it did on him. . . .

"I'd better call in Martin," she said. "I hate speaking to the man, but this is his pidgin. Maybe he can . . ." Her voice trailed off disconsolately.

Jay empathized completely. Even for a PR man, Evelyn Martin was a weasel; you wanted to bathe after talking with him on the phone. But he *was* gifted at spin control—

A metaphorical lightbulb seemed to appear over Jay's head.

"You're not looking at this right," he said suddenly. "This isn't bad news—it's mitigated good news. All it takes is a little spin control."

"Explain."

"Look, all Martin's press release has to say is that Pribhara has canceled for medical reasons, and that Porter has graciously consented to fill out her term. At the end of two months, *maybe* you have to announce that Porter has dropped out too, and let Choy and Mazurski carry on competing from there—a minor kerfluffle. But most likely his wife and kid will love this place as much as everyone else does—

so you announce *then* that he's been given the final position and has accepted. Either way, none of the Board's face is lost."

"Your brother would accept that? Not announce that we've picked him as the final winner until he's committed himself? And not announce that at all, ever, if he decides to opt out?"

"Gladly, I think. It gets him out of an impossible situation too." He had a rush of brains to the head. "But you should bump him to the permanent salary right away."

Her thumbs stopped twiddling. "Done. Mr. Cohn!"

Her AI materialized its lawyer-persona between her and Jay, facing both of them. As always, Mr. Cohn reminded Jay of an impossibly motionless shark. "Yes, ma'am?"

She gave instructions for the amendment of Rand's contract, relying on Cohn's legal software to translate her wishes from conversational English into Lawyerese, and spoke her signature. At Jay's suggestion, she had Cohn upload a copy to Diaghilev so that Jay could pass the document on to Rand later that night. Then she dismissed the AI and turned back to Jay. "Sasaki?"

"Yeah?"

"You've earned your air today."

He smiled; the first sincere smile of the day. He felt as if he had just successfully matched orbits by eyeball, without a computer—a terrestrial analogy might be walking a tightrope over an abyss. "Always nice to hear. I'll let you get back to your meditation."

"Thank you," she said. "But first, your reward. *You* get to tell Martin about all this."

He grimaced. "It's true, then; no good deed goes unpunished."

"Except those committed by Stardancers. They seem to be exempt."

"That's an idea," he said. "I'll go out the airlock without a suit."

" 'In space,' " she said, seeming to be quoting something, " 'no one can hear you scream.' Please yourself—but see Martin first."

Jay sighed. "Yes, boss. After I've eaten."

He had originally intended to call Eva Hoffman and beg off on the chat she had asked for. But now he needed to tell someone how relieved he was, and how clever he had been in wiggling, at least for the moment, off the spot marked X. As he left Tokugawa's office, he consulted the mental list of people he trusted enough to share news like this, and—Ethan being history now—found only Eva's name. She was not an employee of the house, plugged into that grapevine . . . nor did she fraternize much with the other guests, even the other Permanents. Most of them considered her crazy. She was easy to talk to, and in his opinion she had more character and style than any ten other people he knew. He had often thought that if Eva were, oh, say, seventy years younger, he might have considered turning hetero again for her. Hell, even sixty years younger . . .

Telling Diaghilev to call ahead and announce him, he left the Core and jaunted back outboard, through both Deluxe Tier (peasant country, at least in Shimizu terms) and UltraDeluxe Tier (the bourgeoisie;

governors, national-level executives and so forth), all the way to the Prime Tier, the outer suites with the most cubic and a naked-eye view of space. Eva's digs were in the Prime Plus hemiTier: the one whose view included Earth. She had chosen a suite offset from the center of that section, so that the home planet did not completely dominate the view, a choice Jay approved of since he had made the same one himself. Her door opened for him when he reached it, and her voice bade him enter.

Her suite was lavish and comfortable and hushed. As a long-time resident of the Shimizu, he knew the second most expensive thing in it was the hush. The third most expensive thing was the sheer cubic volume, and the air that filled it. Jay was one of the half-dozen hotel staff with enough clout to rate quarters in Prime Plus, and his own suite was a quarter the size of this one. Even by the standards of a permanent guest of the Shimizu, Eva was wealthy. Kate Tokugawa would have said that her assets were "substantial," only a step below "impressive."

His eyes found Eva where they expected to, by the room's *most* expensive feature: floating within the three-meter-across bubble window (called an imax for obscure historical reasons), which made the best Prime Tier suites cost twice as much as Deluxe accommodations. As was her custom when at home, she was wearing only wings and fins, sculling them gently and quite unconsciously to hold her position in space against the gentle current of airflow. It was a sight he had seen countless times, and still found striking and moving: a butterfly with a withered body,

Rodin's *She Who Was Once the Beautiful Heaulmière* somehow given the wings of a swan by the gods in clumsy compensation for the ruin of her beauty. Nobody looked sixty anymore these days—certainly no one whose real age had three digits—and Jay found Eva's defiant decay paradoxically entrancing. Especially juxtaposed against the wings, modern and high-tech . . . and that absurdly expensive surround-window . . . and the stars beyond, their steady fossil light unthinkably older than Eva could ever hope to be. He wished he had the nerve to use the image in a dance . . .

But Eva never missed a premiere. She had been born back in the days when nudity was strongly taboo—and while she'd obviously come into the twenty-first century, he had noted that she was never nude save when closeted with intimates.

Oddly, the thought had never once occurred to him that he would probably be free to use the image as he pleased one day, all too soon—that it could not be long before Eva died. If it had, the thought would have saddened him . . . but there was something about Eva that kept him from having it.

He politely removed his own clothing and let bee-sized tugbots take charge of each garment. He did not bother to remove his own wrist and ankle thrusters. Eva didn't object to their emissions, she just didn't care to use thrusters herself if she didn't have to; and Jay felt far more naked without them than he did without clothes. Nonetheless he allowed other tugbots to give him his own set of wings and fins, slid them on over his thrusters, and used them to join his hostess at the window. He was, if anything, more skillful at air-swimming than she was; he simply preferred the superior kinetic and kinesthetic versatility thrusters offered.

The jaunt to her side was uncomplicated: the room seemed as starkly furnished as a Zen master's cell, all its fabulous conveniences invisible until they were needed. That was its fourth most expensive feature.

She rode the turbulence of his arrival expertly, and helped him steady himself into station beside her, just far enough away to allow them both wingroom, all without taking her gaze from the window. She had chosen a local vertical that put Earth in the lower left quadrant of the window. Perhaps a fifth of the planet was visible, a lens-shaped slice of Old Home. The rest of the view was of eternity.

They shared it in silence for perhaps a minute.

"Drink with me, Jay," she said then.

He didn't care much for alcohol as a rule; he hated what it did to his balance and kinesthetic sense. But he did not hesitate. "Name your poison." He told himself that it would anesthetize him against having to talk with Martin later.

"Jeeves," she called, and her AI shimmered into view, oriented to her local vertical and seeming to be standing on air.

"Yes, madam?"

"The good stuff."

One holographic eyebrow rose half a centimeter. "Very good, madam."

Both of Jay's eyebrows rose at least that much. This was not going to be a casual conversation. He stopped rehearsing his account of how clever he had been in Kate's office.

5

Jeeves moved away without moving his legs, as if he were under gravity and his feet were on wheels, and ceased to exist when he left the humans' peripheral vision. Tugbots delivered an amber bottle, two bulbs and a spherical table to the spot where he had vanished. As they arrived, Jeeves reformed, and picked them all out of the air expertly as he "rolled" back into view. He placed the table between Eva and Jay and told it to stay there, placed a bulb against either side of its velcro surface and the bottle in the center facing them, so that the table looked like a stylized Pinocchio, and shimmied back a pace. Eva thanked and dismissed him; once again he glided out of view before dissolving.

"I never thought I'd see that again," Jay said respectfully.

She nodded. The bottle was an ancient quart of Black Bush, about three quarters full. It was something like a century old, and its contents were twelve years older than that, a blend of whiskey so fine that at the time of bottling it could not legally be exported from Ireland. Its source was the oldest distillery on Earth, whose charter-to-distill had been granted in 1608. There probably was not another bottle like it left anywhere in the Solar System. Jay was the only person in the Shimizu besides herself who had ever seen it; they had shared a dram the night Ethan's goodbye message arrived from Terra.

He steadied her while she poured, a process of pulling the bottle away while chasing it with the open end of the bulb, then pinching off the flow with one thumb while she sealed the bulb with the other. She did it better than the Chief Sommelier in the Hall of Lucullus, losing not a drop of the precious whiskey, fiercely proud of her ability to control her aged fingers. Jay accepted his bulb with thanks. He brought it up past his nose in a slow gentle curve, squeezing slightly so that the nipple dilated and the bouquet came to him. When she had filled her own bulb and replaced the bottle, he raised his in salute, and they drank.

The silence stretched on.

"Silly," she said at last. "I'll never get over how silly it is."

"What's that?" he asked.

"You could blindfold me, tug me around the hotel enough to confuse me, lead me into any room in the place and dock me in front of its window . . . take off the blindfold and *defy* me, without looking away from the window, to tell you which Tier I was in. There is no way to tell a real window from a fake one without instruments. And yet this thing is worth every yen it costs me. About the gross annual product of a medium town . . . and I'd pay three times as much if I had to. Why?"

He seemed to know a rhetorical question when he heard it; he made no reply.

"Why are they so goddam *happy*, Jay?" she asked then.

"Who?"

She gestured at the Earth. "Them." Her gesture widened to take in orbital space, then widened farther. "All of them. Our species. The human race in this year of Our Lord 2064. I think I know why the Stardancers are happy—but why people too?"

"I'm not sure exactly what you mean."

"Exactly. That's what I mean." She squeezed more whiskey into her mouth, rolled it around and swallowed. God, she missed her taste buds sometimes. "They probably don't even seem all that happy to you, do they?"

"I never really thought about—"

"Trust me. I've been watching the human race a long time. At this point we ought to be more traumatized than ever before in our history. The Curve of Change is almost vertical by now, like a goosing finger—you do know about the Curve?"

"Sure."

Of course he did—as a dry old chestnut from a history lesson. For millennia the curve of human social and technological progress had trended upward, but so slowly as to be almost imperceptible . . . then all at once it had passed some critical threshold and begun climbing sharply. Ever *more* sharply, the rate of increase itself accelerating steadily, until the race lurched from covered wagons to spaceships, from kingdoms and fiefs to planetary government, from chronic global poverty to staggering near-universal wealth, in a single century. Remarkable. Inexplicable. Where would it all end? And so on.

But Eva had been born into the middle of that century. Just about the time it was beginning to dawn on humanity just how oddly the Curve was behaving. And humanity's general response had been to run a high fever . . .

"I don't mean trivial things, like conquering cancer. I mean substantive changes in the map of reality. When I was a girl, the phrase 'New World' still meant North America. Now it means Mars. The Old World—that one right there—is just about unrecognizable, if you look at it any closer than this. The population has more than doubled since I was born, and look at that planet: it's still green. All the most fundamental axioms of politics, of economics, of industry, have all come apart since the turn of the millennium, obsoleted by new technology. We seem to have a handle on pollution, for God's sake! After half a century of holding my breath, I'm prepared to admit that it looks like we really may have outgrown war. Thanks to nanotechnology, I'm even getting ready to concede that a day may even come when we'll have outgrown *money* . . . a day when no one alive has to work to earn her living, when nobody will remember—or care—what a 'salary' was, or why people gave up a third of their lives to get one."

"And you wonder why people are happy?"

"*Yes!* Two axioms I cling to are that change is painful and that humans react poorly to pain. Change that radical and fundamental *has* to hurt, to confuse, to anger. For the first seventy years of my life, I watched my species grow ever more neurotic, more sullen, more despairing, more bitter. You know what I'm talking about."

"Well, I've read about it, seen records, old flatscreens and so forth—"

"They don't convey it. Believe what I'm about to tell you: when I was forty-five years old, ninety-five percent of the intelligent, thoughtful university-educated people I knew believed as an article of faith that technology and change were dooming the planet, and that some of us would live to see the Last Days. Just about every one of them had a different candidate for what specifically was going to get us. Nuclear Winter was the big one until the Soviet Union went broke. Within about fifteen minutes, fifty other Ends Of Everything had moved in to replace it: global warming, ice age, the ozone layer, overpopulation, deforestation, dwindling resources, pollution, energy shortage—I can't even remember them all anymore. Pestilence, famine and plague were evergreen favorites, and you could always find someone who was putting his money on a runaway comet. If you had a taste for the exotic, you could be terrified of flying saucers and empires of alien cattle-mutilators. But just about every adult I knew clutched *some* form of Ultimate Paranoia to his or her breast. Almost without exception they chose to believe that the End of All Meaning was just over the horizon. If you didn't know *that*, you were too stupid or naive to be worth talking to.

"I'm overstating it slightly, because the sample I'm talking about consisted almost exclusively of affluent North Americans. But only slightly. In 1991 a major poll asked average Americans if they would like to live five hundred years, assuming that could be accomplished cheaply and comfortably. *Only half of them said yes.* Fully half of that society was looking forward to dying."

Jay frowned and took a drink of his whiskey, forgetting to savour it. "How weird it must have been. To live in an age when the best and brightest worshipped Henny Penny. When the crew of Starship Earth, wealthy beyond the wildest dreams of their ancestors, were on the verge of mutinous panic . . ."

She nodded. "And then right at the turn of the millennium, just as the worst thing possible happened and the wildest of all those paranoid fantasies *came true* . . . just as actual aliens appeared in the sky, changed our destiny for us in great and incomprehensible ways, and vanished again before we could ask them any questions . . . everybody calmed down. The Curve kept on rising faster than ever, and somehow everybody on Earth seemed to heave a great sigh, and kick back, and *relax*. Not right away, no, not all at once—but the damn planet has been getting slowly and steadily *saner* for over sixty years now. And it's driving me crazy!"

He swirled whiskey around in his bulb, stared through and past the oscillating golden liquid to the planet they both had left forever. "It doesn't seem all that sane to me," he said.

"No, I'm sure it doesn't, to someone your age," she agreed. "It *isn't* all that sane. But it's sane-*er*. Do you know that at one time the United States had ten percent of its population imprisoned? Justly? As the best solution they could devise to problems they didn't begin to understand? Every year the papers told you the crime rate was rising. It's been falling for over twenty years, now . . . and somehow that never makes the headlines. The media just aren't geared up to report good news. You have to dig that out for yourself."

"I think it has to do with the Curve you were talking about," he said.

"What do you mean?"

"The latest spike in the Curve. The Nanotechnological Revolution. Molecular-scale machines and computers. It's qualitatively different from the Industrial Revolution or the Silicon Revolution or any of those. For once we got a new technology that cleans up its own wastes, doesn't despoil anything we cherish, and produces so much new wealth nobody could steal it all. Our first *healing* revolution. Take the revolution you grew up with, Eva: nuclear fission. They told everyone it would produce power too cheap to meter. Then it turned out the plants were big kludges, and nobody's power bill seemed to go down a dollar. No wonder they stopped trusting people in lab coats. But this generation got a technology that delivered on its promises." He sipped his drink again, appreciating it this time. "And come to think of it, that was mostly thanks to the Stardancers. Without them and their Safe Lab, we'd still be skirting the edges of nanotechnology, too scared of someone getting a monopoly on it, or scared of the wrong little nanoassembler getting loose and turning all the iron to peanut butter or something."

"Or we might have destroyed the planet in a war for possession of the new technology," she agreed. "Instead we've got a UN that means something—and a repaired ozone layer and a healthy ecosystem and nonpolluting industry and a world so fat and rich it hasn't had even a serious local war for thirty years."

"The Stardancers kept us honest," he said. "Thanks to the Fireflies, we had a precious resource: people we could trust to be above human greed and avarice, people with nothing to gain, people who could not be bribed or coerced."

"Bodhisattvas," she said.

"If you like," he said. "Fair witnesses, anyway."

"No wonder there used to be terrorists trying to kill them. A fair witness can be infuriating."

"Yeah, maybe—but the last serious attempt was about the time I was born. Even a fanatic reactionary can see they're just too valuable to the race now: they can live full time in space with no life support, and space is the only safe place to develop little artificial viruses, the only sensible place to collect solar power. Humanity got lucky. We got just what we needed, just when we needed it."

"Luck, hell," she snarled. He recoiled at her force. "You just said it yourself. Luck had nothing to do with it. It was those damned Fireflies: they saved our bacon for us, brought us the moon-full of Symbiote that makes a human a Stardancer, and *gave* it to us, for free. I could kill them for that!"

She could see that she had shocked him. She

waited, to see how he would handle it. "This is what you really wanted to talk about," he said finally.

She smiled. "Pour for us, please, Jeeves."

When the AI had refreshed their bulbs, she turned to face him directly. He copied her, and they joined a hand to steady themselves in the new attitude. She held on.

"Jay," she said, "I'm old. I was old enough to vote when the first tourist littered the moon. I was spending a fortune on cosmetic camouflage the year the Fireflies showed up and Shara Drummond danced the Stardance for them. I've had a five-cent Coca Cola, and watched the first television set on my block. Flatscreen, monochrome. I've owned 78 RPM phonograph records and a hand-cranked Victrola. I've buried three husbands, three children and two grand-children. One of my great-grandchildren in Canada is dying, and I have to keep asking Jeeves her name. Jeeves, what is my dying great-grandchild's name?"

"Charlotte, madam," Jeeves murmured from somewhere nearby.

"I have been a success in three professions," she went on, "and a failure in two. It's not that most of my life is behind me. *All* of my life is behind me, receding. I always said I was going to check out when and if my clock showed three figures . . . and I came here to the Shimizu for that purpose. I stopped controlling my cosmetic age the day I moved into this suite, as a sign that I was withdrawing from human affairs. I've been saying goodbye for the last sixteen years. You know most of this."

He nodded and sipped the Irish whiskey, still holding her hand.

"Haven't you ever wondered what's taking me so long?"

He shook his head. "Not once. I figure saying goodbye to life could take me, oh, *seventeen* years, easy."

"You'll find out," she said. "Old age is not for sissies. I had all my goodbyes said years ago."

"All right," he said agreeably. "I'll play Mr. Interlocutor. Why *are* you still using up air, Ms. Hoffman?"

"Sheer annoyance," she said. "I'd always expected to live to see the world end. I planned to watch humanity die of its own stupidity and meanness, and chortle at the irony of it all. I expected to enjoy it immensely."

"I can understand that," he said slowly.

"Long before I came up here, I'd admitted to myself that it just isn't going to happen any time soon. Okay: I didn't insist on doom . . . as so many of my contemporaries had. I would have settled for watching us come through in the clutch, reach deep inside ourselves and pull out the best of us and *solve* our damned problems." She glanced down at her bulb, found too much whiskey there and corrected the problem. "What I wasn't prepared for was to have big red Fireflies drop in and fix things *for* us . . . and then scamper off to wherever the hell they came from without telling us *why!*"

She looked into his eyes for understanding, and did not find it. He was too young for questions like this to be troubling in anything but an abstract sense. And he had grown up in a world where telepathic Stardancers—and the mysterious alien Fireflies who

had appeared out of nowhere, created the
Stardancers and their collective Starmind, and then
vanished back into deep space—were prosaic history,
something that had happened sixteen years before
he was born. She saw him try to understand, and
fail.

She broke eye contact and sculled around to face
the window and the world again. "Anyway, it's come
to me in the last few days that what I've been
doing . . . what I've been waiting for . . . has been for
the damned Fireflies to come back from wherever
they went and tell us what's going on. Or for me to
cleverly deduce it for myself. The most important
philosophical question the human race has faced
since the aliens dropped in and out again is, 'What
the hell was *that*?' In sixty-four years we haven't
made a dent in it.

"Realizing that has forced me to face the fact that
I'm wasting my time. If nobody else can figure it
out, I probably can't either. Available evidence indicates the Fireflies drop by once every couple of thousand years at best. I can't wait that long. And this
steady diet of unearned good news lately has just got
me baffled."

"Are you sure it's unearned?" he said. "Stardancers
start as human beings, however different they may
become after Symbiosis. The scientific name for them
is *Homo caelestis*. Humanity birthed them: the Fireflies were just midwives."

"Stardancers do not suffer from fear or hunger or
poverty or lust or loneliness," Eva said. "Thanks to
their Symbiote, they're immortal, effectively invul-
nerable, and perpetually loved. As far as I'm

concerned, that means they're not human anymore. And if things keep going the way they are, it's conceivable that one day nobody on Earth may be hungry or cold or oppressed. If that day comes, by my lights there won't *be* any human beings anymore."

"So you want to leave while things are still miserable," he said.

She frowned at her drink.

"No," she said. "That's my point. Everybody's happy now. I personally think that in time the hangover will arrive, and people will find out that even nanotechnology has hidden costs. No matter how many miracles we come up with, I believe there are *always* limits to growth. I have a friend named Ling who says he can prove it—I can't follow his math, but it sounds convincing. But meanwhile there is peace on the world . . . maybe it's only temporary, but nobody can know that yet. So maybe this is a *good* time to leave, and I should stop dragging my feet."

He kept his face expressionless. "How do you plan to do it?"

His very neutrality cued her that he was angry. It startled her. She precessed to face him again. "Is that relevant?"

"It's closer than anything that's been said since I jaunted in here," he said. "Let's cut through all the bullshit about Stardancers and Fireflies and how happy the world is today. You have obviously decided to check out. For some reason you think I need to know that in advance. That means you have some role in mind for me. I'm curious to know what it is. Do you want me to stand by with the ceremonial sword in case you lose your nerve? Am I

supposed to talk you out of it? Or just be your witness and hold your hand? Angel's advocate, enabler,
or audience—I can go any way you like, Eva. I'm
your friend and I'll try to give you whatever you need
of me, but you've got to tell me the steps."

She let go of her drink and reached toward him
with her withered hands. He abandoned his own
drink and took them in his own.

"In a month," she said, "Reb Hawkins will be
coming to the Shimizu. I want to talk with him one
more time. Immediately after that I plan to go out
the airlock." She gestured toward the window with
her chin. "Out there. When I'm ready, my p-suit will
kill me, painlessly and not abruptly. I want to die
in space. As I die, I would like to watch you
dance . . . if you're willing."

He was speechless. He tried to free his hands, and
she would not let him. He tried to tear his gaze from
hers, and she would not allow that either. "Why me?"
he said finally.

"Dance is the only thing humans do that's *only*
beautiful," she said. "It's the only thing we do that
speaks even to Fireflies, as far as we can tell. I want
to die watching a human being dance. A human, not
a Stardancer. You're the best dancer I know. And
you're my friend. I thought about not putting this
on you until the last minute . . . but I thought you
might want some time to choreograph your dance.
I know how busy you'll be once your brother arrives."

Globules of salt water began to grow from his
eyes. Despite sixteen years in free-fall, she still found
the sight of zero-gee tears simultaneously hilarious
and moving. And contagious. He shook his head, and

the droplets flew away. She blinked back her own, and waited.

At last, with difficulty, he smiled. "I am honored, Eva," he said. He released her hands, plucked his bulb out of the air, and raised his arm in a toast. She reclaimed her own, and they emptied them together. She did not hesitate, spun and threw her bulb as hard as she could, directly at that absurdly expensive window. The bulb shattered musically.

She had startled him. A cannon couldn't have broken that window—but still, what a gesture! He was game, though: his own bulb burst only a second or two after hers. When they had recovered from their throws, he bowed to her, a Buddhist *gassho* she suspected he must have learned from his grandmother. She returned it gravely. "Thank you," she said.

There was nothing left to say. Or too much. After they had watched the tugbots chase and disassemble glass shards for a few moments, he cleared his throat and said, "I've got to see Ev Martin before dinner."

She grinned. "Another argument for suicide. You're right, you wouldn't want to talk to him on a full stomach."

"Not even on a stomach full of hundred-year-old whiskey," he agreed. "But it'll help. Thanks for it."

She made a mental note to leave him the balance of the bottle in her will.

He paused at the door. "Eva?"

"Yes," she said, without turning.

"Is it all right if I spend the next month trying to get you to change your mind?"

"Yes," she said. "But don't be attached to succeeding, Jay. I've been thinking about this a long time."

After a while she heard the door close and seal.

6

Toronto, Ontario
4 December 2064

There is no such thing as a slight flaw in a dance floor.

And all floors have flaws. Anyone but a dancer would probably call them slight: certainly the manufacturers do. Nonetheless, each floor has its own invisible peculiarities, lurking in wait for dancers' feet. Even the floor of Toronto's famous Drummond Theatre. The company had gone through two complete rehearsals, undress and dress, without a hitch; it was in the final onstage warm-up class, a scant hour before curtain, that John DeMarco, who had been dreaming of and working toward this night for all his professional life, found the flaw with his name on it. It broke his ankle.

At any other time it would have been a nuisance. The actual repair could be accomplished in less than ten minutes at the nearest hospital, after two hours of datawork and waiting in the emergency room. And once fixed, you'd be hopping around good as new . . . in a matter of mere hours. . . .

The ugly sound had riveted the attention of all. It took only minutes to establish that the nearest hospital was half an hour away in the best of times, and that everyone in the company seemed to have run out of painblock at once. So had John, of course. Dancers started to drift away to call hospitals and search dressing rooms and find the driver; the AD, watching her company scattering to the four winds an hour before curtain, bellowed them into stasis and bent over John's recumbent form. "Is there any hope at all?" she asked.

It was clearly a break, not just a sprain. John shook his head, and started to apologize.

She waved it away. "Then you'll have to live with it for a while. I can't spare anyone here: I have to recast the whole performance in forty-five minutes, and everyone I can see I *need*. We'll put you in dressing room two. Jacques! Harry!"

The pain was exquisite, almost nauseating. "No! Wait! Put me in the audience. If I can't be in it, I'm gonna see the run-through."

She nodded to Harry and Jacques. "Do it."

Harry, the stage manager, gave him a jacket to put over his warm-up clothes, promised to try and find him some painblock and a ride as soon as possible, and left him front-row center. Not an ideal seat, but convenient. One of the dancers who could be spared momentarily brought him an improvised pack of ice from the concession in the lobby. He concentrated on the frenzied activity onstage to distract himself from his pain.

Shortly after he decided Anna was fucking the whole thing up, he noticed that the pain was gone. Utterly.

He yelped, in astonishment and something like fright. Anna glared at him from the stage. "Harry, take him back-stage—"

"No," he said. "Sorry. I'm fine; won't happen again."

She went back to her work. He bent and looked at his ankle. No question, that was a broken ankle, all right. The swelling was already so advanced that he knew it was badly broken. Now why in hell didn't it hurt?

The swelling began to visibly reduce.

He yelped again. Anna turned and came to the edge of the stage. "John, I'm sorry, but—"

"Look at my foot!"

She blinked.

"God dammit, come down here and look at my fucking foot!"

The dancers followed her. They gathered around and watched his ankle heal itself. After a few murmurs and gasps, no one said a word. In minutes, the ankle looked just like its mate. John flexed it slowly, listening for grating sounds, and then extended it with the same care. Then he circled it, one way and then the other, and started to laugh. Soon everyone was laughing, even Anna. He got to his feet, took a few cautious steps—then took a running start and sprang up on stage. He did a combination on his way to his place for the first piece. "Come on, boss," he said, still laughing. " 'Time's a-wastin'!" It was one of her catch-phrases; the company dissolved into hysterics.

Anna let that go on for a good five seconds. From then on they were so busy that it wasn't until mid-way through the triumphant fourth curtain call that John had time to wonder about it all.

He never did figure it out. He had to be told. But he didn't mind.

PART THREE

7

Logan Airport
Boston, Massachusetts
5 December 2064

Rhea felt as if she were on a conveyor belt, sliding ever closer toward the butcher's blade.

Logan Aerospaceport was used to celebrity press conferences; a soundproof room had been found for Rand, Rhea, Colly and the cronkites and riveras representing the planetary, national and local-birthplace media pools. Cambots swarmed like black-flies, recording the scene from at least eight directions. Once in a long while, one of them would decide the ambient light was insufficient, and turn into a white firefly for a moment or two.

Tough new laws had finally succeeded in taming the media: all four cronkites, and even the riveras, were scrupulously polite. Nonetheless they managed to annoy Rhea—by putting seventy percent of their questions to Rand. In the half-dozen previous press conferences they'd had together, the percentages had usually been reversed. It embarrassed her to be annoyed by that, but she couldn't help it. At least she was able to keep him from noticing . . . though she wasn't so sure about the cambots.

Colly lapped it up. And put on a performance that would have made a child holostar blush. That annoyed Rhea too.

Which made her ask herself why she was so irritable. She realized what bothered her most of all was how much Rand was enjoying the attention and flattery. It scared her. This was going to be a hard thing to undo. It was feeling more and more like a done deal . . . and she still hadn't given her agreement to it. Rand knew that, but he wasn't acting like it. Oh, he told the reporters—and the world beyond them— the assignment was only temporary, just completing Pribhara's season: the story he'd worked out with Jay and that horrible-sounding Martin person. But when he said it, she heard in his voice the quiet certainty that the permanent job was his. She wasn't sure if the cambots were hearing that too, or if she was projecting it.

She felt disconnected, surreal, moving against a tide of invisible molasses. *This is a hell of a way to spend my last hour on Earth,* she decided. "Time to go, darling," she said helpfully, as Rand finished a reply.

"Just one more," the flaky-looking rivera from the planetary pool said. "Do you have any comment on the breaking story about outbreaks of rogue assemblers?"

Rand looked startled. "I'm sorry, I've been too busy packing to monitor news. Nanoassemblers, you mean?"

The rivera nodded. "There seems to be growing evidence over the last few days of random instances of . . . well, of anarchist nanotechnology, all around the globe. Spontaneous healings, spontaneous slum regenerations—sort of little miracles. There's no telling how many, since the tendency is to under-report miracles. Some say there may be some sort of . . . well . . ."

"A conspiracy of rapturists?" Rhea said, thinking of an old story-idea she had never gotten around to developing.

"Rapturists?" the woman from the New England pool pounced.

"The opposite of a terrorist," Rhea said. "But what has this got to do with us?"

The flaky one tried not to look like he knew he was stretching for a tie-in hook. "Well, you're going to space, where nanotechnology comes from. Are you, I don't know, at all afraid some . . . uh, 'Rapturist' might decide to put laughing gas in your p-suit tanks?"

To everyone's surprise, it was Colly who spoke up. "There hasn't been one of those stories in space so far," she said. They all stared.

"It's true," she insisted. "Not one. I watch the news. Anyway, they haven't hurt anybody, have they?"

No one replied.

"Maybe not yet," Rand said. "But anarchy can get pretty scary even when it means well, honey. Maybe especially when it means well." He turned to the rivera. "But no, we're not worried at all. Everybody knows you're safer in space than you are on Earth: look at the stats. We really have to go now. Thank you all—"

On the flight up, Rhea tuned her seatback screen to a news channel, in time to hear herself ask, " . . . a conspiracy of rapturists?" and then, in response to the rivera's prompting, define the term. A few moments later, Colly and Rand's exchange was quoted too.

The piece in which the soundbite was featured might as well have been titled, "Nanotechnology— Threat or Menace?" It was about three times as long as the item she managed to find later on an arts channel, about Rand's return to the Shimizu.

She wanted the flight to be miserable. It was idyllic. No dropsickness in her family—none on the whole plane. No emergencies; minimal, gentle maneuvering; a perfect hop. Superb, pleasant service from human and robot alike. Even the food was excellent: real, microwave cooking rather than flashpak. The Shimizu did not permit clients to arrive unhappy, whether they wanted to or not. The hardest part of the flight was keeping Colly's seat belt buckled once the gravity went away.

The approach was spectacular. The Shimizu looked like God's Christmas ornament, a vast gleaming globe. Its exterior was fractalized for maximum radiating surface, so it sparkled in the sunlight like a vast ball of crinkled aluminum foil. It was girdled by an equator of huge cooling and power-collecting vanes, brilliant silver on one side and space black on the other, that slowly rotated independently as the relative position of the sun changed. A thousand points of light—peoples' windows!—added to the illumination, randomly distributed, going on or off as tenants entered or left their rooms.

The plane crept up on the hotel sideways, spinning slowly around its own axis to distribute the sun's heat, so there were no bad seats. Every time you decided you were there now, the damned thing got a little bigger; it seemed planet-sized by the time they actually reached the spaceport at the "north pole."

After a textbook docking, all four doors opened the instant the seat-belt light went out, so that passengers need not stand in line to debark; customs formalities occurred electronically without any of them noticing. The dock itself was beautiful and impressive, its layout and decor operating somehow on the subconscious to make you feel you were home.

Then Rand muttered, "Oh no—*that* asshole."

A large spider monkey with a head like a red sea anemone sprang at them out of nowhere. At the last possible moment he braked to a stop with smelly, poorly tuned thrusters and flung his arms around Colly. She looked wildly around to Rhea, her eyes asking permission to be terrified.

"I could kiss you," the apparition said, and did so, on the forehead. Colly decided she didn't need permission; the man said "Eek" and let her go and clutched his groin.

"Nice shot, dear," Rhea said, and interposed herself between them before Rand could. She was pleased to find that free-fall reflexes came back quickly to her; she still remembered how to jaunt. "Who or what are you?" she asked him.

He forgot his aching testicles. "The guy who could cheerfully strangle you, Ms. Pash-o," he said cheerfully. "What ever *possessed* you to give them a bite like that, for God's sake? You blew *my* whole story right off the Net with that rapturist line, lady. Who asked you to improvise? If it hadn't been for this little genius here," he said, pointing to Colly, "it could have been a disaster." Forgetting that she had just kicked him, he reached out and tried to pat her head. "You just keep following your mama around, kid, and every time you see her open her mouth to a sniffer, you talk instead."

Colly ducked until he gave up. "Rhea and Colly," Rand said through clenched teeth, "this is Evelyn Martin, Shimizu's publicity chief."

"And people still come here?" Rhea asked. The man was strikingly ugly. His head looked like a large red Brillo pad with bat-ears and pop-eyes. She had not met him on her previous visit, but Rand had assured her Martin was an excrescence; she decided he had understated the case.

Martin didn't seem to hear. "It's okay for you to talk like that now; I'll dub the audio later, give us all beautiful lines for the release. But I've got the top three cronkites in space waiting nearby to do the personal bit, so pee if you have to and we'll—"

Jay arrived. "Rand and his family will be happy to meet with them later this evening," he said firmly, and embraced his brother. "Sorry I'm late, bro."

Martin continued to talk rapidly while Jay greeted Rhea and Colly in turn, but they all ignored him.

"Twenty-one hundred, Ev," Jay said as he led them from the hall. "They'll wait. Nobody ever turned down a free dinner at the Shimizu. Least of all a cronkite." Martin watched speechlessly as their luggage emerged from the plane and began to follow them.

Rhea had known Jay since her courtship with his half-brother over a decade ago, had chatted with him for dozens of hours on the phone since. But since Jay had made the permanent move to space, around the time she and Rand got married, she had only been in his physical presence once, briefly, during Rand's previous residency. In one sense she knew him well already. But to know if you really *like* someone, you have to smell them. As they all relaxed over drinks in their suite—Rhea's new home!—she found herself remembering how much she really liked Jay.

During a visit to the bathroom she took the occasion to summon Diaghilev, Jay's AI, and ask if there had been any recent news of Ethan. "Ethan who, Ms. Paixao?" was the reply, which was all the answer she needed. The relationship was irreparable. A shame; Rhea had liked Ethan, at least over the phone. "Is Jay seeing anyone?"

There was an imperceptible hesitation while Diaghilev made sure she was cleared for that information. "No, ma'am. He dates occasionally, but has not dated anyone twice." She made a mental note to keep an eye open for a nice young man for Jay, and rejoined the others.

The suite was considerably nicer than the one she'd had on her last short visit. It took her a while to note, and a little longer to believe, that the window was real. Earth was centered in the frame, the terminator just reaching what looked like a major blizzard over the northwest coast of North America. This was one of the more expensive suites in the hotel. She hunted for flaws, and cheered up a little when she noticed the furniture was all permanent. Excellent, and fully programmable, but it didn't go away when you were done with it.

But everything else she could see was state of the art or better.

She told herself sourly that the hotel had given them this suite to soften her up—that once Rand signed on for good, they'd be moved to somewhere inboard with the rest of the peons.

It was Jay who snapped her out of her gloomy mood, by asking her about her work. She thought of the story about Mr. Hansen and his beloved nun, but did not bring it up, speaking instead of the novel she had been struggling with for nearly a year now. Jay listened well, widening his eyes at the right spots, making little murmurs of agreement, asked insightful questions with great diffidence. Several of the questions made knowledgeable reference to her earlier works. He was either as much of a fan as he claimed to be, or a gifted actor. Either was gratifying.

Colly jaunted around the room like an old-fashioned maid robot, inspecting everything and trying out acrobatic maneuvers with both her wings and her child-strength thrusters, having the time of her life. Every few minutes she found something that made her giggle and call Rhea or Rand to "Look!"

or "Come see!" Rhea let her roam unchecked, knowing she would tire herself out and nap soundly soon. They'd all had to get up before dawn to make the flight, and it was now nearly 6 PM, Shimizu time. Besides, this suite was safe for kids. It was probably safe enough for a blind hemophiliac epileptic.

One of Rand's early songs, "Blues in the Dark," was playing in the background. It was relatively obscure, but one of her personal favorites, since it was about her and Rand's courtship. Jay had selected it when they came in; either he had remembered some casual reference she'd made in a phone chat, or they shared similar tastes. Either way, it helped her warm to him.

She had to admit, it did feel good to be in free-fall again. She had forgotten how restful it was, how reminiscent of childhood fantasies of being able to fly, like the Little Lame Prince. The drugs had controlled the stuffy-head feeling this time, and her stomach felt fine. Rand had already inserted his personal wafer into a terminal in the suite: Maxwell Perkins, her own personal AI avatar, was again at her beck and call, moved from home into new quarters in the Shimizu's memory cores, as was Rand's version, Salieri—while their original copy still maintained the house back in Provincetown. (Also present, and presently in use, was the persona by which Colly addressed it: a large rabbit named Harvey.) Before long Rhea found herself thinking that this wasn't the worst possible place in the world . . . and then reminded herself sharply that it wasn't *in* the world. Not the same one P-Town was. She glanced out the window at the distant Earth and failed to locate New England.

*Look on the bright side. Your husband might fail
spectacularly. You might get a terrific divorce settle-
ment. You might even convince your daughter to
come back to Earth with you. The damned hotel
could get hit by a runaway planet. Some Rapturist
might put laughing gas in your air tank. The future
holds infinite possibility.*

If Jay was scheming to convert her, his next move
was below the belt—literally. He led them all to
dinner at the Hall of Lucullus. Not the Grand Dining
Room, which peasants like governors and pop stars
had to make do with—where Rhea had dined on her
last visit—but the Lucullus, the most famous oasis
in human space. Rhea had dined well in her time,
but this was something out of the realm of her experience. They did not turn the cherries into beans for
her dessert coffee until she had named the blend
she preferred—then roasted them before her
eyes . . . and under her nose. The coffee waiter—
there was a separate, live coffee waiter—announced
proudly as he was pulverizing them (pausing every
few seconds so as not to overheat them prematurely)
that these cherries had seen the sun rise from a tree
on the island of Sulawezi that very morning. When
she had tasted the result, she believed him.

The meal preceding had been so perfect that Rhea
took the coffee almost in stride, which mildly shocked
her. Lucius Licinius Lucullus, dead over two millennia, would have been proud of what was being done
in his name. She was halfway through her bulb
before she realized how *many* live human beings had
been waiting on them hand and foot throughout
dinner, with only the maitre d', wine steward and

coffee waiter ever coming to her conscious attention. Zero gee left a lot of ways to skirt the edges of peripheral vision, but still . . .

Jay saw her glance around and read her mind. "They're a highly specialized breed of dancers," he said, grinning. "A few of them take class with me. The standard joke is, if you can see one, you don't have to tip him."

Rhea was used to superb service from machines. From human beings it was *much* less common, and a bit unnerving. It made her feel a little like a plantation owner before Civil War One. She reminded herself that these serfs almost certainly made more money than she did—and didn't have to keep thinking up new ideas.

Even Colly, who hated restaurant dining, was impressed. The peanut butter and jelly sandwich she was served (by yet another waiter! They couldn't keep one around just for that; he must be a kind of utility infielder) precisely matched her specifications down to brand and relative proportion of ingredients, and when she challenged the kitchen by impishly requesting an obscure brand of ice cream only sold in Provincetown, they accommodated her without batting an eye.

For all of Rhea's life, "cooking skill" had consisted of selecting the right equipment. It still tended to be the wife who told the equipment to start working, but it had been half a century or more since women's sense of self-worth had depended to any significant degree on the results. Nonetheless, she was mildly irritated to see Rand put away twice as much food as usual.

She managed to find a more acceptable reason to be disgruntled almost at once. A glance around the sumptuous room reminded her of how terrifyingly easy it was to get fat in free-fall. A fat person floating overhead will never again be able to impress you face to face. She had heard that plumpness was fashionable in space—at least among those raised in gravity—but she didn't care if it was.

For his pièce de résistance, Jay let Rand pick up the check . . . making the point that he could now afford to. Colly's eyes grew round at that, and Rand swelled visibly as he thumbprinted the pad.

What can I do? What can I possibly do?

The second press conference was a little more fun than the first, because at least half the time was devoted to asking her to expand on her comments about Rapturism, which by now had acquired an audible capital letter. The fun part was ignoring Martin's frantic attempts to change the subject or put words in her mouth. Book interviews were wonderful training for that sort of thing. And Rand didn't seem to mind sharing the camera—perhaps because this time the implied larger audience was spacers, people he didn't identify with yet. Or perhaps, she had to concede, he was just being in love with his wife.

An hour later, on that assumption, she gave him the fuck of his life in the ingeniously designed bedchamber of their lavish new suite, using tricks only possible in free-fall, and drifted (literally) off to sleep curled around his back, furious at him.

The next day she and Colly were peeled away from Rand, and sent on a tour of the hotel with a slender, frail-looking, yet strikingly handsome young Orientator, while the two brothers holed up in Jay's studio to try and salvage what Pribhara had started.

Colly gaped at him when he stated his name. "Duncan *Iowa?*"

Rhea started to chide her, but Duncan only grinned broadly. "My mother was a Frank Herbert fan." Seeing that she didn't get it, he went on, "He wrote a book called DUNE with a character named Duncan Idaho. So she always wanted a son named Duncan . . . and then she married my dad, Walter Iowa, and just couldn't resist."

Rhea noticed that he did *not* go one step too far, and explain to an eight-year-old Terran that Idaho and Iowa were both the names of states. That was careful diplomacy. He was spaceborn, and would have explained it to another spaceborn, to whom states were distant and remote abstractions. But he could think like an earthborn, well enough to preserve a child's dignity. She decided she liked him.

So did Colly. "I have the same problem," she said solemnly. "My own parents thought it would be fun to name me after a breed of dog."

Duncan nodded gravely. "That's something to bitch about."

She burst into giggles, and they were friends.

The tour was not the standard first-time first-day grand tour Rhea had taken on her previous trip here. This seemed more like a kind of VIP, behind-the-scenes version. It was still quite impressive, but more intimate, somehow, conveying the added message that only special people got to be impressed in this particular way. "Of course, you'll still be learning things about this place the day before you go back home," he said at one point. "I'm still learning things about it."

"How long have you had this job?" Rhea asked politely.

"I just got it. But I've been coming here since I was a kid."

That long, huh? she thought ironically, but kept the thought to herself.

She swapped bio synopses with Duncan as the tour progressed. He was twenty, bisexual, single, and had a bachelor's degree in molecular electronics from U.H.E.O. which he hoped to parlay into a Master's once he had earned the tuition. If only he had been fifteen years older, massed twice as much, had a hairier torso and been muscled more like an earthborn, she would have considered trying to pair him off with Jay. His parents were both spacers who worked at Skyfac.

Colly's favorite part of the tour was what she instantly dubbed the Blob: the Shimizu's famous zero-gee swimming pool. Located at the very center of the hotel for reasons of orbital stability, it was essentially a large spherical tank, thirty meters across, containing 210,000 liters of crystalline water and happy people.

Of course Colly insisted on going in. You donned breathing and comm gear and four fins, and entered through an air-lock. Inside, it was preternaturally beautiful: artistically colored lights were deployed all around and blended to produce shifting effects, and the tank was stocked with multihued fish of tropical breeds—robots, of course, but no less brilliant or beautiful for that. They were absolutely impossible to catch, or even touch: Colly spent a happy time trying. Rhea enjoyed herself almost as much as her daughter. Afterward in the dressing room, Colly announced that air bubbles were prettier in free-fall—and acted more interesting too.

What Rhea thought was that swimming in P-Town was better—whether you did it on the ocean or bay side. But she kept the thought to herself.

When they rejoined Duncan, the first thing Colly said was, "Duncan, how come you don't have muscles, like Daddy?"

"Colly!" Rhea began.

But Duncan cut her off, smiling. "I know that would be a rude question on Terra—but things are different in space. Here it's just a good question."

Colly looked pleased. "So what's the good answer?" she asked.

"Because I don't need 'em. Earthworm muscles—excuse me, Terran muscles—are worse than useless up here. You don't need that much power, and you keep hurting yourself, by pushing off too hard."

"Oh." Colly looked down at her skinned knees, and rubbed a banged elbow thoughtfully. "I knew that: I was just testing you."

"Can I ask you a question now?"

"Sure."

"Back there in the pool—why did you like those angelfish so much?"

"They kept making, like, a flower," she said. "You know, tails together but each head pointing out a different way, like a puffball."

"Don't real angelfish do that on Terra?" he asked.

She stared at him. "How could they? Some of them'd be upside down!"

He blinked, and grinned. "Isn't that funny? I knew real fish can't live in free-fall, because they die without a local vertical to align to; I've read that. But I didn't follow it through and realize they wouldn't ever make puffballs down there."

"That's the difference between book learning and experience," Rhea said, seeing a chance to make this a lesson for Colly. "Duncan was born in space. He knows a lot, but you know things he doesn't."

"And vice versa," he agreed. "That's why I'm here. Over the next couple of days you're both going to get real tired of hearing me repeat certain things. Free-fall safety, vacuum-drill, flare-drill, p-suit maintenance, things like that. And you'll tell me that you know all that stuff, and you'll be right. You know it as book learning. So let me keep bugging you, okay? Otherwise you may get in some kind of trouble, from expecting an angelfish to make a puffball."

Colly nodded solemnly. She had been watching the way he handled himself in zero gee, and trying to copy his movements, but from then on she would ask his advice, and take it.

"For instance, both of you put in your earphones for a second."

Rhea and Colly both complied.

"I want you to hear a sound without others hearing it. Listen—" He touched a pad at his wrist, and they heard a distinctive warbling shriek. "If you hear that, you have less than twenty minutes to get here to the pool. If you're late, you'll die. It means a bad solar flare is on the way—and this pool is also the Shimizu's storm shelter."

"How long do they last?" Colly asked.

"Anywhere from eighteen hours to three days or so."

"We might have to swim for three *days*?" She didn't seem alarmed. Rhea certainly was.

"Oh, no! They pump the water into holding tanks all around the pool, so it'll do the most good as shielding."

"That thing is huge," Rhea said, "but is it really big enough to accommodate twelve-hundred-odd people for up to three days?"

"If they're friendly," he said with a grin. "Don't worry: most flares you're ever liable to see, you can deal with by just getting into the radiation locker in your suite. It takes a Class Three flare to empty the pool, and that hasn't happened in my lifetime. Doesn't mean it couldn't in the next ten minutes— but they've got some real sharp folks modeling the sun nowadays, plus the Stardancers keep a couple of angels way in past the orbit of Venus all the time, keeping an eye on the old girl. They can send a telepathic warning back to Earth orbit *instantly*, a lot faster than a radio or laser message: when Mama Sol clears her throat, we get a lot better warning than you get of a quake in San Francisco. And in any emergency, trained men in radiation suits will chase down stragglers and sleepers. *But*—and this is what I was talking about before—you can't ever leave safety to machines and other people. Sometimes they goof. If you ever start seeing green pollywogs—little green flashes in your vision—get into that locker, fast.

Don't wait for the central computer to tell you to . . . and don't stop to pee."

After lunch he took them to Wonderland. Both ladies found it delightful. As you approached it, the first thing you noticed was a child-sized white rabbit a little ahead of you, wearing a vest and consulting a pocketwatch. You followed him as he jaunted feetfirst "down" a long tunnel; onrushing air gave a reasonable illusion of falling in a magical sort of way.

The place into which you emerged lived up to its name.

Colly wanted to stay—forever. After an hour, Rhea was sick of rosy cheer and wanted to go be sullen with her husband. She left Colly with Duncan, made an agreement to meet them at suppertime, and followed Maxwell Perkins's excellent directions through a maze of unfamiliar corridors to Jay's studio. One thing about AIs: they made it hard to be a stranger in a strange land, even if you wanted to be. As long as there was a local database for your AI to invest, wherever you went, you were home.

She paused outside the door, and had Max ask his alter ego—Rand's AI avatar Salieri—whether she could enter without disturbing her husband; with his assurances she thumbed the door open and jaunted in. The work in progress looked so odd that her eye ignored it, noting only that it seemed to involve some sort of pseudo-underwater visuals and twelve-tone music. She had been married to a shaper too long to expect a rehearsal to look or sound like much.

Rand was drifting a few meters off to her left, upside down with respect to her local vertical. His body was derelict, relaxed into the classic free-fall crouch, all his attention focused on the dozen writhing dancers who filled the cubic before him. Even upside down she could see that he was scowling so ferociously his forehead looked ribbed. He was making little growling mutters deep in his throat, shaking his head from side to side.

She knew she had never seen him happier.

Dammit.

In that first glimpse of him, utterly intent on his work, she knew deep down, below the conscious level, that she was doomed. She could either live the rest of her life here, or start reliving the glorious single years . . . with an eight-year-old. Her subconscious thought about it, decided her conscious mind did not require this information just now, and tucked it away in the inaccessible node where stories got worked out.

It stayed there for the next month. Every time it tried to get out, she went to work on a story instead. It was a very prolific month.

8

The Shimizu Hotel
7 January 2065

Rand became aware that a fragment of his attention was needed somewhere. His wife was present, and speaking to him. He played back mental tape and found that she had asked him if he would be free for dinner.

The question confused him. It called for speculation, and contained a word with at least six different meanings. He searched for a proper response, and selected, "Hah?"

She understood perfectly. "Thanks, darling. I'll have Salieri ask you again later. Listen to Salieri, okay? He'll know where we are."

There were so many words, he decided a nod would be safest. It seemed to work: she went away, and though she was frowning slightly she did not slam anything on the way. Relieved, he relaxed and let his eyes and mind go where they needed to. *Damn* Pribhara anyway! Thanks to her, he had been placed in a position where his triumphal first achievement as Resident Shaper would be to wash someone else's laundry. He had been doing so for a month, and all he had to show for it was a mountain of wet laundry.

The thing was worse than awful: it was more than half done. Pribhara might not be good, but she was fast. There was no hope of scrapping it altogether and doing something completely new; deadline wouldn't allow it.

Ah well—the ones he should feel sorry for were Jay and the dancers of his company. They had already wasted hours and liters of sweat trying to make this dopey idea work . . . and were committed to performing the results in public, unarmed. All he had to—

She didn't say, "I love you" before she left.

He was going to give that some serious thought—but just then it came to him in a clap of thunder how something might be salvaged from this fiasco. Steal from that weird dream he'd had last night: scrap the fakey underwater visuals completely . . . and substitute mid-air. Instead of sea-bed, substitute a city-sized carpet of clouds, backlit. Individual clouds could billow and move *almost* the same way the stupid seaweed did, the way the dancers needed it to for the choreography to work. From time to time, clouds could part to reveal the ground far below. Sure, it had been done before—but not lately, and not by him. God damn, that might just make the nut. But could he get away with it? What about the abominable shark in the second movement?

Substitute a roc, perhaps? No, screw the details—
what did it do to the overall *feel?* Did the dance still
work with the music?

Well, hell, just about anything worked with that
twelve-tone noise. Or didn't, if you asked him. No,
it felt feasible. The essential artistic *wrongness* of
dancers moving normally while supposedly deep
underwater vanished now. If he had to, he'd write
all new music to match the dance—he could almost
hear it now, he certainly knew the choreography well
enough. "Jay! *I got it!*"

It took a while to establish communication; Jay was
in work-mode himself. But eventually they had recognized each other and agreed on a common language, and Rand floated his concept. Jay liked
it—said, in fact, that he had had a vaguely similar
dream himself only the week before. He sank a few
experimental harpoons into the idea before he would
get excited, but when it continued to hold air he
became nearly as elated as Rand.

But not quite. There is a special pleasure in solv-
ing a difficult puzzle that has baffled your big
brother. Jay had always been thirteen years older,
stronger, smarter and more successful. Rand did not
resent him, exactly: he had always been kind, sup-
portive and generous with his time and attention.
That they had had a childhood relationship at all had
been primarily Jay's doing; he'd seemed to really
enjoy having a brother to teach things to. He had
doubtless influenced Rand's career choice, and had
never (Rand was sure) insulted him by using his own
artistic clout to pull strings on Rand's behalf. And
they were as easy in each other's company as brothers

were supposed to be; the difference in their ages had not been relevant for decades.

And still, it was always pleasurable to pleasantly surprise the man.

Jay handed the group off to Francine, his dance captain and assistant choreographer, and took Rand to his own suite. Along the way they tossed the new concept back and forth like an intellectual medicine ball, firming it up considerably in the process.

"One thing that helps a lot," Rand said as the door sealed behind them, "this crew is really good."

Jay nodded enthusiastically. "Best of the two. They actually enjoy the pony shows as much as the art." The Shimizu offered two streams of dance entertainment to its guests: the high art on which Rand and Jay were collaborating, performed in the Nova Dance Theatre, and the "pony show"—essentially cabaret dance adapted for free-fall, sophisticated T&A—performed in the Dionysian Room. "I think of the two assistant ADs, Francine is the one who'll take over my job when I retire. The team you worked with last time is good too—but this team is the original. It's not just more hours logged: about a year ago something clicked and they meshed." He tossed Rand a bulb of cola, got a root beer for himself.

"That must be rare," Rand said.

"About like the odds of any twelve people in the same occupation falling in love and making it work."

The analogy, with its reminder of the collapse of Jay's relationship with Ethan, made Rand's good cheer begin to evaporate. Work had driven the crisis in his own marriage clear out of his mind—as he had hoped. Jay must have seen something in his face, because his next words were, "So how are things going with Rhea?"

"Honest to God, I don't know what to tell you, bro. She's adjusted to free-fall now, and she seems to like it here okay—but it's going to take more than that. All I can do is cross my fingers and pray that she falls head over heels in love with the place before the next month is up. Because if she doesn't, I'm screwed."

"It happens," Jay said sadly. "Happened to me: *I'm* in love with this dump. It sort of creeps up on you. Don't— "

"You weren't born in Provincetown." But he knew Jay was trying to cheer him up, and did his best. "That kid you picked to show her and Colly around *is* a good salesman, though."

Jay grinned. "If you're not careful, she'll fall head over heels in love with *him*. I'm kidding! As a matter of fact, I have it on good authority that he's, well . . . at least bi."

"That was my guess . . . just how good is your authority?"

"Don't be silly. A twenty-year-old? I'm old enough to be his . . . his . . ."

" . . . best lover yet. Come on, what have you got to lose?"

"A lot. You obviously haven't tried to keep up with a twenty-year-old lately. Anyway, I like 'em with muscles. We're wandering. Look, what I started to say was, don't change that diaper until you smell it. I know how much that house means to Rhea, and I know Provincetown is the most amazing place on Earth. But this is the most amazing place in space. Give her time."

"Well . . . I've got a surprise I've been working on for her in my spare time; I plan to spring it on her soon. Maybe tonight. It might just—"

"Phone, Jay," Diaghilev said. "Eva Hoffman, urgent."

Jay's face changed. "Oh, shit. Excuse me, bro. Sergei, give me privacy." Tugbots brought him earphones, hushmike and a monitor screen. He tossed Rand his holo remote and took the call. Rand passed the time by not-quite-watching flatscreen music videos from the Old Millennium, with the sound off, trolling for images to swipe.

He killed the screen when he heard Jay say, "Jesus Christ."

"Something wrong?"

His brother looked stricken. "One of my closest friends just decided not to die after all."

Rand looked at him. "Yeah, that'd be hard to take," he said solemnly.

Jay grinned, then frowned, then emitted a short burst of nervous laughter. "God, that sounds dumb, doesn't it?" He shook his head. "Maybe I've got the same problem she has. I just don't know how to deal with good news."

"Who are we talking about? Or should I ask?"

"Eva Hoffman."

Rand was shocked. "*She* was thinking of catching a cab? I always figured her for an honored guest at the Party at the End of the Universe. I'm glad she changed her mind. I like her a lot."

"Me too. She'll be at the special, tomorrow night."

"What special?"

The company was presently performing *Spatial*

Delivery, the piece he and Jay had co-created during his earlier residency; it would be played three nights a week and Sunday matinees until the new piece replaced it a month from now. But this was the first Rand had heard of a special performance.

"Oh shit, I haven't told you yet? Sorry; too many things on my mind. We're doing a command performance. A private concert. In the same theater, of course, but the rest of the goats get told the show is cancelled. Only uips and a handful of peasant vips admitted."

" 'Whips'?"

"Spelled *U*-I-P. Ultimately Important People."

Rand prepared himself not to be impressed. "Like who?"

"Chen Ling Ho. Imaro Amin. Grijk Krugnk. Chatur Birla. And Victoria Hathaway. The Fat Five, I call 'em."

It was hard to get air. "All of them? In the same room at the same time? They're gonna see my—our—piece?"

"Yep. Kate Tokugawa's been working on this visit for a month, in secret, and she wants all the trimmings. She authorized me to tell *you,* of course, but I plain forgot."

"What the hell are five of the most powerful people on Earth all doing here at the same time?"

Jay shook his head. "My guess is, historians will just be getting really involved in arguing about that forty years from now. Probably no one will ever know. Those folks can edit reality. And they do not like people knowing what they're doing. Especially before they've done it. Make damn sure you tell Rhea and

Colly not to tell anyone about the special until all five are dirtside again."

"Tell two women not to talk about the most exciting thing that's happened to them in weeks. Yeah, that'll work."

Jay grabbed him by the upper arm. "Listen to me. This is serious. If the presence of those five guests becomes public knowledge, while they're still here, you and I could both become unemployed real fast. If not worse. People have accidents in space."

Rand shook his arm free. "And an ordinary hotel guest like Eva Hoffman is invited to this top-secret performance?"

"Oh Christ, Rand, Eva isn't any ordinary guest, you know that. Eva is Eva. Even Kate is afraid of her. As a matter of fact, I think Eva's going to be there as a guest of Chen Ling Ho. Her and Reb Hawkins-roshi. Look, just trust me on this, okay? Tell Rhea and Colly not to discuss this, even with Duncan. After the Fat Five have left, they can brag all they want; by then security won't matter anymore. Between you and me, I suspect the news will be all over Shimizu within five minutes after they dock—but I do not want any leaks traceable to *us*. I like this job. And I'd like to get back to it, okay?"

"Okay. I'll tell them. Boot up Terpsichore and let's see how the new idea is going to work."

While Jay brought up the holographic choreography software, a collateral descendant of the original twentieth century Lifeforms program, and set up the parameters of Pribhara's wretched piece, Rand checked in with Salieri.

"How'm I doing, Salieri?"

"Rhea and Colly are expecting you for dinner at 19 o'clock in the Hall of Lucullus, but they will understand if you are late. I will remind you at 18:45. If you elect to keep working, I will inform them, and remind you to stop work and eat at 21 o'clock, using extreme measures if necessary."

"Excellent. Whenever I go home, remind me about that new window program just before I get to the door. Dismissed. Let me at that interface, Jay—see how you like this . . ."

Extreme measures proved necessary. By the time he got back to his suite, Colly was fast asleep, dreaming of angelfish making puffballs.

He was eager to show Rhea the surprise he had prepared. But she had a surprise of her own to show him first. "I was checking on . . . oh hell, what I was doing was snooping," she said gleefully, tapping a keyboard. The file she wanted displayed on the nearest wall. "And I found this in Colly's partition." It was a text document. At first he took it for one of Rhea's manuscripts, since it had been created with the same arcane, obsolete word-processing software she used. But then he saw the slug at the top of the file: *The Amazing Adventure,* by Colly Porter."

"It's a short story," she said, her delight obvious. "About a little girl who goes to space and defeats spies."

He grinned. "Oh, that's wonderful. And she didn't say anything to you about it?"

"Not a hint. Wait, let me show you the best part. . . ." She scrolled the document a page or two, found the place she wanted, and highlighted a portion of the text. It read: "But the truth was far from reality."

His bark of laughter triggered hers, and then they tried to shush each other for fear of waking Colly, and broke up all over again. The sequence ended with them in a hug, looking at the screen together in fond appreciation. "Is it any good?" he asked.

"Hard to tell; she hasn't finished it yet. But so far . . . for an eight-year-old . . . it's terrific."

"How long has she been working on it?"

She punched keys. "File created three days ago."

He was impressed. "And she's got, what, eight pages down? Jesus, that's amazing."

She nodded vigorously. "Damn right. Eight pages in three or four days is good output for *me*." She frowned. "Could we have raised one of those freaks who actually enjoy writing?"

He gave a theatrical shudder. "Could have been worse. At least it isn't heroin."

"That'd be cheaper. Ah well, she'll grow out of it. At her age I wanted to be a gymnast."

"Sure, I know. But it's still cute as hell. And you should still be flattered."

She hugged him closer and nuzzled his ear. "You watch: in another year or two, she'll be shaping. I'll go snooping through her files, and a monster will appear and bite me on the ass."

"And it'll serve you right," he said, nuzzling back. "Snooping. Despicable. You haven't been snooping in my partition, have you?"

She snorted. "As if I could outhack you. Why, is there anything interesting in there?"

He smiled. "Never accuse your husband of having a boring diary. Salieri!"

"Yes, Maestro?"

"Run file 'Home.'"

"Yes, sir."

"Take a look out the window, love." He pulled his head back slightly so he could watch her reaction. He was really proud of this idea, and had high hopes for it. He had set himself the question: *my wife is suffering, and it's my fault. What can a person of my special talents do about that?* This was the answer he had come up with after three days of thought. Because it was just a rough first draft, the visual image took a few seconds to coalesce and firm up, pixel by pixel. But somehow he got the idea she guessed what it was nearly at once, the moment she heard the soundscape. She stiffened in his arms.

Outside the window were Cape Cod Bay and Provincetown. The view from Rhea's upstairs turret writing-room window, back home. Bay to the left, stone dike sticking its tongue out at the horizon; P-Town in the center, the Heritage Museum's spire rising above the jumble of rooftops; and off to the right, the Pilgrim Monument. It was early evening there; a crescent moon was just rising over the water.

"That's not a simulation," he said quickly. "It's live, and real-time. Well, three-second switching delay." Somewhere a dog yapped. "See? That's the Codhina's rotten little Peke."

Something told him to shut up now. He studied her face. It was as though a gifted actress had been asked to do the audition of her lifetime in fifteen seconds. Every expression of which her features were capable passed across it in rapid succession. The only sounds were distant waves, winter winds, a few gulls, a passing car with a bad gyro and, over all, the sound of Rhea's deep breathing.

And when she finally settled on a reaction—silent, bitter tears—he only got to see it for a second before she left the suite at high speed.

Nice work. He breathed deeply himself for a minute. Then he jaunted to the window and gazed hard at Provincetown for a measureless time. Finally he shut down the display. "Salieri, let me speak to Rhea."

"She is not accepting calls, sir."

"Where is she?"

"Privacy seal, sir."

He nodded. He knew a couple of ways around that . . . but he decided he had already done enough stupid things for one day. If Rhea had wanted him to find her, she wouldn't have taken the trouble to invoke privacy seal.

He was too tired to deal with this much misery, and could not diminish or share it, so he took his work to bed with him, and fell asleep on the back of a cloud, winds whistling past his ears.

9

The Ring
Saturn

The Stardancer was unplugged from the Starmind, thinking with only her own brain. The vast System-wide flow of telepathic information from the millions of Stardancers who made up the Starmind passed through her, but she did not pay any conscious attention to it, and sent nothing back out into the matrix.

A year ago, something she still did not fully understand had told her that she needed to be still and meditate. She had been engaged in the form of meditation that worked best for her—dancing—continuously ever since. This sort of unplugging was not unusual; at any given time, as many as several thousand Stardancers might be out of rapport, dropping in or out of the matrix as suited them, and as they could be spared from ongoing tasks. Having accepted the alien gift of Symbiosis, they were all untroubled by the need to eat, drink or sleep, and were impervious to fatigue. Furthermore they were effectively immortal, or at least *very* long-lived, which tended to produce a meditative state of mind.

To an observer unfamiliar with Symbiosis, she might have seemed to resemble a human being in an old-fashioned, bulky red pressure suit—without air tanks or thrusters or transparent hood. But she was not human, anymore, and the red covering was literally a part of her; the organic Symbiote with which she had merged forty-four years earlier. Designed by the enigmatic alien Fireflies to be the perfect complement to the human metabolism, Symbiote protected against cold and vacuum, turned waste products into fuel, could be spun out at will into an effective solar sail . . . and conferred telepathy with all others in Symbiosis.

It also required sunlight, of course, like all living things. She was now, orbiting Saturn, almost as far as she could get from Sol without artificial life-support in the form of a photon source. But she did not feel cold . . . any more than she had felt hot when, decades earlier, she had traveled to the other extreme end of her range, the orbit of Mercury.

She had selected an orbit high enough above Saturn's mighty Ring to free her from concerns about navigational safety in that endless river of rock. Her visual field was perhaps the most beautiful the Solar System had to offer, so beautiful that she had almost ceased to see it. And even her harshest critic—herself—could not have said that her presence there detracted from the view, for she had been a gifted dancer even before she had entered Symbiosis. A tape of the past year's dancing would have fetched a high price on Earth. But this was hers and hers alone. As her body flung itself energetically through the near-vacuum, her mind was utterly still; she had long since reached that much-sought state in which one is not even thinking about not thinking. She was pure awareness, fully present yet leaving no trace.

Since she had once been a human being, there was a very primitive part of her mind which was never still for long, and in that part something like daydreaming took place from time to time. Sometimes it reached out across the immensity that engulfed her and touched the similar places in the minds of her most beloved ones, as if to reassure itself that they still existed and that all was well with them. As it went down the list, brushing against each mind, her dance unconsciously changed so as to express them and her relationship with them. Thus an occasionally recurring series of motifs ran through the dance: a sort of kinetic giggle that was her youngest child Gemma, followed by the syncopated, slightly off-rhythm movements that represented Olney Dvorak, the Stardancer she had conceived Gemma with . . . and so on, down to her eldest, forty-three-year-old Lashi, and his human father—

—it was at that point that her back spasmed and she screamed.

Any telepathic scream is strident and shocking enough; when it comes from one who has been in deep meditation for a year, every Stardancer in the Solar System flinches. And comes running to see what is wrong and what must be done about it. At once, the Starmind enfolded her like a womb, probing gently to learn the nature of her hurt.

But even she did not know.

The only clue was the word she had screamed: the name of her first co-parent. *I just touched him,* she told the others, *and suddenly I knew something was wrong. Everything is wrong.*

He was in the hookup, of course, and as baffled as she was. He reported that as far as he knew, nothing specific was wrong. He was in a region of great potential danger, but he had been there for half a century now. He was presently engaged in a delicate and complex task, with elements of almost inconceivable danger in it, but as far as he could tell it was shaping correctly.

Since there was absolutely no explanation for her terror, she could not shake it off. Unreasonable fears are the hardest to conquer. She wanted to scan and analyze every second of his memories of the last several weeks at least, looking for clues to the danger, but since he was not a full-fledged Stardancer she could not probe as deeply as she wanted. Their son Lashi joined her, and they probed together.

The results were still ambiguous.

So Lashi turned his attention to his mother. *When did you first become aware that something was wrong?*

When I screamed.

But how long before *that could something have gone wrong? When was the last time you had monitored Father?*

She thought about it. *Yesterday, I think. And everything was fine then.*

And we know what has changed in the last twenty-four hours. So we know where the danger lies.

Lashi's father said, *But why are they any more dangerous to me today than they were yesterday?*

I don't care, she wanted to say. *Can't you get out of there?* But she could not ask that, because she already knew the answer.

I don't know, she said instead. *But dammit, you be careful!*

You know I will, Rain, he replied.

PART FOUR

10

The Shimizu Hotel
7 January 2064

By the time Jay and his brother had finished a room-service dinner and separated for the night, it was 21:45. Jay tried to call Eva, but her phone was not even accepting messages. He and Rand had accomplished so much work that he decided to celebrate. He jaunted to Jake's, in the Deluxe Tier, one of the livelier of the Shimizu's twenty-one taverns—and one of only three in which off-duty employees were welcome. There he found some friends, and settled down to matching orbits with them.

He liked Jake's; he had become a semiregular there since Ethan left him for an earthworm. The management frowned on spilled blood or broken bones, but was tolerant of merriment short of that point. It was a great place to hear extravagant lies. One red-faced old man, for instance, a wildcat asteroid miner named Wang Bin who had come to the Shimizu to drink up a lucky strike, insisted on telling the whole room about a "white Stardancer" he claimed to have seen on his last trip out. "Damn near ran into him, no beacon or anything, spotted him by eyeball. Just like any other Stardancer, but white as a slug. Didn't even have the manners to acknowledge my hail." And a groundhog dancer from Terra who had joined Jay's table told them all a whopper about a broken ankle that had healed itself just in time for a curtain.

The dancer was attractive, close enough to his age and well built—but as Jay thought about making an approach, he realized he still wasn't ready. The memory of Ethan was still too clear. A few abortive experiments had reconfirmed for him that casual sex is best with oneself—certainly simpler.

A sense of duty made Jay leave sooner than he wanted to. As soon as he got back to his room, he tried Eva again. Considering the late hour, he did not expect to reach her; he hoped to leave a message requesting an appointment for a chat tomorrow. But the face that appeared onscreen was not Jeeves. Instead he saw a bald and beardless man who had done nothing to disguise the fact that he was well over ninety years old, dressed in black loose-fitting tunic and trousers.

"Hi, Reb," Jay said after a moment of surprise. "I heard you were coming over. How are things in Top Step?"

Reb Hawkins bent forward in the Buddhist *gassho* bow, then smiled warmly. "Hello, Jay. It's good to see

you again. Things are well in Top Step, I'm happy
to say. How is it with you these days?"

It had been a long day; Jay was too tired for tact.
"To be honest, Reb, I'm consumed with curiosity. Is
Eva still up?"

"She's gone to bed, but she told me to expect your
call. Why don't you come over for a cup? We haven't
talked in a while. Or are you too tired? I know you've
been working hard on the new piece."

Jay was torn. His brain hurt. But he did want to
know why his old friend had decided not to die after
all, and it was not the sort of question that could
be dealt with over the phone. "I'm on my way."

Hawkins-roshi was something of a legend in space.
He was a Zen Buddhist monk, and the oldest continuous resident of Top Step, the Earth-orbiting
asteroid where human beings came to enter Symbiosis. For over forty years, until his retirement, he
had helped hundreds of thousands of postulants make
that profound transition, from *Homo sapiens* to *Homo
caelestis*, with minimal psychological and spiritual
trauma. A cronkite had once referred to him as the
Modest Midwife to the Starmind. During those four
decades, he had also made regular visits to most of
the other human habitations in High Earth Orbit,
including the Shimizu, dispensing spiritual sustenance
and friendship to Buddhists and nonBuddhists alike.
He and Eva were old and close friends, had known
each other since they'd been groundhogs. Jay had
met Reb through her.

Almost the moment Eva's door had dilated behind
Jay, he was glad he had come. He had forgotten how
soothing Reb's presence could be. It was not merely

his obvious years; Jay was pretty sure Reb had had the same effect on people when he was a teenager. He simply had an almost tangible aura around him, projected a zone of serenity, of clarity, of acceptance. There is a quality dancers call "presence," and Jay was very good at achieving it onstage. Therefore he knew how amazing it was for Reb to have it all the time, every day. Presumably Hawkins-roshi had an automatic pilot, like everybody else . . . but he never seemed to use it. He would surely have long since been abbot of his own monastery somewhere down on Earth by now, if he had not found a career more important to him in space; helping human beings become something more.

"How long are you here for?" Jay asked him. "Can that big rock get along without you?"

Reb smiled. "Top Step can get along just fine without me. I'm retired, remember? It's Meiya's headache these days. I'll be here for a week, or until Eva throws me out, whichever comes first. I can use the vacation."

"I'm glad. I'd like to have a long talk with you sometime."

Reb nodded. "But not tonight. You're exhausted. You don't want any tea, do you? I'll make this as quick as I can. You want to know why Eva has changed her mind."

Jay nodded gratefully. "She told you she'd confided in me, then."

Reb nodded. "We talked for a long time. About suffering, and what it is for. About friendship, and what that is for. About what she has done since she came here to space, and what she might do yet. About samsara. In the end I was able to persuade her that to end one's life when one is not in mortal pain or fear is a kind of arrogance."

Jay stared. He had said much the same thing to Eva, in one form or another, at least a dozen times in the last month. "But Eva *is* arrogant," he blurted out.

Reb said nothing.

It came to Jay that perhaps Reb was just better than he was at teaching people about arrogance. Come to think of it, he was doing it now. . . .

"Well," Jay said lamely, "that's great, then. I'm glad you managed to get through to her. But I still don't see how you—"

"How do you *feel* about Eva's new decision?" Reb interrupted quietly. "If you don't mind my asking."

One of the problems with talking with holy men was their uncanny habit of putting a finger—gently, nonthreateningly—right on your sore spots. Another was the difficulty of successfully bullshitting them. "Ambivalent," he admitted.

Reb nodded. "I can see why. What a mix of emotions you must have felt, when she asked you to dance at her dying."

Jay nodded vigorous agreement. "Oh God, yes! Sad, of course, but also proud to have been asked, and annoyed at the extra workload, and creatively stimulated, and . . . and Reb, I'm almost as confused right now. I'm glad we're not going to lose her. But I've just gone through a month of trauma and grief reconciling myself to the idea that we were . . . and I've wasted hours of work on a piece that now may never get performed, at a time when I was already up to my ass in alligators . . . and—"

"And?"

"—and if you want to know the truth, a part of me resents the hell out of *you,* for accomplishing in one conversation what I've failed to do in a month of trying. I mean, I know this is your line of work—but she and I have been friends a long time. Part of me wants to kick you—and then go wake her up and punch her in the nose."

Reb grinned. "You're welcome to kick me. But if you feel you must wake Eva, make sure your insurance is paid up first. Whatever Eva's brain may be thinking at any given moment, her body's survival instincts are strong . . . and I happen to know she fights dirty."

"Yeah, I know." Jay had once seen a foolish person behave rudely to Eva. He lived.

"Think of it this way. A man tries to split a tough piece of wood with an ax. He strikes again and again, day after day, with no result. Then another man comes along and takes a tentative swing. The wood splits with a loud crack. Did the first man play no part?"

"Well . . . sure, he did. But he's going to feel frustrated as hell."

"So you didn't just want Eva not to die; you wanted the credit for changing her mind. Be content with partial credit, all right?"

Jay laughed ruefully. "You're right. I'm being silly."

"Also known as the human condition. You're tired and high. Go to bed, and in the morning you'll be a much more admirable human being. I'll be impressed, I promise."

Jay laughed out loud. Reb could always jolly him

out of a sulk. "You're right. Uh . . . look, tomorrow's going to be hectic. Could you ask Eva if she can set aside time for a visit with me the day after tomorrow?"

"I'll tell Jeeves."

"Thanks. And could you and I have a talk the day after that?"

"Whenever you like. I'm going to be busy myself tomorrow, but the rest of the week is pretty much open. Diaghilev and Rild can work out a time."

"Good. I'll see you then."

"And I'll see you tomorrow night at the performance," Reb said.

"Oh, right. I should have known you'd be on the comp list."

They exchanged bows, and Jay left. On the way home his thoughts were so scattered that he let Diaghilev navigate for him. Eva's sudden flip-flop just seemed so weird, so . . . arbitrary. Rhea would have said that it didn't ring true artistically. *Eva spends sixteen years making up her mind, withstands a month of argument from me . . . and then Reb shows up and tells her suicide isn't nice, and she folds?* There had to be more to it than that. What else had Reb said to her? All Jay could think of to do was to ask her at his first opportunity.

As he jaunted along, he remembered some of Reb's closing words. "Diaghilev and Rild can work out a time." Jay was struck by that now. Reb met thousands of people a year, juggled trillions of details . . . and had remembered the name of Jay's AI without checking. He himself had forgotten that Reb called his own AI "Rild"—and had never gotten around to following up his original mental note to find out what that name signified. Whereas he was willing to bet that Reb knew not only who Sergei Diaghilev had been, but exactly what he symbolized for Jay. Perhaps here was a clue as to why Reb had succeeded with Eva where he had failed. Reb retained every detail of what people told him, and followed them up, thought them through. "Sergei," he said suddenly, "who did Reb Hawkins name his AI for?"

"I don't know, Jay. Shall I find out?"

"Please."

"Waiting . . . The only match I find on file is a character in a twentieth-century novel called LORD OF LIGHT, by Roger Zelazny. Rild was student of the Buddha, a former assassin who came to surpass his master in enlightenment."

The answer was interesting—but what caught Jay's attention was its first word. It had taken Diaghilev a startlingly long time—nearly two whole seconds—to tap into the vast memory cores of the Net. It was late at night; most guests and staff were asleep. Someone must be using a hell of a lot of bandwidth and processing power for something.

Of course. The Fat Five were inboard. When Leviathan swims under your boat, the sea swells.

He was essentially asleep before he reached his suite; Diaghilev guided him inside, sealed the door, undressed him, administered hangover preventative, and strapped him into his sleepsack so that he would not wake with the classic free-fall stiff neck. His dreams were full of Stardancers . . . millions upon countless millions of them, swarming around Terra like moths around a fire, staining the ionosphere red with their numbers.

The next day began with an omen, to which he paid insufficient attention.

"Huh? Whazzit?"

"I'm sorry, Jay," Diaghilev said, "but Evelyn Martin insists on speaking to you at once."

Jay suggested some other things Martin could do instead; Diaghilev pointed out that they were physically impossible. "Not for him they aren't. All right, all right: audio only, accept. What the fuck do you want?"

"You're not archiving tonight, right?" Martin's nasal voice demanded.

"Oh, for Christ's sake." From time to time, especially if he had made any alterations in the choreography, Jay would have a concert recorded for archival purposes—and some of the camera angles would include the faces of the audience. Martin was afraid he might do so tonight, with the Fat Five in the house. As a matter of fact, he had been planning to. "Of course not. Anyway, what's the difference? By the time the tapes are edited, the uips will be long gone, and the fact that they've been here won't be secret anymore."

"Doesn't matter," Martin said. "Just promise me the cameras stay off tonight. If you want to swear it on your mother's grave, I won't mind."

"Do you have any idea what time it is?"

"I don't give a shit. I've been up all night, swimming in a river of shit upside down, and the tide's still coming in: they come aboard in a couple of hours. I feel like that little Dutch kid that used to go around sticking his finger in lesbians; if it ain't one thing it's six others. On top of everything else I had a guest croak on me a couple of hours ago, like I got nothing else to do—"

"A guest died?" That was unusual. The Shimizu had diagnostics and emergency medical facilities as good as anything on Terra; it would take something like an exploding bullet to the brain to defeat them. The saying was, *You couldn't die here if you tried.* "How did he manage that?"

"Genius. Apparently he built the comm gear in his p-suit himself. So he's outside taking a stroll, and he goes to put in a call to his heap, up at the dock. Only his homemade antenna slips out of alignment when his homemade power supply blows up, so he microwaves his frontal lobe instead. So now I got to grease all the news weasels to forget to file the story, and rummage through the antheap down there to find his dirtbag relatives and grease *them*—"

Jay did not want to hear about french-fried brains and PR men's problems before coffee. "Who was he?" he interrupted. "Anybody I'd know?"

"Nah—just checked in yesterday. Some old rock rat who struck it rich, and decided to spend his fortune and the last minutes of his life making mine miserable. Why the hell couldn't the inconsiderate bastard have poached his brains out there in the Belt somewhere, where it wouldn't have been my problem?"

Alcoholic memory stirred. "Wait a minute. Chinese guy? Wang something?"

"How the hell did you know?" Martin sounded suspicious.

"I ran into him at Jake's last night. He was telling us all some yarn about a white Stardancer."

"Jesus Christ—keep that quiet, will you? It's gonna
be hard enough sitting on this, and those bastards
love anything with a Stardancer hook, gives 'em great
visuals to cut to. 'White Stardancer,' my ass—the old
fart's probably been sautéeing his cerebrum for weeks
now, and only just finished the job this morning. Hey,
that's it—if he was already brain-damaged when he
got here, we got no liability at all—"

This triggered Jay's gag reflex. "I'll keep the cameras off tonight, Ev," he said, and cut the connection. Getting back to sleep was out of the question
now, so he called for coffee, unstrapped himself from
his sleepsack, and began his day.

Twelve extremely hectic hours later, he met Rand
and his family at their suite and journeyed with them
to the Nova Dance Theatre. All were dressed in their
finest, and the adults were as nervous as if they were
about to go onstage themselves. They chattered along
the way, and fiddled with their seams and fastenings,
and inspected each other for unseen flaws in cos-
tume or makeup. Only Colly seemed to take it all
in stride; money and power did not impress her, since
she did not use the former and had all she presently
wanted of the latter.

They had to pass a checkpoint to reach the foyer,
manned by six very serious-looking guards, each
wearing different-colored armbands. No weapons
were visible, but it was clear that they were available. Jay noticed with amusement that the guards
seemed to watch each other as carefully and

constantly as they did the civilians. Five private security forces, plus the Shimizu security, and none of them trusted any of the others.

And indeed, when they had passed thumbprint and retina checks and entered the foyer, Nika, the tech director, approached them before Jay could even begin trying to spot the uips. "Boss," she said, "how the hell am I supposed to call the show with a six-pack of gorillas looking over my shoulder, frowning every time I touch something?"

"Jesus," Jay muttered. "They're even back in the tech hole?"

"They seem to think it's their fucking command center," she said bitterly. "And there's more six-packs at every entrance and exit to this area, plus one at each stage wing. I don't care about them, as long as none of the dancers crash into them when they exit, but can't you get me a little elbow room in the hole?"

Jay thought about it. "I don't think so, Nika. They're right; that area has to be secured. If I were an assassin, backstage is the way I'd come in. Do the best you can, okay? At least Rand and I won't be in there with all of you; we're watching this one from the house. Just tell the goons not to touch anything while the concert's running."

"None of them would dare. The other five would shoot him. They get nervous every time *I* touch a control. Honest to God, I never saw such a paranoid bunch in my life."

"If you needed bodyguards, wouldn't you want them to be paranoid? I have to go—"

Nika jaunted off, frowning, and Jay caught up with

Rand and his family. They were just being presented
to the honored guests by Katherine Tokugawa.

"Mr. Imaro Amin . . . Pandit Chatur Birla . . . Honorable Chen Ling Ho . . . Ms. Victoria Hathaway . . .
Citizen Grijk Krugnk . . . please permit me to present
the Shimizu's Co-Artistic Directors: our resident choreographer, Mr. Jay Sasaki, and our resident Shaper,
Rand Porter." All bowed. Jay was amused again. Kate
had solved an impossible protocol problem in the only
way she could—by introducing the five uips to her
vips in alphabetical order. . . .

"We bid you welcome to Nova Dance Theatre,
lady and gentlemen," Rand said smoothly. "It gives
me great pride to present my wife, the author Rhea
Paixao, and our daughter, Colly."

More bows all around. "I read your last book,
AND CALL HER BLESSED, with great pleasure,
Ms. Paixao," Birla said.

"So did I," Hathaway said, "and it was wonderful. Even better than THE FREE LUNCH."

"I would have to agree," Birla said, "although it
is a close call. I have conversations with characters
of yours all the time."

Rhea thanked them, turning a fetching shade of
pink. The compliments had to be genuine: the uips
had not expected to meet her, and had no reason
to stroke her if they had. Jay was stunned to learn
that people as rich as this read fiction for pleasure—
two of them, anyway. And while Rhea had a good
and growing literary reputation, she had never yet
had a top-ten bestseller: you had to *care* about good
books to know of her work. Interesting. Uips were
not automatically philistines. Rand caught his eye and

grinned, and Jay knew precisely what he was thinking: *if they like Rhea's stuff, they'll like ours*.

While the conversational pleasantries flowed back and forth, Jay studied these five people who could make Kate Tokugawa snap to attention. He had never met a whole handful of trillionaires before.

Amin was a Kikuyu financier from Kenya, said to be the only African trillionaire. Of average height and mass, he was in his early forties and looked thirty, except for his eyes; he was the most obviously vicious of the five. His hair was straightened, but paradoxically his skin tone was artificially *darkened*, to a Bantu black which did not match his nose and cheek structure. His fortune was based on Earth-to-orbit shipping. He ignored the arbitrary local vertical which everyone else had adopted—the Terrans from habit, the spacers out of politeness—and just let himself drift free.

Birla, a swarthy Marwari from Rajputna, was the talker of the group, which made him seem more trivial than he could possibly have been. He was a hundred and twenty—four years older than Eva!—and looked forty. According to the bio Jay had scanned, he was ostensibly a devout Hindu, but he seemed in no hurry at all to reincarnate. The friendly twinkle in his eyes had to be fake, but it was a good fake. He owned as large a proportion of the Terran and orbital media as the UN would let him, and influenced even more; Evelyn Martin hovered near him solicitously, ready to open a vein on request.

Chen Ling Ho, a Mandarin from Beijing, was fifty and looked fifty. He was short to the point of tininess, smaller than Kate, and looked as benign and childlike as Colly. Jay had read that his enemies called him The Krait. He was also the Zen Buddhist at whose request Reb Hawkins had been invited to the Shimizu. That interested Jay: there were many Chinese Buddhists, but few who followed the Soto path, which had originated in twelfth-century Japan. Chen was a grandson of the legendary Chen Ten Li, the twentieth-century statesman who had been present at the creation of the Starmind; heavy (and early) family investment in nanotechnology had made Ten Li rich beyond measure. In defiance of tradition, it had been the *second* generation—his son Chen Hsi Feng who had nearly succeeded in destroying the family name and fortune, by becoming an antiStardancer fanatic and launching a treacherous and doomed attack on the Starmind. Ling Ho, the third generation, had miraculously managed to salvage most of the wreckage, largely thanks to adroit fence-mending with the Starmind. That doubtless accounted for his conversion to Reb Hawkins's faith. Jay wondered how many trillionaire Zen students there were.

Victoria Hathaway was a WASP from New York; calendar age eighty-seven, apparent age just under thirty. She looked like holo stars wished they looked—but there was a coldness in her eyes and mouth that made Jay think of her as a long sleek shiny pair of scissors, with a carefully trimmed little tuft of pubic hair just at the place where the blades joined. Most of her money was said to be in real estate, on and off Terra, and she was famous for both her ruthlessness and her absolute lack of any vestige of a sense of humor—though no one dared mention the latter quality to her face.

Grijk Krugnk was by far the ugliest of the lot, a Slav of some kind from Votoskojek who was sixty-six and looked fiftyish. He was built like a power plant, but not as pretty, so obviously a brute that many had found him fatally easy to underestimate. His wealth sprang from power generation, most of it spaceborne. Oddly, he was the only one of the five whose English was utterly unaccented, like a cronkite's. He handled himself in free-fall as well as Amin, but made less of a point of it. His complexion must have been ruddy on earth; in zero gee his face looked like a tomato.

Each of the five had a personal bodyguard, and all but Chen had an additional companion as well. These latter were introduced, but Jay didn't bother to remember any of the names; they were obviously AIs with a pulse. The killers were not introduced, as it might have distracted them. Chen's bodyguard seemed to be the only one with any extensive space experience: Jay noticed that he watched feet as well as hands. That made his boss the smartest of the five uips.

"Is there anything you would like to tell us about the work we are about to see, Mr. Sasaki? Mr. Porter?" Birla asked, snapping Jay out of his reverie. Rand let him take it.

"No, sir," he said. "If it doesn't speak for itself, then nothing I could say will help. Shall we go in?"

Perhaps taking their cue from Tokugawa's introduction, the five uips entered the theater in alphabetical order. Once inside, things got briefly complicated again.

This piece, *Spatial Delivery*, had been staged for

proscenium performance, rather than in the sphere. That is, it was designed so that the audience used only half of the available "seating" area, strapping their backs to a common hemisphere, and the piece was performed against the backdrop of the other half. This cut audience capacity in half, but was a lot easier to choreograph and shape than a spherical piece which had to look good from all possible angles at once.

But if five people sit against a hemisphere, and keep pretending that there is a local vertical, then some of them must sit "above" others.

After a few seconds of backing and filling, the five decided face was more important than up and down, and solved the problem by making a puffball, like a two-dimensional version of Colly's beloved angel-fish. Lesser mortals filled in the gaps between them in whatever orientation suited them. Jay sat with Rand and his family in the center. He saw Eva nearby, and waved; she waved back.

The house lights dimmed, Rand's overture began, and Jay forgot anything as trivial as trillionaires.

The first half went very well. Emerging from his warm fog to the realization that he must make small talk during the intermission was like being dumped from a snug bed into an icy vacuum.

And indeed it developed that the intermission chatter of uips was every bit as inane and clumsy as that of the mere vips Jay was used to. They all liked it so far, of course, and said so—but for all the wrong reasons, some that Jay would never have thought of in a million years. Intermissions always made Jay wish he had taken up engineering, or any trade where the customer's wishes were possible to fathom. Talking to civilians usually reminded him forcefully that no artist ever succeeds save by dumb luck. Since he believed the purpose of art was to communicate, this tended to depress him slightly.

Five minutes before the end of the interval, he excused himself from the gathering, saying that he needed to check something with his technician backstage. Rand seized the opportunity to accompany him, ignoring his wife's brief look of dismay, and they jaunted back into the empty theater together.

There were four "wings," short cylindrical tunnels of invisibility created by Rand's shaping gear, at the four cardinal points of the terminator that divided audience from stage. Dancers seemed to materialize as they entered, vanish as they exited. Knowing that two of the wings would be blocked by knots of dancers nerving themselves up to go on for the second act, Jay and Rand picked one of the other two at random.

And nearly got themselves shot by trigger-happy guards. "Jesus, folks, relax," Jay said. "There won't even be anybody out there to protect for another five minutes yet. Why don't you safety those damned things until then? I don't want you drilling one of my dancers on their way to the can." Shaking his head, he passed on until he came to the tech hole, which was located at the farthest point of the theater, so that its one-way glass looked out past the dancers toward the audience. In fact, he and Rand had nothing to accomplish here; Nika had this piece on tracks by now. The tech hole was simply the nearest place to hide for a few minutes.

Not wanting to risk being shot again, he paused at the door and touched the intercom button. "It's me and Rand, Nika," he said. "Coming in."

The door opened on horror.

Five bodies, drifting limp in free-fall crouch. Jack-in-the-box effect made them move toward him as the door swung open. Nika was one of them. A barely perceptible bitter odor preceded them; Jay could not identify it but knew it was trouble. "Oh, *shit,*" Rand said behind him.

"Hold your breath," he snapped, and leaped into the hole. The room's air system had already scavenged up most of the bitter gas, but who knew how much it took to immobilize a man?

He did not have time to find out if any of the floating bodies were alive; more urgently he needed to know who was missing. Sure enough, the worst possible: the Shimizu's man. His brain raced. The assassin had planned to kill from here, firing through the one-way glass into the house. At Jay's announcement he had bolted out one of the other two doors from the hole—seconds ago. His only move now was to cut through another six-pack somehow, enter the theater through one of the four wings, leave by the audience entrance, and try to kamikaze whomever his intended victim was out in the foyer. But *which wing?* Presumably he knew which two were mobbed with dancers; he had been hanging out in the hole. And if Nika had had her mikes hot . . . he knew which wing was guarded by a six-pack *who had just been told to safety their weapons.* By Jay! The son of a bitch could have circled around behind them while they were gaping in the open door of the hole. . . .

"Make an announcement," he brayed at Rand, and pointed to Nika's board and mike.

"What do I say?"

"Run for your fucking lives!" He left the hole at full thruster power.

He began deep breathing as he left the hole—can't have too much oxygen in a crisis—but within seconds he held his breath again as he detected more of that bitter smell ahead. The assassin had had a second gas-bomb—and kept it to use where it would do him the most good. As Jay came around the curve he saw the six-pack he had passed moments earlier, drifting with the air-currents. He wanted to decelerate to a stop and peer cautiously into that magic tunnel before entering it—but he was traveling so fast he'd have had to overshoot it and beat back, and he just didn't have the time. Instead he threw himself into a power turn and rocketed right into it at max acceleration.

That probably saved his life. The assassin was still in the tunnel, waiting to scrag Jay the moment his head showed. But Jay arrived like a right hook, smashing solidly into him before he could fire. They recoiled from each other violently, and the assassin lost his grip on his weapon, a hand laser. But there was no gravity to take it away; it kept station with him as he tumbled, and he grabbed it again on the second flailing try.

The assassin was a very good shot. But Jay was a very good dancer—and fortunately the gun was a pulse job rather than a garden-hose-type continuous-beam laser. He twisted, arched, feinted, leaped, contracted, and bolts of shining death missed him by centimeters. He had one further advantage: he could use all four thrusters, while the assassin had to reserve one wrist for aiming. Thank God the man seemed to be out of knockout bombs.

But Jay could not hope to close; it was all he could do to stay alive. And any second his luck must run out. He could leap through the imaginary wall of the tunnel, but the killer would only follow. Any minute now the nearest six-pack would arrive behind him, and none of them would hesitate to fire through him even if they identified him as a friendly. Jay had time to realize that he was going to die protecting people he did not like or even respect, and then the tunnel had a blowout. A hole the size of a Frisbee appeared in its wall with a plosive *phuff*, jagged metal teeth pointing outward; the shriek of escaping air tore at their ears and pressure began to drop.

Of course it is impossible for a holographic cylinder to have a blowout, and in any case the nearest vacuum was hundreds of meters away. But both men were spacers; they reacted quite instinctively, dropping their quarrel and leaping for the hole together to seal it with their bodies if necessary. Only one of them remembered on the way that the greatest shaper in human space was presently in the tech hole, and that this tunnel belonged to him.

11

Eva was the first to enter the tunnel; nearly at once she reversed thrust and recoiled backward into Reb, who was at her heels. A weapon she was not licensed to possess vanished from her hand. Jay had clearly coped. Even her atrophied sense of smell could detect the odors of burned metal and burned meat.

"Nice work," she said. "Remind me not to piss you off."

Jay's eyes met hers, but it took him a second or two to recognize her. "I got him," he said wonderingly.

That much was clear. The body that floated between them was so obviously a corpse that Eva's subconscious had ignored the gun it still clutched in one hand. Boiling brains leave a skull any way they can. Jay had a small smear of suet on his right cheek that must have burned him as it struck, but he didn't seem to be aware of it. Eva threaded her way through horrid drifting tendrils of brains and blood and took Jay in her arms. "That you did," she said soothingly, wiping his cheek. "That you did."

Rand arrived just then; at Eva's signal he left Jay to her. She gestured again, and he and Reb took charge of the body, towing it backstage, shooing its gore along with it.

Sure enough, Rhea and Colly were the next to arrive. At the alarm, all five uips had ducked for cover and their guards had clustered around them, and mere vips had struggled to get away from them, and Tokugawa and Martin had called for information—but Rhea and Colly had both realized they had family in the firezone. Rhea hadn't been able to stop her daughter, but had gotten—barely—ahead of her to shield her from possible fire. Eva moved so that she and Jay blocked their way. "He's fine," she said quickly. "Wait here for him."

Rhea was frantic. "I've got to—"

"You've got to wait here," Eva said, indicating Colly with her eyes.

"I—yes, okay." She got a firm grip on Colly. "He's really all right?"

"Not a scratch, truly."

"He saved my life," Jay said.

"And others," Eva agreed. "Both of you did. I'm surprised at you, Jay—I thought you had more sense than to be a hero."

"I had to," he said. "It was partly my fault."

She put a hand over his mouth. "He's delirious," she said to Rhea. "All the adrenalin." She turned back to Jay, put her lips to his ear. "As your attorney,

I advise you to shut the hell up. You are not competent to assess blame."

He blinked at her. "You're not an attorney, Eva."

"The hell I'm not. I'm licensed for the High
Court—and if you don't start zipping your lip I'm
going to need to be. When they get here, you tell
them facts only, get it? Facts only. You can draw
conclusions when you're thinking more clearly.
Okay?" She shook his shoulders. "Okay?"

"Sure, Eva. Facts only. That's good." She studied
him carefully, decided he was not quite in shock in
the medical sense—but close.

The tunnel went away; Rand must have reached
the tech hole. Almost at once they were hip-deep
in people, all talking at once—all five uips, assorted
assistants and bodyguards, the Shimizu's security
chief, the house physician. The loudest by a good
margin was Martin. Eva bellowed for silence, but her
tired old lungs weren't equal to the task.

Reb's amplified voice filled the theater like the
voice of God. "Ladies and gentlemen, please compose yourselves. There is no longer any reason for
alarm. An attempted assassination has failed, and the
situation is under control. Please return to the foyer
as quickly and quietly as you can; emergency personnel will be arriving and you are in their way. You
will all receive a detailed report when things have
clarified."

Rand's voice joined him. "Dancers, please join our
guests in the foyer and escort them to the reception room. The rest of tonight's concert is canceled."

The tumult of attempted conversation became
even louder—but at Martin's physical insistence, they

at last began moving away, with Tokugawa in the lead. Rand told Rhea to take Colly back to their suite, and she agreed without argument. Dr. O'Regan and Chief Cruz remained behind. "Who was it?" Cruz asked.

"One of yours," Eva said. "Dunno which—he didn't have his face with him."

Cruz's face darkened. "I know which. Shit. Where'd they take him, the tech hole?"

"I think so." She turned to Jay. "Can you stand another look at the son of a bitch? Chief Cruz needs you to show her what happened."

"Oh sure," he said.

As they left the tunnel, they had to duck around tumbling bodies and a few severed limbs—but fortunately no more horrid trails of blood, as laser amputation tends to self-cauterize. Eva noticed how hard Cruz had to work to ignore the one in Shimizu livery.

Cruz made them wait briefly outside the tech hole. Two crime-scene technicians and three interns all arrived at once; she and the doctor went inside with them. The security chief emerged with Rand in less than a minute, scowling blackly. The conference took place there in the corridor. Cruz—mortified that one of her own people had been the killer—obviously wanted Eva gone, but did not dare try to chase her out. Eva did not even have to claim status as Jay's attorney of fact; a steely glance was all it took. She and Cruz had taken each other's measure a long time ago.

So she was able to ride herd on Jay. She was fond of the boy, and his raving about the attempted assassination being partly his fault had unsettled her. If Cruz had heard that, the questioning might well have taken place under drugs. At Eva's direction, Jay gave a baldly factual account of what had occurred. She spotted what he had meant as soon as he said it—"I told them to safety their damned weapons and continued on to the hole"—but of course no one else saw any blame in that. It was what anyone might have said in his place. She was glad she had gotten to him first.

"Pity you couldn't have taken him alive," Cruz said, when Jay had finished the story and Rand had added events from his perspective. "I hate to let someone kill a dozen people in my care without asking him who paid for it."

"I was dead," Jay said, "and then Rand gave me a split-second advantage. I didn't think about it. I grabbed his gun hand and made him shoot himself under the chin. I'd do it again."

"Oh, I wasn't criticizing! *Do* it again, if there's a next time."

Eva snorted at that. If Jay had not gotten lucky, Cruz would have had more dead—and perhaps a dead uip or two as well—and would have been looking for work tomorrow.

"I wish he was still alive too," Jay said. "So I could kill him again. Nika's . . . Nika was special." Suddenly he shook his head with great violence. "Jesus! Did that really happen?" He giggled.

"You've got everything you need for now, right, Chief?" Eva said.

Cruz frowned, but nodded. "I may want to hypno him tomorrow."

"Gotta wait for it to seep into long-term storage for hypno to do any good," she agreed. "Jeeves—"

"Yes, madam?" He shimmered into existence, urbane and unflappable.

"Take Mr. Sasaki home. My place, not his. Bunk him down in my bed and make me a doss in Guest Room Two."

"Very good, madam. If you would be good enough to follow me, sir . . ."

"Half a mo." She motioned Jay close and murmured in his ear. "Want Jacques to join you?"

He blinked at her and struggled with the question. Jacques's job description read, "hedonic technician"—but Eva happened to know that he was more artist than technician, a natural healer and comforter. "No," Jay said, and then, "I don't think so," and then he blushed slightly and said, "Uh . . . yes. Please."

She nodded. "Tell Jeeves. Run along now."

Once he was gone, she turned back to Cruz. "How did you know who the assassin was?"

"Eh?"

"You said, 'I know which.' How did you know?"

"Oh. Savannavong only joined the force a month ago. I wouldn't have used him on this job, for that reason—but Hanh came down sick this afternoon and I was stretched thin."

"Savannavong was real good at making people come down sick," Rand said bitterly. "Hanh got lucky."

"So did you two," Cruz said. "You both reacted like trained cops. Either of you ever in service?"

"I did two years with NYPD. Draftee. But that was over twenty years ago, and I never drew my

weapon in the line of duty. Jay's never had any kind
of combat training, to my knowledge. We just kept
making mistakes until the bastard was dead."

"You'd better get home," Eva said. "Your wife still
doesn't know the details."

"Chief?"

"Go ahead."

Rand threw her a grateful glance and made his
escape.

People were coming and going from the tech hole
now, bringing in forensic equipment and taking out
corpses. But they gave the glowering Chief Cruz a
wide berth; for the moment Eva was effectively alone
with her. "Does your thumb hurt, Chief?" Eva asked
suddenly.

"Eh? Yes it does—why? How did you know?"

"Because I figure you for an honest cop. The
moment that alarm sounded, an honest cop in your
shoes would have pushed a button and flooded the
whole damn theater and backstage area with sleepy
gas."

"I did! Some son of a bitch had—"

"I know. It didn't work, so you kept pushing; that's
why your thumb hurts."

Cruz nodded slowly. "I see." She thought some
more. "Well, it wouldn't have helped anyway; the
bastard obviously had nose filters in."

Eva nodded. "Like you do. But you didn't know
that at the time. An honest cop couldn't have."

"But why disable the sleepy gas if he had filters?"

"So he'd have maximum confusion to escape in
after he made his kill? Squawking civilians in all
directions."

"God dammit, Eva—"

"Relax, Rani—I'm on your side. I know this whole episode makes you look like a horse's ass, but I can't think of anything you could've done better. And I'll tell Kate Tokugawa that, if you like. But if I were you, I'd have Dr. O'Regan document that thumb sprain."

She left Cruz and went to the reception, curious to see how the ultimately rich responded to a brush with death. Six cronkites ambushed her just outside the door, looking like children who needed to urinate; the first in line named a figure. "No comment," she said. He named a second figure, and when she refused that too, a bidding war developed. She brushed through them grandly and entered the hall. Guards prevented them from following; frustrated, they all jaunted off to file what little they already had.

The party had that slightly forced gaiety which screams of fear just past. But the uips themselves seemed the calmest people in the room—except for Reb, of course. In fact, the only person who still showed any overt signs of fear was Evelyn Martin, grinning and sweating and talking even faster than usual. He spotted her, detached himself and came over.

"Hi, Eva," he said loudly. "So glad you could make it." Sotto voce he added, "Anything else gone wrong out there? Any more assassins come to squeeze my ulcers? Fresh stiffs? Other major felonies? Chief Cruz find out the assassin is a High Council member or anything like that?"

"Good news," she said. "No news." Louder, she added. "Awful to see you, Evelyn. You're looking uglier than usual tonight."

He beamed. "Thank you, dear——have you met our honored guests? Chen Ling Ho, for instance?"

"Get a grip, Evelyn. I introduced *you* to Ling. Why don't you go take a trank?"

"I'm at system max now," he said.

"Take stimulants, then. Your voice will rise above the audible range and you won't be so conspicuous." She drifted away, and joined her escort, Dr. Chen. He was chatting with Reb and Victoria Hathaway. Chen introduced her to Hathaway—who regarded her aged features with barely concealed horror.

"Hello, dear," Eva said. "It's nice to see you again."

"We've met?" Hathaway said, disbelieving but polite.

"I knew your grandmother. You peed on my lap once."

Hathaway gave the only possible reply: dead silence.

Chen intervened. "Eva, have they determined yet who was the assassin's intended target?"

She shrugged. "For all Cruz can tell at this point, he was a good guy, come to take out Evelyn Martin on behalf of all mankind."

That got a laugh; even Hathaway almost smiled. "I assume the man's background is being checked?"

Eva shrugged again. "Sure. But it's a waste of time. The background check you have to go through to get hired for Shimizu security can't be improved on. Serious money went into this." She made sure her gaze was not resting on either Chen or Hathaway.

"I will bet cash the person who hired it done is in this room."

Hathaway flinched, but Chen only nodded. "The probability is high," he agreed.

"Was it you, Chen?" Hathaway asked bluntly.

Again Chen looked as if he were remembering what it felt like to smile. "Twelve dead, none of them the right one? I'm offended, Victoria. Can you truly believe me so inartistic?"

"Oh, but you can believe it of *me*, right?"

"Since you ask, yes. Now we are both offended. Shall we seek another topic of conversation?"

Eva had a mischievous thought. "Unless you'd like me to narrow the list of suspects for you," she said.

"How?" Chen and Hathaway and Reb all asked simultaneously.

"Well, only theoretically. I don't actually expect, uh, people of your caliber to submit to a body search. But I'll bet a dead frog the person who hired that killer is wearing nose filters. He or she knew the killer would be covering his escape with death gas, and might have been forced to flee past his employer. Nose filters that go in far enough to be invisible aren't easily removed."

Hathaway objected. "That wouldn't prove a thing. Any of us might be wearing nose filters out of simple paranoia. In light of events, it would seem an intelligent precaution."

Eva nodded. "But you're probably not *all* filtered. I said 'narrow the list,' not nail it down. Irrelevant anyway; none of you will tolerate a search on principle—and I don't blame you."

"Then why did you bring it up?" Hathaway snapped.

Eva did not answer. But she was already enjoying the mental picture. As the word spread, the five would spend the next hour discreetly trying to peer up each other's nostrils. Victoria Hathaway might actually not look down her nose at anyone for the rest of the night.

Reb escorted her home. They took double-bulbs of Irish coffee to the window, and sat looking out at Mother Terra in companionable silence for some time.

"Jeeves," she said then, "is Jay awake?"

"He and Master Jacques are both sound asleep, madam."

"Thank you. Let me know if he wakes." He shimmered away again, and she turned to Reb. "That bedroom is soundproof anyhow."

Reb nodded. "Go ahead."

"I need a better cover story for him. About why I'm still using up air. Oh, you did a good job. But I heard his voice, and he didn't really buy it, deep down. I'm afraid I shot my mouth off to him about why I was planning to take a cab. He's not going to be satisfied with what you told him. And I don't know what else to say. The boy knows me too well. And he spent a whole month trying to change my mind: his pride demands a convincing explanation."

"Not just pride, Eva. He loves you."

"So what do I tell him? I *can't* tell him about—"

"No. I suggest you stall as long as possible. With everything that's happened tonight, he'll be too busy to remember the question for a few days. When he does, you can be unavailable for some additional time. It may be weeks before he has time and opportunity to brace you about it."

"And what then?"

"You tell him I promised you entertaining surprises were still in store for you—and proved it the very next day."

"And if he persists?"

"Let icicles form on your brow and tell him it's personal. A shame to hurt his feelings, of course, but I don't see what else you can do."

She sighed, and sipped her drink. "You're right. I can't tell him."

"No, you cannot. I should not have told *you*, Eva. But you are my oldest living friend, and I could not see you leave just before everything changed."

She found her eyes stinging, and shut up. They shared more silence for a time.

"Do you think it was Chen?" she asked at last.

"Behind tonight's violence, you mean? I don't know. What do you think?"

"I think an inartistic hit would be a very artistic touch indeed. But it's hard to refute his essential point. If he'd done it, it would have worked, however garishly."

"Apparently it was only by incredible chance that it didn't."

"And I tend to find incredible chance incredible. But I'd bet my life both Jay and Rand are straight." She glanced over her shoulder at the bedroom door. "You know what I mean. They're both honest."

"The gods have blessed us," Reb said cheerfully.

"They have?"

"Of course. How often does life hand you a really good puzzle?"

She blinked, and grinned. "You're right. Not often enough these days. I feel like a sixty-year-old again."

12

Kechar Dzong
Lo Monthang
The Kingdom of Lo, Nepal
12 January 2065

"There was a time," the old monk said above the howling of the late afternoon wind, "when this kingdom controlled all trade throughout the Himalayas. It was the top of the roof of the world."

Gunter Schmidt thought, *I will not kill my travel agent. That is far too merciful. I will sue him until he bleeds from the eyes.*

"Of course," the old man said with magnificent redundancy, "all that was long ago." He underlined the unnecessary words with a sweeping and equally superfluous gesture. Every square inch of the immense fortress-cum-temple within which they stood shouted that the structure had already been

155

a long-abandoned ruin on the day Johann Sebastian Bach died.

From their vantage point on one of its flat rooftops, they could see Lo itself laid out below them in the merciless sunlight of a cloudless December afternoon, a collection of flat-roofed, log-laddered earthen dwellings at the base of the hill on which this crumbling castle of Kechar Dzong stood. Even by Fourth World standards, the Kingdom of Lo was unimpressive. The land was parched, supporting nothing higher than thornbushes; a few carefully nurtured stands of poplar and willow saplings were to be found in the village itself, but wood had been too precious to burn here for centuries. The brief growing season was over, and even the Himalayan vista in the distance could not overcome the bleakness and desolation of the landscape. The kingdom was permitted to exist, semiautonomously with its own king and queen, within the larger kingdom of Nepal—largely because there was nothing here worth arguing over.

"What happened?" Gunter asked, not because he wanted to know, but because he wanted to hear the old monk say something he didn't know already.

"Calamity. The Kali Gandaki moved."

"I hate when that happens."

The old man actually seemed to catch the sarcasm. "The Kali Gandaki was the river from which the strength of Kechar Dzong flowed. It once passed by right there—" He indicated a vague gully meandering through a section of rocky outcroppings no more or less desolate than any other, a few hundred meters downslope. "But when it changed its location at the end of the sixteenth century . . ."

Gunter understood now, and his anger deepened. "And ever since, you have been praying for its return—"

"—in the Tiji ceremony, the elaborate and beautiful ritual I told you of earlier, yes," the old monk agreed happily. "Dorje Jono, the son of the demon who moved the river, repels his father with the power of his magical dancing, and brings water back to the land. The Tiji ceremony takes three full days, and involves every member of the kingdom who is well enough to travel. We summon them with the two mountain horns I showed you downstairs, each of them four meters long. For three days Lo becomes the most magical place in the Himalayas, with *damyin* music and feasting and dancing and singing and beautiful costumes and pageantry and—"

"In *May*," Gunter said through his teeth.

His rhapsody interrupted, the old man blinked at the venom in Gunter's tone. "Well, yes, as I said, that is when foreigners usually visit us. We seldom see a European this late in the year."

"Really?" Gunter said, pulling his parka tighter at his throat against the sharp and icy wind. He mentally replayed the conversation with his travel agent, realizing in hindsight that while the man had waxed eloquent about the Tiji festival, he had never specifically said when it was held. He had only seemed to suggest, somehow, that Gunter barely had time to book his passage if he wanted to be there in time. The trip here had been quite arduous. The last fifty kilometers had been accomplished on horseback, following a guide with whom Gunter had no languages in common. *So I can't sue the bastard, and killing him is too good for him. Ah, but what about torture?*

From somewhere in the far distance to the north came the half-mournful, half-comic sound of a Tibetan mountain horn like the two Gunter had been shown downstairs, a sustained baritone bleat that made him think of a brontosaur dying in agony. It made the mountains ring with echoes. "What's that?" he asked idly. "Call to prayer? Some sort of religious ceremony in another temple?" Perhaps this trip need not be a total loss. Exotic religions were a hobby of Gunter's; having had his mouth set for a grand festive colorful Buddhist ceremony, he was now prepared to settle for the local equivalent of Vespers, rather than go home empty-handed.

But the old man was shaking his head. "I have no idea."

For some reason, this irritated Gunter. "Well, who lives up that way, then?"

The old man looked sore puzzled. "Hardly anyone. There is an old hermit who lives in that general direction . . . and I know he has such a horn, because I have seen it outside his home. But I have never heard him blow it—if indeed that is his horn."

Gunter lost his manners. He had wasted a week and a fortune to see something exotic, and now he was freezing his buns off in a crumbled ruin—an *empty* crumbled ruin—that would be deserted for the next six months, with a canny native guide— clearly one of the oldest inhabitants of the area— who could not even tell him the significance of a simple mountain horn signal. "Perhaps it is Charlie

Parker," he snarled, "practicing in secret until the day when Kansas City needs him again!"

He did not expect the monk to get the reference, of course—but the gesture the old man made indicated that he had not even heard the remark. The wind had redoubled in fierceness and volume. "Never mind!" he said, louder, and could not even hear himself this time. Again the monk pantomimed, *Excuse me?* Gunter's temper boiled over; he waved his arms angrily, gave a wordless shout of exasperation, and set off toward Lo, below. He deliberately left the ancient ruin by a different exit than the one by which he and the monk had entered, one which was more difficult to negotiate, and once he had reached the ground he continued at a pace which he knew the old man would be unable to match. He had forgotten how difficult the climb up had been.

Within a few hundred meters, he was breathing hard. It occurred to him suddenly, as he was negotiating a two-meter drop-off, that in his irritation he was about to leave here *completely* empty-handed. He stopped and took his camera from his shirt pocket. At least he could get some good shots of the ruined temple itself. He had purchased enough memory for five straight days of shooting; might as well get a few minutes. He turned and grunted with satisfaction: the decaying temple really did look striking against the sky. It somehow gave Gunter the impression of a fortress built to defend men against the gods. Unsuccessfully. He backed off a few steps for a better angle, and checked the camera's charge. To avoid wasting power, he disabled the audio pickup. The wind was really roaring now, and he could

overdub the audio later, with something suitably timeless and melancholy.

He peered through the viewfinder and panned
across the face of the ruin, left to right and then back
again. He did not see the old monk anywhere, and
wondered if he were still within the walls, paralyzed
by Gunter's rudeness. Then he did see him—and
sure enough, he was standing in the same window
they had both been looking out from, minutes earlier. He appeared to be doing jumping jacks.

Gunter grunted in surprise, and zoomed in. No,
the old man was hopping up and down and flapping
his arms, but not in any organized fashion. He
seemed to be waving at Gunter. Gunter zoomed in
farther, and became even more puzzled. The old man
appeared to be laughing like a loon. And he was
pointing now, pointing to the north. Was he trying
to say something about that silly horn blast? In sign
language, at this distance? Gunter waved back with
his free hand, signing, *forget it*. This seemed to con-
vulse the aged monk; he held his ribs and roared
with silent laughter.

Gunter had heard of this: Himalayans were known
to go into spontaneous laughing jags, due to the low
oxygen content at this height. He found it annoy-
ing: here he was trying to get an imposing shot of
this ancient temple, and its caretaker was capering
like an ape in the foreground. *Go away,* he gestured.
Get out of the window!

The monk nodded at once, still laughing merrily,
and vanished from the window. Gunter kept shooting. Now the wind began to devil him, increasing its
force until it was tugging at his clothes, pressing at

him like a Tokyo commuter, hammering at his eardrums. The camera was just big enough to present sail-area to it; the wind kept trying to force it to the right. Gunter had image-stabilization circuitry, but knew that this much wavering was taxing it. He twisted slightly to his right to put his back toward the wind, shielding the camera with his hunched left shoulder. The wind pressed especially hard at his ankles, for some reason, and his feet began to feel chilly. *Oh fine,* he thought, *defective boots on top of everything else. I am definitely going to sue* somebody *when I get home!*

But almost as he finished the thought, he realized that his feet were actually *cold,* colder than they should have been even if the boots' heating systems had both failed completely. He glanced down, and discovered that he was standing ankle deep in crystal clear water. It rose as he watched, climbing his shins.

He looked to the north, and saw the Kali Gandaki river returning, after five centuries, dividing around his feet. Now his ear could distinguish between the sound of its passage and the similar sound of the wind. For no reason at all he remembered the damned travel agent saying that the Tiji festival was also known as the Festival of Impermanence.

From above him, in the temple, came the continuous *BBBRRRRRAATTTTTTTT!* of a mountain horn, cutting cleanly through the wind and water noise to alert the village below, and this horn sounded to Gunter more like a brontosaur laughing. . . .

PART FIVE

13

The Shimizu Hotel
18 January 2065

Rhea was drifting helplessly in deep space, her air supply almost gone, her thrusters dry, gasping for air that wasn't there, when windchimes sounded in the distance. She sighed, came back to reality, saved her changes, folded the typewriter and tucked it in her pocket, and went to answer the door.

It was Duncan, of course—the only person besides Rand, Colly and Jay for whom the doorbell would function while she was working. "Is Colly ready?" he asked.

His eyes seemed to ask several other things, and Rhea sighed again. *I wonder what my eyes are answering,* came the sudden thought. "Come in," she said, and looked away. "Max, please tell Colly Duncan is here."

"Beg pardon?" the AI said.

"Sorry. Tell Colly *that* Duncan is here." Rhea hated making syntax errors; it was professionally embarrassing.

After a pause, her AI said, "Colly says to tell you she's changing clothes and will be with you in two seconds."

They looked at each other. "Five minutes," they chorused together, and shared a grin.

Almost at once something about that trivial event bothered Rhea. It was a domestic little moment, something she and Rand might have shared, a small intimacy. Rand had in fact been doing his best to generate such moments, lately—probably because the deadline for her Big Decision was approaching. That underlying awareness had been making the return grins she gave her husband slightly forced. The grin she had just given Duncan was quite genuine. She realized she was drifting just perceptibly toward him, and overcorrected. "Come on in," she said to cover it. "You know where everything is."

"Are you working?" he asked, entering the suite.

She hesitated. The question meant, do you want to be left alone? Duncan was very understanding of a writer's problems; if she said yes, she would cease to exist for him. "No," she decided. "Can I get you anything? There's time for coffee."

"No, thanks," he said. "How's the work coming?"

"Not bad, thanks to you. I really struck ice with Buchi Tenmo."

He grinned again at the spacer expression. Spacers didn't give a damn for gold or diamonds or oil: for them a new source of potable water was real wealth. She had picked up the idiom from him—and it seemed to please him that she had. "Yeah, she's pretty amazing . . . when you can tell what the hell she's talking about."

"Yes, there is that. It's like talking to an angel on psychedelics sometimes. Would you mind sitting in on the conversation once or twice? You've been talking with Stardancers a lot longer than I have."

"Sure—but don't expect that to help much. Buchi's just *different*. Even for a Stardancer. The ones born that way, who've never breathed, are the weirdest . . . but the most interesting too, I think."

A week ago, Rhea had asked Duncan how one got to know a Stardancer. She knew it could be done simply and easily, even from the surface of Terra—but how did one scrape up an acquaintance? It turned out Duncan was friendly with several Stardancers. Most spacers were. And one of his personal friends among *Homo caelestis* happened to be physically located near enough to the Shimizu to allow for something very like a face-to-face meeting . . . through Rhea's own window. Duncan had made the introduction a few days earlier, then politely left them alone. "When would be good for you in the next few days?"

"Any time; when's good for you?"

She thought about it—and suddenly realized that the search criterion with which she was examining her calendar was "times when Rand and Colly won't be around." That made perfect sense: the conversation would be confusing enough without distraction. Nonetheless it struck her all at once that she was making a date to be alone—or almost alone—

with a handsome young man. One who, if she wasn't misreading signals, was interested in her.

It's for work, *for heaven's sake!*

Yes . . . but is it prudent?

Oh, shut up. "How about tomorrow night, after twenty?"

He nodded. "Program loaded."

There was a brief silence. Rhea felt compelled to break it. "So how are things with you?"

"Pretty good, actually. I made another piece last night, and it turned out well."

Duncan's hobby was vacuum-sculpture. To Rhea the artform seemed to consist of assembling ingredients in various combinations, exposing them suddenly to vacuum, and then taking credit for the weird and beautiful shapes chemistry caused to occur. But vacuum-sculpture could be very beautiful—and she had to admit that Duncan seemed to produce aesthetically pleasing results more often than chance could account for. Didn't photographers throw out twenty prints and take credit for the perfect twenty-first? Come to think of it, wasn't her own storage cluttered with drafts that hadn't quite gelled?

"I'd like to see it," she said politely.

"No problem. We'll talk to Buchi from my place, then."

She opened her mouth . . . and then closed it firmly. He was pointedly not looking in her direction.

"I thought I'd take Colly to the pool again," he went on.

Rhea laughed. "You think you have a choice, huh?" The laugh sounded too loud in her ears. "She's a born water baby. You couldn't keep her out of the surf, back ho— . . . back in Provincetown. You know, I've always thought it's ironic. As far back as history goes, the Paixaos have made their living on and from the sea—and my mother was the first one in the family that ever learned to swim. How could you spend all that time on the water and not know how to swim? Weren't they scared?"

Duncan shrugged. "I've lived all my life in space— and I don't know how to breathe vacuum."

"But that's not possible—and it is possible to learn to swim, and it doesn't even take much time."

"Look at it from your greatest grandfather Henry's perspective," he said. "Suppose you're off the Grand Banks and the ship sinks. How much good does it do you to know how to swim?"

It occurred to Rhea that Duncan knew a lot more about her family than she knew about his. She was not normally so forthcoming; had he been making an effort to draw her out? She reviewed memory tape, and could not decide. "I guess. It still seems odd. Maybe we should ask Buchi to teach you how to breathe vacuum."

And now I've drawn the conversation back to our rendezvous. . . .

Colly appeared just then. How she could have spent five minutes dressing was something of a mystery, for she was dressed for the pool, in the ubiquitous guest robe and nothing else. Since so many nationalities and cultures mingled in the Shimizu, all guests conformed to a minimal nudity taboo in politeness to the less civilized nations; one did not jaunt down public corridors naked. But a guest robe was sufficient, and even those could be dispensed with once one reached the pool—or any other nonpublic location. "Hi, Duncan! Come on, let's go!"

"Sorry to hold you up," he said sarcastically, and made way so Colly could hug her mother goodbye.

As Rhea handed the child off to Duncan, their hands brushed briefly. Rhea had gotten used to casual touching in space, even from strangers; free-fall made it necessary in close quarters. But this touch she felt from her scalp to the soles of her feet. It seemed to her that he made it linger.

She was glad then for Colly's eagerness to be in the water; the two headed for the door before the blush reached her cheeks.

I should have said yes when he asked if I was working.

In fact, she *should* be working. She took her keyboard from her pocket and unfolded it. Work would be a wonderful distraction from the trend her thoughts were taking.

Almost at once she found another distraction. The virtual screen that sprang into existence over the keyboard was preset to display her calendar as its boot document, so she wouldn't start sinking into the warm fog if there was some imminent obligation scheduled. It showed the next thirty days, and the box for 5 February was highlighted—it leaped out of the screen at her, as it had been doing ever since she had highlighted it.

I have two more weeks to make up my mind whether I'm going to stay here, was what she had thought when she first started work that morning. Now, perhaps because of what had just transpired, it came out, *I have two more weeks to make up my mind whether I'm going to stay married to Rand.*

She entered her date with Duncan into the calendar, put the typewriter away again, and went to the window. She watched the majestically turning Earth for a measureless time, trying to put names on her feelings, and failing. They would not hold still long enough.

Finally she looked around her, as if to make sure she was alone . . . and checked her watch to make sure Rand was not due home . . . and spoke to her AI. "Maxwell: window program 'Home.'"

"Yes, Rhea."

Terra went away, and was replaced by Provincetown.

She was back in her own writing room in her own home, looking out of the turret through her favorite window, hearing the sounds of the street below, hearing the gulls and the distant surf, seeing Mrs. Vasques, her neighbor, haranguing yet another motorist who had clipped her fence in trying to negotiate the insanely narrow street. The illusion was nearly perfect—except for the same flaw it had had weeks ago, when Rand had first sprung it on her. This time, she was able to identify the flaw. *This Provincetown didn't smell.* There was no salt tang in the air—none of that rich aroma that the landsman calls the smell of the sea and the sailor calls the smell of the land, the shore smell of decaying vegetation and sea creatures at the border between two incompossible worlds.

Maybe I could get a steward to bring me some fish leftovers, she thought, and began to cry. Fetal position is hard to achieve in free-fall, but she managed it.

She never did get back to work that afternoon. But she did manage to stop crying an hour before Duncan was due to bring Colly home for supper, so that her eyes wouldn't be red when they arrived.

Rand showed up just as they did. He had been making a major effort to eat most meals with his family these days. For some reason, his arrival relieved her. Duncan declined an invitation to join them for dinner, and that relieved her too. During the meal she found herself paying more attention than usual to her husband, asking questions about his work and listening attentively to the answers, making little excuses to touch him. Before she knew it they had made a nonverbal contract, entirely by eye contact, to make love when he got home again that night. He went off to Jay's place whistling.

She managed to get a little work done after supper, while Colly was off playing with a friend. She didn't understand where the story was going, but it wouldn't let her alone; its disturbing central image—adrift, running out of air, no direction home—had been recurring in her thoughts for weeks now. The question was, of course, *who* was adrift, and why? She had no clear idea as yet, but she knew if she kept playing with the situation it would come out of her eventually.

As she was putting Colly to bed that night, she said, "So—was it fun playing with Jason, honey?"

"He's okay, I guess," Colly said. "For a boy,

anyway. At least he's gonna be here a whole two weeks." For Colly, the biggest flaw in the Shimizu's accommodations was its criminally inadequate and excessively fluctuating supply of eight-year-olds. Children of transient guests rarely remained aboard more than a few days; permanent guests tended not to have small children, and by evil luck all the spacer children of hotel staff were either over ten or under six—less use than a grown-up. Colly still had all of her phone friends, of course, and her Provincetown chums were all phone friends too, now . . . but she was chronically short of playmates she could smell and touch.

"Oh, that'll be fun," Rhea said.

"I guess." Suddenly Colly looked stricken. "Hey, Mom?"

"Yes, dear?"

"I just thought of something. My birthday comes in two and a half weeks, right?"

Rhea did mental arithmetic. "That's right, honey. Why?"

Colly sat up on one elbow. *"How am I gonna have a party?"*

Rhea started to answer, and stopped.

"You can't have a birthday party on the *phone,*" Colly said. "And all my friends are back on Earth! I'm not gonna get to have a real party, am I?" Her voice was rising in alarm.

"Uh . . . sure you will, honey. There'll be kids aboard then, I'm sure there will. One or two, anyw—"

"But I won't *know* them," Colly insisted. "What good is a party with people you don't even know?" She started to snuffle.

Rhea was tempted to join her. Instead she took Colly in her arms and rocked her. "Don't cry, baby. It won't be so bad. All your friends can be there on the phone—no, you know what? I'll tell you what: we'll get Daddy to merge all the phone signals into his shaping stuff, and your friends can be here almost like real, holographically, walking around and everything." As she spoke, Rhea was estimating the cost of such an event: assuming Rand had time for this, and valuing his time at zero, it came to roughly the price of two luxury automobiles back on Terra. They could afford it, now—but still . . .

Colly considered the offer for a moment, then resumed snuffling, softer than before. "That'd be better . . . but you can't tickle a holo, Mom. You can't throw pieces of birthday cake at a holo."

"Sure you can—only it's even better, because nobody really gets messy. You wait and see: it'll be fun."

Colly was dubious, but after ten minutes of rocking and cuddling and soothing she allowed herself to be mollified, and went to sleep. Rhea left her bedroom exhausted and heartsick. Colly was right: a birthday party aboard the Shimizu probably wasn't going to be much fun.

Less than a minute later, Rand arrived home, shiny-eyed and eager to make love.

Since adolescence Rhea had known that a contract with a man to have sex at an appointed time *must* be honored, if at all possible. Feeling martyred, she pasted a smile on her face and cooperated. But she made a mental note to discuss Colly's birthday party with him as soon as they were done; she was not a hundred percent sure the consolation prize she had promised her daughter was technically feasible.

It was just as he was entering her that it dawned on her that the question might be moot: their child's birthday came *after* the date on which she was to give Rand her final decision. . . .

It was not a terribly erotic train of thought. The act was technically successful for both of them, for they had been married for a long time—but for the same reason, Rand asked, "Want to talk about it?" when their breathing had slowed.

She burst into tears. "I don't even want to *think* about it."

He held her close, but said nothing. He knew, in general, what was on her mind—and knew that she knew he knew. What was there for either of them to say?

What could Donny Handsome have said to Patty?

She untucked her chin from his neck and pushed at him with her hands; he rose far enough on his elbows so that she could see his face. She looked at it a long time . . . not just the eyes or the mouth, but the whole face. He waited. "You're staying?" she said finally.

His face went blank. He was silent an equal time. She waited.

"Yes."

She nodded, and pulled him back down to her. They lay there together in silence, breathing in the same rhythm and thinking the same thought.

What did that nod mean?

Twice, she felt him start to ask her. Each time he changed his mind. She couldn't blame him—but part of her wished he had asked. If he had, perhaps an answer would have come to her.

She forgot to ask him about Colly's birthday party that night.

Rhea knew that a real window like the one in her suite was supposed to be much better than a fake one—she knew, to the yen, how much more the former cost. But she was a shaper's wife: to her Duncan's fake window was just as good. Better, for she could shift to a view in any direction at all simply by touching a control. Somehow it felt more correct to talk with a Stardancer *without* Earth in the background, overshadowing everything.

And Buchi Tenmo did not appear to mind talking to a camera rather than a person in a window. She did not need to see Rhea; she already had. She must be used to talking with Duncan this way too.

Insofar as she was used to talking at all. So far Rhea had found it always took the first few minutes of the conversation for Buchi to become even partly comprehensible. That did not surprise Rhea. To temporarily "place on hold" an ongoing conversation with millions of others, and funnel consciousness down to only one or two nontelepathic minds must be a disorienting experience—especially for a spaceborn Stardancer, who had never been such a limited being herself. The wonder was that the trick was possible.

And already Buchi was winding down, only minutes in. She had progressed from incomprehensible polyglot babble to a lock on English—of a sort. Any minute now it would start conveying information.

"—*as the world whirls around peg in a square holy cowhide it from yourself-esteem cleaning up your action figures it would be that's entertainment to tell you but I forgot is a concept by which we measure painting the town read all of your books now, Rhea, and they're very beautiful . . . the gostak distims the doshes . . . eftsoons, and right speedily . . . don't blame him for not being careful in the beginning . . . a straight hook basically seeks fish who turn away from life . . . there: subject, object, predicate . . . am I getting there, Rhea? Duncan? Can I hear you, now? Are we having fun yet?*"

"You're getting there," Rhea agreed. Things always improved dramatically, she had found, once Buchi reinvented the sentence. She found herself asking the question she had suppressed during her previous encounters with the Stardancer. "Buchi? Does it hurt? Doing this, I mean, talking with us—is it hard?"

"*It's fun!*" For that moment Buchi sounded remarkably like Colly. "*Is it hard to talk with me?*"

"A little," Rhea admitted. "But you're right, it's fun. But then, I'm only doing what I do all the time: talking, in my own language. You're doing all the work."

"*By 'work' I understand you in this context to mean 'energy expenditure regretted or begrudged.' By that definition I have never worked in my life. Although I'm always busy.*"

"I wish I could say the same." A light dawned somewhere in the back of Rhea's head. "But you've put your finger on something, Buchi. I've been thinking about our conversations, and why they haven't satisfied me, and I think you just gave me a handle on my problem."

"Problems are better with handles on them?"

"For me they are. Looking back over it, everything I've been asking you has been about . . . has had to do with things that a human supposes would be disadvantages of being a Stardancer. The bad parts. I've been asking you about the bad parts—and for each one I come up with, you explain how it's not a bad part. Some of the explanations I just flat don't understand—"

"I always have trouble conveying the idea of self generated reality," Buchi agreed. *"To a human it seems a flat contradiction in terms."*

Rhea had asked in her first conversation whether Buchi ever missed being able to "really" walk the surface of a planet, as opposed to "merely" reexperiencing it through the memories of those Stardancers who had lived on Earth before joining the Starmind. Communication had broken down when Buchi insisted that she could, really, walk on Terra any time she wanted—that she could "really" experience things she had never personally experienced—knowing the difference, but unbothered by it. Rhea, who had never confused even the best virtual-reality environments with real-reality, was baffled by this. She had spent most of her own professional life battering at the interface between almost-real and real, trying to make words on a screen sound and smell. She had to tiptoe around the thought that anyone for whom reality and imagination were interchangeable was someone who was not quite sane.

"—but that's not the problem," she went on, but Duncan interrupted her.

"It's like this window, Rhea," he said, touching her wrist and pointing.

"Huh?"

"You know that to most of the people in this hotel, this window we're looking out right now isn't as good as the one you have back in your suite. God knows it costs a lot less. But we've talked about it, so I know you agree with me that this one is actually better. It may not be 'real'—but it can look in any direction you want, or show you anything you want to see, flatscreen anyway. I know yours can do even better, the way Rand has it tricked out now . . . but most people who pay a premium for one of those windows do it so they can tell themselves that what they're looking at is 'real.' They care a lot about 'real.' You and I care a little less. Buchi cares not at all. Think of it as a spectrum rather than a discontinuity."

Rhea looked at him, surprised and a little impressed by his insight. "I think I see what you mean," she said.

He flushed and went on. "With total control of her brain and body, reality can mean whatever she wants it to mean. She can *experience* the touch of someone half a light year away, feel it on her skin. Or feel the touch of someone long dead . . . as long as someone in the Starmind holds the memory of how it feels to be touched by that person. Not one coffee molecule has ever passed her lips her whole life long, but she's probably tasted better coffee than you or I ever will."

"I'm doing it now! 'Bean around the Solar System...'" Buchi let the song parody trail off after a few more hummed bars.

"But with reality that slippery..." Rhea began.

Duncan interrupted. "...how do they make sure they don't lose track of the one you and I believe in? What do they do for a reality check, you mean?"

"Yeah, I guess that's what I mean."

"We are many," Buchi said. "And we are one. E pluribus unum. Alone/All-one. Consensus reality is very important to us. If we ever lost it, we would come apart. It is the same with your own neurons. We put about as much effort into it as they do. And about as often, we fire randomly—we make things up, we vacation in realities of our own fashioning, singly or in groups. The universe is always there when we return. It is not a problem."

"Now there," Rhea said triumphantly, "is my problem. As I started to say before, I can live with the fact that I have trouble grasping your explanations of why assorted aspects of being a Stardancer aren't problems for you. What's driving me crazy is that you just... don't seem to have any problems!

"None of the ones I envisioned. None of them has even triggered mention of any problem you do have. I'm a writer: to me a character is his or her problems; if they don't have any, they're no use to me, I've got nothing to work with, no way to motivate them. I guess what I'm asking is, don't you people— you Stardancers—have any problems? I know you never get hungry or thirsty or cold or lonely or lost or have to go to the bathroom at an inappropriate time. But Jesus, Buchi—isn't there anything you fear?

Or miss? Or yearn for? Or regret? Is there anything you lust after? Or mourn?"

"*Must your characters always be driven by the lash?*"

Rhea thought about it. "Pretty much, yes. That's what the audience wants to see. How someone like itself reacts under the lash. Because it helps the reader guess and deal with how she would react under the same pressure. The rule of thumb is, the sharper the lash—the tougher the antinomy—the better the story. For us humans, life is suffering, just as the Buddhists say. Is that really not true for you?"

The answer was almost a full minute in coming. It was the first time Rhea could remember Buchi hesitating even slightly in responding. Two or three times she began to speak, but each time decided to wait for an answer.

"*The Starmind suffers,*" Buchi said at last, "*as sharply, as deeply, as keenly, as you yourself. But in different ways ... for different reasons ... and I cannot explain them to you. No terrestrial language contains words that will convey the necessary concepts: you do not have the concepts. Every human language contains the implicit assumption that individual minds have bone walls around them. It would be much easier for me to convey color to a blind man.*"

Rhea was frustrated ... but if there was anything her work had prepared her to believe, it was that some things simply could not be put into words. "What are you all *doing?*"

"*What are you asking?*"

"What is the Starmind doing? Are you doing

anything? Did those Fireflies have any *purpose* in creating your kind? Are you all working toward something together . . . or just floating around like the red blobs in a lava lamp, marveling at the Solar System and unscrewing the inscrutable?"

"You know hundreds of things we do. I can download a summary list to your AI if you wish. It runs about a terabyte."

"Then I've seen most of it. Well, scanned it." Even that was an absurd claim. "All right, I've scanned the superindex, tiptoed through some of the subindices, and jumped in at random here and there a few hundred places. And one thing I noticed."

"Yes?"

"Most of the things you do come down, in the long run, to helping *us*. Helping humans. Helping Terra. Some of it benefits us directly, like nanotechnology, and some it just seems to happen to work out to our benefit way down the line, like that Belt-map hobby of yours that kept us from getting clobbered by Lucifer's Hammer in '32. Even the 'pure-science' researches you're engaged in always seem to benefit us more than they benefit you, when the dust settles."

"Can we ignore suffering at our own heart, at our roots? We may not be of humanity . . . but we are from humanity."

"I'm not complaining. I'm just asking: is that what you Stardancers do for problems? Borrow ours?" She had an image of the human race as endearingly dopey pets, who could be relied upon to produce fascinating but trivial problems, supply life's necessary irritant. "If some cosmic disaster wiped us all out . . . would the Starmind go crazy from boredom? Or would you still have things to *do?*"

Another pause. This one was only ten seconds or so. *"We would still have a nearly infinite number of things to do. And again, I despair of finding words that will successfully hint at their nature."* Another five seconds. *"One subset may perhaps be intelligibly outlined, at least. You are aware, are you not, that the Starmind is not alone in the Universe?"*

"Huh? Sure. So what?" It was a classic insoluble problem. Within a few years of its initial formation, the Starmind had reported to humanity that it was receiving telepathic broadcasts from numberless other Starminds throughout the Galaxy and Magellanic Clouds—a potential source of inconceivable wealth in any terms. But it came in *all at once*, at the same "volume," from all quarters—and none of it appeared to be in any known or decipherable language or concept-system. The Starmind did not even know how to say, "Quiet, please—one at a time!" The best it had managed, according to all reports, was to learn to ignore the useless infinity of treasure, as a geiger counter suppresses its "awareness" of normal background radiation. "What good does that do you if you can't *communicate* with anybody?" Rhea asked. "You can't, right?" She knew the answer—but from books and media accounts, and knew how much that was worth.

"No, we cannot," Buchi agreed. *"But that may not always be so."*

"You think the problem might actually be solvable?" Duncan said excitedly.

"Our seed has been awake for less than seven

decades," Buchi said. *"There are yet far fewer of us
Stardancers than there are neurons in even the most
limited brain. Yet our numbers grow—and the
Starmind grows wiser every nanosecond. It is certain that we live longer than you, and we do not
waste a third of our lives in stupor and another third
working at life-support. We have time. Time has us.
We use tools you cannot understand to build tools
you cannot conceive to solve problems we ourselves
cannot name. It is not a thing to trouble yourself
over."*

"Do you know anything at all about where it's all
going?" Rhea asked. "That you can explain?"

"Yes. Wonderful things are going to happen."

Rhea blinked. "But *what?*"

The silence went on until she realized no answer
would be forthcoming. "When?" she tried then.

That answer came at once, startling her.

"Soon."

"How soon?" she blurted.

Again, silent seconds ticked by.

"Within my lifetime?" she tried.

"I cannot be certain, but I believe so."

"Will you be able to explain these things to us
humans when they happen?"

"When they happen, you will know."

"And you can't give me any idea what it will be
like?"

More silence.

"Why doesn't anybody else know about this?" Rhea
said irritably. "I've read—scanned—everything I could
get my hands on about you Stardancers. This is the
first hint I've heard that the galactic signal-to-noise

problem might be susceptible of solution. Is it a secret, or what?"

"Would I have burdened you with a secret without warning you? The reason you have not heard of this before is that you are the first to have asked about this in many decades, the first since we began to be sure of it ourselves."

"Really?" Rhea asked. "That's hard to believe."

"Yes, isn't it? Rhea, answer me two questions. First, regarding the Fireflies, who made us: is there any characteristic commonly associated with the term 'gods' that they lack?"

Rhea thought hard. Apparently omniscient, apparently omnipotent, apparently benevolent but absolutely unknowable . . . long gone and not expected back soon . . . "No," she admitted. "Wait: two. They seem to have no desire at all to be worshipped . . . and they haven't instructed anyone to kill anyone else in their name."

"You anticipate my second question: do you know of any religion on or off Terra which worships them?"

It startled her. "Why, no. There are cults who worship *you* . . . at least one large one. And up until forty-odd years ago there was a small one trying to kill you. But I don't know of any Firefly-worshippers, now that you mention it."

"Rhea, humanity can just barely live with the mere memory of the Fireflies. They are too vast to think about. From the human point of view, the best thing about them is that they were in the vicinity of Terra for a matter of hours, at the orbit of Saturn for a matter of months, and left promising my father not to return for a matter of centuries. We Stardancers

are tolerated, for all our alienness, because we were once and still partially are human. Beneath my Symbiote are flesh and blood, born of woman. But of all the things we are asked—and we are asked many things by many humans—we are rarely asked about the Fireflies . . . and almost never about other Starminds, circling other stars. Your governments and philosophers were overjoyed to learn that the galactic surround is incomprehensible to us, and have been happy to tiptoe around the sleeping dragon ever since."

"If that's true, I'm pretty disgusted with my own species," Rhea said.

"You need not be. Think of it from a historical perspective. After two millions of years of slaughter, humanity has just learned how to live with itself in peace, and has done so for a time measured in mere years. Can you reasonably expect it to be prepared to deal with a galaxy of unknown strangers? So quickly? I can tell you that we the Starmind tremble at the thought of the Fireflies returning—and we could at least talk with them if they did. Why should you not 'pretend it never happened'? It seems to me a healthy psychological adjustment for your race at this time."

Rhea started to reply, but Duncan interrupted her again. "Excuse me, Buchi—I want to backtrack a second. Did you say when the Fireflies left, they made a promise to 'your *father*'?"

"Yes."

That had caught Rhea's ear too. "Who is your father, Buchi?" she asked.

"Charlie Armstead."

Rhea's eyes widened. "And your mother?" she managed to ask.

"Norrey Drummond."

She heard a singing in her ears, like a Provincetown mosquito. The second and third Stardancers who had ever lived, founders of Stardancers Incorporated, as famous throughout even the human race as Shara Drummond herself! "My God! I never dreamed—"

"Me either," Duncan said in awed tones. "You never told me that, Booch."

"You never asked. What's your father's name, and why haven't you told me?"

"It's 'Walter.' But you're right. His name only comes up if someone finds *my* name funny and I have to explain the story."

"I saw the humor in your name the moment you told it to me," Buchi said. *"But I assumed you were tired of explaining its origin, so I did not comment."*

"And bless you," he said. "It's just that I keep forgetting you folks don't use last names to indicate either paternal *or* maternal descent."

"There is no need to. We know our lineage, and each of the other's—it need not be encoded in our names. We choose names purely for their meanings."

The humming in Rhea's ears was beginning to diminish. "What does your name mean, Buchi Tenmo?" Rhea asked.

" 'Dancing Wisdom Celestial Net,' " the Stardancer answered.

"That's beautiful!" Duncan said . . . an instant before Rhea could. "I wish I had a name that good."

He turned to Rhea. "Or like yours. 'Rhea'—'earth' or 'mother,' two of the most beautiful words there are. And 'Paixao,' just as beautiful: 'passion.'"

The mosquitos resumed their attack on Rhea's ears. She could feel the lobes turning red, offering blood. "What does *your* name mean?" she asked quickly, aware of the significance of his having looked up the meaning of her name, but unwilling to acknowledge it.

He made a face. "I got the booby-prize. 'Duncan' means 'dark-skinned warrior'"—Rhea found herself thinking that he was dark-skinned even by Provincetown standards, though he certainly wasn't *muscled* like a warrior . . . and forced herself to pay attention to what he was saying—"and 'Iowa' . . . well, there's the political district in the North American Federation, of course, the province or state or whatever . . . and at least one writer once confused that with Heaven. But actually it comes from 'Ioakim'—apparently an official at someplace called Ellis Island made Greatest Grandad change it. It's Russian Hebrew for 'God will establish' . . . which I for one find wishful thinking."

Rhea found that she wanted to change the subject from Duncan's name, from Duncan, and suddenly remembered a question that had ghosted through her mind perhaps a dozen times over the course of her life. "The word 'God' makes me think of Fireflies again," she said. "Buchi, there's one more question I've always wondered about. Why did the Fireflies come when they did?"

"They came when it was time."

"Yes—but why was it time? The generally

accepted answer is that they came 'at the dawn of space travel.' But it was more like brunchtime. Humanity had been in space—had been established in space—for years when they showed up. We'd been to Luna decades before. Did it take them that long to notice? Or that long to arrive? If we could establish a time-duration for their journey, it might be a clue to where they came from."

"Their arrival was instantaneous," Buchi said flatly.

"Then what triggered it? Do you know?"

"The signing of a contract. An agreement between Skyfac Incorporated and Shara Drummond."

Details from a history lesson came back dimly to Rhea. Sure enough, the way she remembered it, the Fireflies had first been sighted in the Solar System about two weeks before Shara Drummond left Earth to create the Stardance. They had flicked into existence around the orbits of Neptune and Pluto (at that time very close together), the outer limit of the System, and then moved in as far as the orbit of Saturn a couple of weeks later . . .

. . . the day Shara reached Skyfac! Where they stayed, until she was on the verge of being sent home again with her dream unfulfilled—then arrived just in time to force the performance of the Stardance . . .

"They came to us the moment that a human being came to space for the express purpose of creating art," Buchi said.

The words seemed to echo in Rhea's skull.

"How they knew of that, even the Starmind cannot yet imagine—but the fact is unmistakable."

She felt as if her head were cracking. The insight

was too immense and powerful to deal with—yet so obvious she could hardly believe no one had worked it out ages ago.

"Thank you, Buchi," she said quickly. "You've been very gracious and helpful, we'll talk again another time, I hope you'll excuse me now but I need to get to my typewriter so I can—" She stopped babbling when she noticed that she had already switched off the window.

She turned from it, and there was Duncan.

At once he turned away, which relieved and annoyed her at the same time, and jaunted across the room . . . but in seconds he was back, bearing a strange and uncouth object, waving it at her as he braked himself to a halt at her side. "I promised I'd show you this, Rhea," he said.

It was his manner more than anything else which cued her. This had to be the new piece of vacuum sculpture he had mentioned. Resolving to find something polite to say about it, she began to scrutinize it for material to work with.

A timeless time later, she began to experience perceptual distortion, and slowly figured out the cause. Her eyes were beginning to grow tear-bubbles. . . .

What it was made of she could not guess. The subtleties of its composition process were a closed book to her. But what it looked like, to her, more than anything else she could think of, was a piece of driftwood she had once brought home from the Provincetown shore. It had a similar shape, twisted on itself, asymmetrically beautiful, and it had the stark bleached color and polished appearance of very old driftwood. Washed up on an alien shore . . . like herself.

"It's very beautiful," she said, and heard a husky note in her voice. She searched for polite small talk. "Does it . . . do your pieces have names?"

"It's called 'Driftglass,'" he said. His own voice was hoarse.

She flinched slightly. "It's very lovely. It reminds me—"

"—of home, I know," he said quickly. "It's yours. I made it for you."

The mosquitos at her ears had brought in chainsaws. "I . . . I really have to go," she said. "I promised Rand—" She was already in motion, three of her four thrusters firing at max acceleration, past him before she could see his reaction.

"Sure, of course, good night," she heard him say behind her as the door got out of her way, and as she came out of her turn and raced down the corridor, she was for a time very proud of herself. Until she noticed that she had Driftglass in her hand . . .

And I didn't even thank him.

"You are going too fast," came a voice from all around her. "Please slow down." She flinched, and then realized it was only an AI traffic cop; she was exceeding the local jaunting speed limit. She decelerated at once.

"Thank you," she said. "That is very good advice."

14

Rand had come to feel that his favorite part of the Shimizu was the corridors. They were designed to be visually appealing, padded enough for the most inexpert jaunter, and offered an ever-changing parade of rich and almost-rich people to gawk at. They were the place where one flew, where you could enjoy the sensation of a jaunt that was not over within seconds. Most important to him, they represented the blessed hiatus between the problems of the studio and the problems of the home. They were the equivalent of a solitary drive from office to home back on Terra: the place of unwinding from work, and of winding other mechanisms back up again.

But sooner or later the corridors always led him back to his door. He was coming to think of it as the Place of Sighs; whichever direction he was going, he always seemed to pause just outside the thresh-old and sigh, first.

He did so now, decided he was ready to enter his home, and thumbed the doorlock.

Before he could enter, something burst from the room and enveloped him. Its first effect was as invigorating as a cool rain on a dry afternoon: his wife's laughter . . .

As a musician he found it one of the Universe's more glorious sounds; as a husband he found it exhilarating. In either capacity, he had been missing it lately. Like an addict following the smell of smoke, he followed it inside, seeking the source.

Rhea was in the living room, a little northeast of the window. She was sitting in the piece of furniture in which she usually did her writing—she moved around as she wrote, and hated the sound of Velcro separating as she did—but her seat belt was not fastened. And she had configured the furniture in the shape which its menu called "love-seat." In its other corner, also unstrapped, was a broadly grinning Duncan Iowa. He had just opened his mouth to say something, to make Rhea laugh again, when he caught sight of Rand in the doorway. "Hello, Rand," he said.

Rhea turned, smiling. "Hi, darling," she said. "You must be exhausted—would you like a drink?"

He controlled a frown. "Why would I be exhausted?"

She looked surprised. "Well . . . the premiere is only a week away, right?"

"Sure—but my part was done yesterday. Jay and the dancers will be killing themselves from here on in, muscle-memorizing it, but I'm just there babysitting the software and looking for holes. I told you that last night."

"Oh. I forgot."

"Never mind." He had been hoping to hear some more of her laughter, and now she wasn't even smiling anymore. *Nice work.* "What were you guys laughing about? I could use a giggle."

She shook her head. "It'd take too long to explain it. Duncan just came up with a neat way to improve some comic business in a story I'm working on."

"Oh. I see." In ten years of marriage, Rhea had never permitted Rand—or anyone—to see or hear about a work-in-progress. It was one of her many writer's superstitions. "A story is like a soufflé," was the line he had heard her tell people a hundred times.

"Where's Colly?"

"Studying." She glanced at her watch. "No, by now the terminal has unlocked, so she's probably playing games or watching a movie."

He nodded. "As long as she's not on the phone again. That kid will talk away our air money one of these days."

"Oh, no, she can't be—I've got the White Rabbit set to warn me if she asks for a phone circuit."

"The which?"

"The White Rabbit," Duncan said. "It's her new name for Harvey. He's still a rabbit, but he's shorter, and dressed like the Tenniel version. You know, the guy who illustrated the original Alice books."

Rand was doubly irritated: that a strange man knew more about his daughter than he did, and that this young lout thought the best damn shaper in human space needed to be told who Tenniel was. But he still had faint hopes of hearing Rhea laugh again sometime tonight, so he pasted a big happy smile on his face. "Ha ha," he said, as if reading the words from a page. "That's cute. Pocket watch and all, eh?" *I know the fucking books, sonny.* "We'd better be careful what she eats and drinks. If she starts to grow, we'll need a bigger suite."

He was rewarded with a grin from his wife. "I don't think there is such a thing. If she does, we'll have to put her in the pool: she can have it all to herself."

"I think Colly would really like that," Duncan said.

"Can you stay for dinner, Duncan?" Rand asked, in the tone of voice that both sounds perfectly sincere and conveys the subtext, *a negative answer is expected.*

The lad was not completely mannerless; he pushed himself away from the love-seat and looked around for anything he might have left. "No, thanks, I have to—"

A braying sound interrupted him, for all the world like a burro's mating call. All three froze.

"FLARE WARNING, CLASS ONE," said a very loud voice. "THIS IS A SAFETY EMERGENCY. ALL GUESTS MUST GO AS QUICKLY *AND CALMLY* AS POSSIBLE TO THE NEAREST RADIATION LOCKER, AND REMAIN THERE UNTIL FURTHER NOTICE. THERE IS NO CAUSE FOR ALARM AS LONG AS YOU SEEK SHELTER *NOW.* IF YOU HAVE A SPECIAL PROBLEM, ONLY, PHONE 'FLARE EMERGENCY' AND HELP WILL ARRIVE AT ONCE.

WAVE-FRONT X-RAYS EXPECTED IN NINE MINUTES, TWENTY SECONDS. CLASS ONE FLARE WARNING—" It began to repeat.

"Volume mute!" Rand barked, and the voice went away. "Duncan, you're staying."

"I shouldn't," he said. "I've got my own bolt hole, two minutes away—that's seven minutes cushion."

"Don't be silly," Rhea said. "There's plenty of room in our locker, I've seen it. This suite was built for up to six." Still Duncan looked hesitant. "For heaven's sake, we're going to be in there with Colly for what, three hours to three days? With no phone, no TV, completely cut off from the Net? We *need* you, Duncan."

He grinned. "That logic I understand."

"We're wasting time," Rand snapped, and led the stampede.

By thoughtful design, access to the radiation locker was through Colly's room. They expected to find her in a panic—but as they cleared the door they found her oblivious, wearing earphones and fixated on a screen, talking on the phone with a hush-filter. She flinched sharply when she became aware of them; on Earth she would have jumped a foot in the air. In free-fall the same reflex causes one to tumble erratically; she flailed like an octopus to regain her balance. *"It was just for a minute,"* she cried. *"I was just gonna hang up, really!"*

Rand got a grip on an ankle as it went past, swarmed up her and yanked the earphones out. "Quiet, Colly!" he said, trying to control his voice carefully so as to command instant attention without scaring her.

It seemed to work. "What is it, Daddy?"

"It's all right, baby—there's a flare on the way, but it's only Class One. We're all going on a picnic together for a little while. Wanna come?"

Her eyes got big and round. "Sure, Dad. Can I bring the White Rabbit? Harvey, I mean? I changed his name."

"So I hear. I'm sorry, honey—radiation lockers are meant to keep electrons out, and that's pretty much what the White Rabbit's made of. We're going to have to rough it, like they did in the Olden Days. Do you have any books around?"

"Hard copy, you mean? None I haven't read a jillion times. You mean no games, or *anything*?"

"Only if they're free-standing, hon. Nothing that uses the Net. Get your Anything Box." It was a nanotechnological toy-set, which could be caused to become a range of things, from a 3-D chess set to a Monopoly board to Scrabble game.

"I forgot to charge it," she wailed.

Duncan already had the locker hatch open, and was waving Rhea to enter; she held back. "Come on, Colly," he called. "You don't need machines to play games."

"You *don't*?" She looked dubious. "Okay." She started for the hatch. "Hey—what about supper?"

"That kitchenette will make sandwiches in under two minutes," Rhea said, and began to turn toward the door. "We've got about seven left—"

"No, Rhea!" Duncan ordered. "That was a best-guess, and you don't screw around with a flare emergency, for *anything*. There's food and water in the locker—come on!"

"Go ahead," Rand said. "I've got Colly."

Rhea gave up and went to the hatch. Duncan caught her as she arrived, and handed her through the door. To guide a body from behind in free-fall without causing it to tumble, one pushes the buttocks. Rand had been in space long enough to know that, so he couldn't even be annoyed. He put his attention on his daughter. "Push off on me, hon," he said, and spread-eagled himself facing the hatch. Colly doubled up, put her feet against his stomach, and jumped. He used his thrusters to recover and follow her. Her aim was superb; she went through the hatch like a perfect slam-dunk and into Rhea's arms.

Duncan seemed to have assigned himself the role of doorman; he waited for Rand to precede him. "After you, son," Rand said gruffly. And as Duncan turned, he pushed the lad in, the same way he had done for Rhea.

The next few hours were not particularly pleasant ones.

Perhaps no one has ever spent a really comfortable three hours in a radiation locker. They were the only cubics in the Shimizu which could reasonably be called "spartan," being simple boxes designed to keep a human alive for up to three and a half days despite the best efforts of energetic protons to kill him. (X-rays, although they arrive first, and keep coming as the following plasma cloud of electrons and protons strikes hull metal, are not a problem: a mere millimeter of aluminum will stop most of them.) A radiation locker is very easy to get into, impossible to get out of until the emergency is past, and will supply breathable air, potable water, digestible food substitutes, basic emergency medical care, and plumbing facilities. Period. If one wishes to make it congenial, one can stock it with one's own free-standing computer gear, library of music and literature, programmable furniture, or a supply of gourmet delights, for there is a fair amount of room. But almost no one ever does . . . for the same reason that people still build at the base of volcanos. Bad solar flares are quite uncommon for about nine and a half out of every eleven years. When the tornados come once every decade or so, it is easy to forget to keep the storm shelter adequately stocked. So most visits there begin with a mournful inventory that is finished all too soon, followed by the dawning realization that this will be a sentence.

In this case, Rand decided early on not to dwell on the dark side of things, and resolved instead to concentrate on what *could* be accomplished while in here. So he checked his mental buffer, and found a task waiting: chewing his daughter out for using the telephone against express orders. But to his intense annoyance, Duncan interceded on her behalf ("butted in," was how Rand phrased it to himself), claiming that she deserved praise for having figured out how to circumvent an AI lock. When he rejected this as irrelevant, Colly took over her own defense, presenting in a shrill voice the novel theory: "Anyway, I'm not even getting a real birthday party; space stinks and I want to go home."

Since Rand had been counting on Colly's enthusiasm for space to help win over Rhea, he took recourse in a strangled silence. Rhea had privately asked him, several days ago, about interfacing his shaping equipment with the phone so that the friends at Colly's party could at least be convincing fakes. At the time he had been too busy, and said he would "think about it," but later he had thought it through in financial terms only, and rejected the idea on those grounds. He wanted mightily now to promise—to have promised—to do it . . . but he could not construct a logic-bridge that would get him from "You're spending too much money on the phone" to "I'm going to help you spend a king's ransom on the phone," and did not have Colly's daredevil indifference to logic to help him. He made a firm private resolution to tackle the project and banged his nose on the fact that he could not even begin for . . . how long did Class One flare emergencies generally last, anyway? He was forced to ask Duncan. And the answer—three hours to three days; we'll know when the door opens—did not please him. It began to dawn on him that he was going to have to fill an indeterminate time with small talk, with a wife whom he had hurt, a child he had disappointed, and a young man who was beginning to annoy the hell out of him.

In the end, it was only eight hours, and even they were not the horrors they might have been. But only because Rhea rose heroically to the occasion, and almost singlehandedly carried the group on her shoulders, quelling negative emotions by sheer force of personality. She changed subjects, she suggested topics, she refereed potential disputes before they could occur, and she took upon herself any housekeeping task that might otherwise have brought Rand and Duncan into contact.

Eventually she bullied them all into the proper bomb shelter spirit. She told them endless stories, some pirated and some improvised. She cajoled Rand into singing the songs he sang best. Duncan reached back into the memory banks of a childhood in circumstances so primitive (by contemporary Terran standards) that he had frequently been deprived of amusement facilities, and pulled out game after game that could be played without tools or power. Before long Colly too was making her unique contribution: giggling. Not long after her usual bedtime, she fell asleep, but a child's snores and other sleepsounds are nearly as uplifting as her giggles. And it is difficult for a conversation to turn to an argument if there is a child sleeping in the room. Before long, Rand had regained his original impression of Duncan as a decent enough young man—just needed a little seasoning among Terrans to learn the fine points of good manners, that was all. After all, Rhea seemed to like him, and she had good people radar.

Good spirits might not have lasted, but luck was with them: just as group morale peaked, the locker door opened and a loud voice began reassuring them that everything was fine. They managed to silence it before it could wake Colly, and emerged smiling together. Duncan had the grace to make his excuses and leave nearly at once. By the time Rand had finished seeing him out the door, Rhea had put Colly into her sleepsack and gone to their bedroom; he put the suite to sleep and joined her. He was quite tired; the only things he intended to do before sleeping were check to make sure their AIs were still sentient, and make sure that if there were any casualties, no one he knew was on the list.

But by the time he reached the bedroom, Rhea was more than halfway out of her clothes.

"Uh..." he managed to get out before the process was complete, and then she advanced on him like a cloud of electrons and protons. His own clothing was no protection at all. His next syllable was some five minutes later, and was even less spellable; he repeated it several times over the next few minutes, with increasing volume and decreasing period. The last iteration was a shout, which by then seemed to him to contain all the information the universe out there desperately needed to hear—until he heard Rhea shriek the message's other half in harmony with him.

Before he fell asleep, he regained enough intelligence to compose a platitude, something along the lines of "Out of adversity comes fortitude." Maybe... just maybe... Rhea was going to snap into it.

Talking work with Jay wasn't as much fun as it had been; with four days left before the premiere of *Kinergy* (as they had decided to name the new work) Jay had too much else to do, Rand had too little else to do, and there was nothing to discuss together but things that might go wrong. And the incessant ego-struggles and other personal frictions among the dancers—but Rand hated that particular topic. He had himself pointedly chosen a field that allowed him to work alone when it suited him.

So he had no digression to propose when Jay said, "How's it going with Rhea, bro?"

He decided to tackle it. "You know, last week I'd have said it was fucking hopeless. But it's the funniest thing: somehow that flare emergency seems to have turned things around. At least a little, anyway. She came through it like a trouper, never complained once, never even frowned—and as soon as it was over, so was she: *all* over *me*. We haven't had a session like that since . . . Jesus, I don't know, but whenever it was, it was back on Earth. It felt . . . it felt like christening the Shimizu, christening space. Do you know what I mean?"

Jay nodded at once. "Ethan and I christened High Orbit that way, once."

Rand winced away from the thought. Obviously the event had not cemented Ethan's commitment to living in space very effectively. "I mean, it's like when I first moved to P-Town. I'd never lived by the ocean, and I wasn't sure if I could take that much horizon. And the storms, you know, the winds. And then we went through our first hurricane together, and it was hard, but when it was over I felt like, 'Well, that wasn't so bad; I can live here.' Sitting in a radiation locker isn't fun . . . but it's a lot more fun than sitting in a singles bar. Maybe she's going to steady down and learn to live here."

"But it's still that much up in the air, is it? With four days to curtain? You have to give Kate an answer one way or another the following week."

"I know, I know. But it's the kind of problem where you can't push for an answer, no matter how urgent it is."

"Well, all I'm saying is, if she bails out, don't necessarily assume that you have to follow her—for keeps, I mean. Just because Ethan and I couldn't make it work on a commuter basis doesn't mean it can't be done. Look at that Philip Rose and *his* wife—and he's a writer, like Rhea. Quite a few spacers have made marriage with a groundhog work."

"You really think it's an option? After what happened to you?"

"Well, maybe not a great one. But it might be worth giving it a year and seeing how it works." He seemed to start to say something, and then changed his mind. "I'm just being selfish, bro. *Kinergy* is a good piece. I like working with you; I don't want to give it up. Losing partners is a habit I'm trying to break."

Rand thought about it, and shook his head. "I hear you. But I just can't see Rhea and I staying married that way. Besides, it's not fair to Colly to yo-yo her that way, uproot her every three months."

"There are other rotation schedules."

"Doesn't change anything. If Rhea goes, my choices are her—and Colly—or my work. So you can imagine how relieved I am at any hint that she might be willing to stay."

Again Jay seemed to choose his words carefully. "Rand? Suppose she does go? Suppose the wild sex after the flare was just the bomb-shelter reflex to celebrate not having been killed after all? Suppose your choice *is* Rhea or the Shimizu: what then?"

"That I can answer concisely and with absolute certainty. The answer is, it beats the shit out of me." He picked at a cuticle. "I really like this place. I

really like this job. I really love working with you.
But I *really love* Rhea and our kid. All I can tell you
is, I'm praying it never comes up. And all hopeful
omens are welcome."

15

Assorted Terran Locations
19 January 2065

Hidalgo Rodriguez woke from a troubled sleep. His nightmares had been stranger and more unsettling than even a full gourd of *wheero* could account for. But opening his eyes was less than no help. He shrieked, and sprang to his feet even faster than he had on that distant childhood day in his father's goat shed when he had learned empirically that a human sneeze means "Run for your life!" in Goat.

The shriek woke Amparo and the children; within seconds they were harmonizing with him.

Their homey familiar hovel was gone. It had been replaced, by something indescribable, almost literally unseeable. It was everywhere, on all sides, had no apparent openings, and no features that any of them could identify. The light by which they saw it had no detectable source. Their first and best guess was that it was some kind of magical trap.

This diagnosis caused Hidalgo to utter a bellow of what he hoped sounded like rage, and throw himself bodily at the nearest part of the thing he could reach. He did not really expect to break through, but he had to try. He struck hard with a hunched shoulder, rebounded and gasped. He had not produced an opening or even a dent—but part of the omnipresent . . . *stuff* . . . had suddenly became transparent.

A window . . .

Outside it Hidalgo saw the familiar landscape of his home region, with some odd alterations he was too busy to study. He grabbed up a rag, wrapped his fist in it, and smashed at the window. It emphatically refused to break. His hand was more equivocal; he swore foully.

His son Julio followed Hidalgo's example, racing full tilt into the nearest wall to him. When nothing happened, he picked another spot and tried again. This time he was spectacularly successful: a door appeared in the stuff. He tested it; it worked just fine . . . and the entire Rodriguez clan joined him at high speed.

They stood outside the thing for a minute or so, all talking at the top of their lungs, none of them hearing a word—or noticing the sounds of similar loud "conversations" in the near distance.

The thing was still unidentifiable. It certainly did not look like a house, or even a building—not any that they had ever seen. It did not seem to have any straight lines or perpendiculars or right angles to it; there was no chimney.

Curiosity—and the growing realization that it was *much* hotter out here than it had been inside—finally caused them to reenter it.

They tried poking it some more. Finally Luz let out a scream. She had found a spot which caused it to grow a basin. Shouting at her to get away from it, Hidalgo cautiously approached the thing. For some reason, it had an extra faucet. He tried the one nearest him; its mechanism was unfamiliar to him, but not hard to figure out. Water came out, and swirled away.

Hidalgo gaped. His family had never, as far back as history recorded—yes, even unto his grandfather's day!—had access to running water in the home. He was rich! And there were *two* of the things. He tried the other one—and when he had grasped what it produced, he fainted dead away.

Hot water . . .

When he awoke, his new house was talking to him, telling him cheerfully of traffic conditions in a city he had only heard of. It showed him pictures. . . .

Hidalgo was a little comforted when he learned, shortly, that all of his neighbors in the hillside shanty-community were undergoing essentially identical experiences. So, elsewhere around the planet, were the family of Nkwame Van der Hoof, and *their* neighbors . . . the family of Algie Bent and their neighbors . . . the family of Trojan (his parents had named him after their hero) Khamela and their neighbors . . . the family of Lo Duc Tho and their neighbors . . . the list went on. Indeed, it was never completed.

A plague of houses seemed to be loose on the world. . . .

It took much longer for it to become apparent—
and longer for it to be believed by anyone with an
education—that people who lived in those toadstool
houses could not get sick.

PART SIX

16

The Shimizu Hotel
20 January 2065

Jay was watching the first full tech run-through of *Kinergy,* and wistfully praying God to strike him dead, when the alarm went off.

"FLARE WARNING—CLASS THREE—"

"Again?" someone groaned.

"—REPEAT, CLASS *THREE!* THIS IS A SAFETY EMERGENCY: ALL GUESTS MUST GO AS QUICKLY *AND CALMLY AS* POSSIBLE TO THE POOL AREA, AND REMAIN THERE UNTIL FURTHER NOTICE. THERE IS NO CAUSE FOR ALARM AS LONG AS—"

"Jesus, Class Three!" Francine said. "All right, everybody: drop what you're doing and *move*. Quietly! Rand, Andrew, kill the holo and sound—"

It vanished, and the theater reappeared.

"—PLEASE REPORT ALOUD WHEN YOU

HAVE LEFT FOR THE POOL; THE SHIMIZU WILL HEAR YOU AND NOT WASTE TIME SEARCHING FOR YOU—"

"Nova Dance Company, all members, leaving the theater now," Jay barked.

Andrew, the tech director who had replaced the murdered Nika, was a spacer: he came popping out the hatch from backstage like a cork leaving a champagne bottle. Jay suddenly remembered that Colly was back there with Rand, and headed for the tech hole to see if his brother needed any help. On the way it dawned on him that his troubles were over, or at least postponed: the company—and everyone else in the Shimizu—would all still be in the pool when the curtain was supposed to go up on *Kinergy*. Rescheduling after the emergency would take days. The Sword of Damocles had extended its expiry date.

Rand and Colly were emerging from the tech hole as he reached it. Colly seemed frightened, but not panicked; Rand was looking grim. "Honey," he said to her, "Uncle Jay is going to take you to the pool. Mom and I will join you there in two seconds."

"Daddy, no—"

"Take her, Jay."

"Rhea will be *fine*, bro," Jay began, but Rand cut him off.

"I tried to phone. Not accepting calls."

"At worst, somebody in a rad-suit will fetch her—"

"It's only a little out of the way—*take Colly.*" He kicked off and fired his thrusters. Jay found himself reassuring Colly, which helped calm himself; they jaunted for the pool together.

So did most of the population. The crowd of course thickened as it neared the center of the hotel. Some had a festive, holiday spirit; some were manic; some were silent and terrified; some were being dragged, protesting bitterly, by employees in bulky anti-radiation gear. Those whose protests became loud were sedated. Every corridor seemed to have a calm, competent employee whose sole job was to keep traffic flowing, and another who said reassuring things to anyone who would listen. Colly was actually enjoying herself by the time they reached the pool area. A smiling employee gave her and Jay ear-buttons to insert; at once a calm voice was murmuring instructions in their ears. "The pool is nearly empty now. When you are told to enter, do so promptly. Look for your last initial in the large green letters on the pool wall, and jaunt to that area so we can sort you out. Look for an employee with red arm- and leg-bands. If you have any emergency—first aid, medicine, need for a toilet, a missing loved one—report it to that employee—" and so on. The whole thing was well thought-out, well rehearsed, and worked wonders in holding down the general confusion; the Shimizu had been doing this, successfully, every eleven years for the last half-century. In under a minute, all of the pool's large doors opened at once, and they were told to enter. The ear-buttons became strident on the subject of not stopping in doorways to gawk. Jay and Colly were swept along with the flow, and found themselves inside the pool, with hundreds of chattering guests.

Jay looked around, located a green "P" on the wall a few hundred meters away, and took Colly there, breathing a sigh of relief that both Rand's and Rhea's last names happened to end with the same letter. "We'll wait here for your folks, pumpkin," he told the child. "This is gonna be lots more fun than a dumb old rad locker, huh?"

"Sure," she agreed, counting the house. "Wow! Kids I don't even know! There's one that looks *my* age—over there, see? Uncle Jay, can I go say hi?"

"Later, honey. Let's wait for your parents, okay? We've got three days, you know."

"Oh . . . okay." Suddenly she was horror-struck. "Uncle Jay—*what about the show?*"

He grinned. "The concert, you mean. Colly, do schoolkids back on Earth still get 'snow days'?"

She blinked. "Oh. No—but Mommy told me about them. You mean like 'sunspot days,' when the school system crashes, and you don't have to study."

"That's right. Well, your Dad and I, and the whole company, are about to have three 'sunspot days' in a row. And believe me, we can all use the rest."

"Oh. Hey, well that's great, then. Boy, it's weird to be in here without any water . . ."

"That's right, I hear this is your favorite place, isn't it?" Jay said absently. His watch said there were a little less than five minutes left before the doors would seal; he was scanning all the door areas at once for Rand and Rhea. At this point the majority of the new arrivals were being dragged by no-nonsense employees; Jay tried to mentally subtract them from the view, and so he didn't see Colly's parents right away.

Then he did. They and Duncan were just being released by the trio of chasers who had hauled them in. They must have come peaceably, for they were all still conscious—but as Jay opened his mouth to call Colly's attention to their arrival, he noted their respective body languages, integrated them, and closed his mouth again. Something was wrong. . . .

He squinted. Duncan seemed to be saying something—whether to Rand or Rhea or both was unclear. Whatever it was required gestures to get across. Rand's reply was so emphatic that even at that distance Jay could hear it, though not what was being said, amid the general din. Rhea and Duncan both answered at once and at length. This time Rand's reply was inaudible. A few seconds' pause . . . and Duncan spun around and started to jaunt away. Rand thrusted after him, overtook him, grappled with him, both their voices were heard shouting, Rhea chased them doing some shouting of her own—

For some reason nine groundhogs out of ten who attempt to fight in space make the same mistake: intuiting that a straight punch will push them away from their opponent, they instinctively go for an uppercut. But this only sends them sliding *past* him, toward his feet. Spacers know this, and are generally ready to meet the descending chin with an upthrust knee. Jay saw his brother begin an uppercut, and winced in anticipation. Rand massed much more than Jay—a terrible *disadvantage* under these conditions.

—but for some reason Duncan did not make the obvious counter. He took the punch, failed to lift his knee, and he and Rand went past each other like tectonic plates. That was all they had time for; the three chasers who'd fetched them here had already left in search of remaining stragglers, so it was a couple of the ear-button vendors who handled the job of sedating Rand and Duncan and, since she was still shouting, Rhea. In seconds, all three were at peace or a convincing imitation. The whole brief incident had gone largely unnoticed in all the general confusion.

"Do you see Mom and Dad anywhere, Uncle Jay?" Colly asked.

"No, honey," he said gently. "But I'm sure they're just fine. They've probably volunteered to help out with crowd control, since they know you're with me."

"Oh, I'll bet you're right," she said. "Daddy's real good at getting people to stay calm in a 'mergency."

"Yeah." He looked around and located an employee without arm- and leg-bands, a roving problem-solver, and waved her over. "How about this, pumpkin? How about if I stay here and wait up for them, and you go with this nice lady here, Xi—hi, Xi!—and meet some of those kids you saw? Xi, this is Colly Porter."

"Hi, Colly."

"Hi, Xi. Hey—get it? 'High-gee,' like the Space Commando's ship."

"That's a good one," Xi said patiently.

"Wow, suppose your parents really liked the Oz books, and they picked 'Wiz' for your last name? I have this friend named Duncan Iowa, because his parents—" They drifted away together; Colly forgot to say goodbye to Jay.

As soon as they were out of eyeshot, Jay made a beeline for the area where Rand, Rhea and Duncan had been towed and secured. A banded employee whose name Jay couldn't recall was trying to ID them so that they could be processed. "Those two are mine," he said. "Family."

"Fine by me, Sasaki-*sama*," she said respectfully. "Wrap 'em up and take 'em home. What about the Orientator?"

After a split-second's hesitation, Jay said, "Process him."

"You got it." Duncan would regain consciousness in the presence of a proctor, receive a ringing lecture—and a large black mark would be entered on his record. It might even be a firing offense, if the cause of the fight had been what Jay suspected it was. His first instinct had been to cover for Duncan . . . but if it turned out that his brother had not had some good reason to take a poke at the boy, the record could always be jiggered retroactively.

"How're you fixed for antidote?" he asked the woman.

She started to say something, then shrugged and tossed him a pair of infusers from her pouch.

He towed the sleeping Rhea and Rand slowly to the "P" section—an awkward task, especially in a crowd, but not difficult for a dancer. On the way he thought things through; when he got there he left Rhea in the care of the banded employee in charge, told him to let her sleep for now. Then he located a glowing letter whose adherents chanced to include few children and none near Colly's age, and towed Rand there. He Velcroed his brother to a support, bared his arm, triggered the infuser, and backed off a few meters.

Rand woke as quickly and seamlessly as he had

fallen asleep—and looked around wildly for his opponent and prepared another punch. In moments the world snapped back into focus for him. He groaned; his shoulders slumped and his head bowed. Then he drew in breath for what was going to be a great bellow of either anger or grief—but by then Jay was close again, and clapped a hand over his brother's mouth.

"Easy," he murmured. "You don't want to get dosed twice. You might—" Some mental censor made him decide not to name the most common consequence of a double-sedation: temporary impotence. "—regret it. Calm down . . . and tell me what happened." He took his hand away.

Again Rand slumped, this time all the way into free-fall crouch, a position halfway to fetal. He said nothing for long moments.

Jay already knew the general shape of what Rand was probably going to say, but it was important that Rand say it. "Well?"

His brother looked up with the expression of a man who has just lost a limb, and is trying to integrate the intellectual knowledge with his emotions. "When I got there . . . they were together."

Jay thought of six or seven things to say, hundreds of words. "So?" was the one he chose.

Rand struggled to keep his voice down. "Come on, Jay, do I have to show you a graphic?" he said in strangled tones.

Jay frowned. "You caught them in the act? They ignored a Class Three alert? I don't believe it!" *Even if it really happened,* he thought, *there simply had to be time for them to at least throw a goddam robe*

*on—they're dressed now, for Christ's sake!—and if
they did, there's no way to* prove *anything—this can
still be fixed—*

"They were fully dressed. It took me nearly two
full minutes to get there. But Jesus, Jay—*I've got
a fucking nose,* okay? I've got eyes. It happened.
Something happened."

"—and you don't know just what. Do you?"
When there was no answer he rushed on. "It
could have been a passing thought, a fleeting
temptation, and some very bad timing, okay? It
happened to me once: I was flirting, like you do,
you know . . . and just as I started to realize it was
getting to be more than just flirting, just as I was
deciding to back off, his wife came in and caught
us both with boners. It didn't mean a thing; it
blew over. There's no way to be sure this meant
anything. Give her a chance to explain, when she's
over the embarrassment."

Rand looked away. "I will." He looked back again.
"But Jay, I've lived with her for ten years. I've seen
her look embarrassed. I've even seen her look guilty.
But this is the first time I've *ever* seen her look
ashamed. I already know all I want to know. And I
thank you for your counsel and support, and I would
greatly appreciate it if you would leave me the fuck
alone now, so I don't have a fight with you, okay?
Wait—where's Colly?"

"She's covered," Jay said. "Take it off your mind.
I'll go get her as soon as I wake Rhea up. You sure
you'll be okay here?"

"No, but moving won't help. Go."

"Listen to this when you're ready," Jay said,

handing Rand his own ear-button. "It'll tell you the procedures." And he left his brother alone to mourn.

As Jay was returning to "P" section, he found himself humming a tune in a minor key, and suddenly recognized it as a nearly century-old Stevie Wonder song called "Blame It on the Sun." The irony was too unsubtle for his conscious mind; he stopped humming. He knew he should be sad for his brother, he intended to be as soon as he could, but for now he was numb. Too much going on; too much still to do; an eight-year-old still his nominal responsibility—to whom this all must somehow be explained before much longer. Then, three days or more locked in a can with the problem. His head began to throb.

Rhea came out of it as quickly as Rand had—and began blushing the moment she focused on Jay's face.

"What happened?" he asked. "No, forget that: *how much did he see?* How much can he prove?"

Her eyes widened as she took his meaning. "Oh, Jay—"

He turned away. "Dammit, Rhea . . . dammit to hell . . . *fuck* it to hell—"

"Where's Colly?"

"Having a jolly time in the company of a very nice lady, meeting other kids," he said bitterly. "I'd say we have at least another ten minutes before you're going to have to explain to her why Mommy and Daddy aren't talking to each other. And why Uncle Duncan has a bruise on his chin. But you're a writer: I'm sure you can improvise something."

"She doesn't call him 'Uncle Duncan,'" she said absurdly. And then: "Oh . . . my . . . God . . ."

"MAY I HAVE YOUR ATTENTION, PLEASE,"

said a loud and omnipresent voice. It repeated twice, as the hubbub dwindled, then went on, "WE ARE VERY PLEASED TO REPORT THAT THE CLASS THREE FLARE ALERT WAS A FALSE ALARM— REPEAT, THE ALERT WAS A FALSE ALARM." The hubbub became an uproar; the voice got louder to compensate. "THE EMERGENCY IS OVER. TO MINIMIZE CONFUSION, PLEASE RETURN TO YOUR STATEROOMS BY LETTER-GROUPS, BEGINNING WITH THOSE WHOSE LAST NAMES BEGIN WITH 'A' AND THEIR FAMI- LIES. PLEASE DO NOT TRY TO LEAVE UNTIL ALL THOSE IN THE PRECEDING LETTER- GROUP ARE GONE. THE SHIMIZU APOLO- GIZES FOR ANY INCONVENIENCE, AND THANKS YOU ALL FOR YOUR COOPERATION DURING THE EMERGENCY—"

"Jesus Christ—" Jay began.

"Take her home for me, Jay," Rhea blurted, and jetted away before he could object. She mingled with the crowd whose last names began with "A," and was lost from sight. Jay stared after her, feeling his head- ache gather force.

Within moments, Colly appeared, trailing a frantic Xi. "Did they show up yet, Uncle Jay?"

He started to say no automatically. But then he had the thought that in the near future, a lot of people were going to be lying to this child, and he didn't want to be one of them anymore. "I caught a glimpse of them," he said, then skated quickly off the thin ice. "But we'll never find them in this madhouse now. That's okay; I'm sure we'll meet them back at your suite"—whoops, hitting thin ice again—

"eventually. Say, did you meet any interesting kids?"

"Wow, yeah—I met a boy my own age, named Waldo, and he's a spacer, like me: *he's* gonna be here forever too! I never saw him around before because he's got something wrong with his muscles and he can't go out and play—but who cares? I can go to *his* house and we can be friends *forever*! I invited him to my birthday party—"

Don't count on it, pumpkin, Jay thought, but all he said was, "He sounds nice."

A lot of people's plans were going to be changing soon.

He had already left the pool with the rest of the S's, and was in the corridors with Colly, before it sank in: *Kinergy* was going to go on at the appointed time after all. . . .

In common with most of the choreographers who had ever lived, Jay had, two days before curtain, no idea whether he was on the verge of artistic triumph or disaster. It was no longer possible for him to evaluate the work, either objectively or subjectively. He was prepared to take the most ignorant amateur criticism to heart, or discount the most informed professional praise. The final, and only important, verdict would come two nights from now, in the form of applause or its embarrassing absence or—God forbid!—active booing. He burned to know what that verdict would be . . . and feared to find out. The only thing he knew for certain was that he could definitely have used another week to polish the damned thing. That was why he had welcomed the flare emergency.

And all the fucking emergency had accomplished was to cost him his tech rehearsal—and to shatter his brother's world.

Well, perhaps there was a relatively bright side to all this—at least from Jay's point of view. Presumably Rhea would go back dirtside now—that might even be why she had done it. That would leave Rand no real choice but to stay here in space! The only place waiting for him on Terra was Provincetown, Rhea's town. He'd be miserable for a while, sure . . . but as Sam Spade had once said, that would pass. He'd heal. A season of his own original work, some media massage courtesy of Ev Martin, a few standing *O's* . . .

Oh, shit! Would Rand be in any shape to come to the premiere?

Jay assumed his brother would not make the remaining two days of rehearsals—and that would hurt, but Andrew could probably handle things alone. Jay also knew he would miss Rand's companionship, his services as a sounding-board, the last-minute inspirations he might have contributed—and that wasn't fatal either.

But Kate Tokugawa would be livid if Rand did not appear at the premiere. His presence was *required*. All the media would be there. It was a matter of face. Hers, and the Board's.

In his heart, Jay knew face was as low in Rand's present scale of values as it was high in Kate's. Oh, this was more than a tragedy: it had all the makings of a catastrophe. . . .

"I wish that dumb old flare wasn't a false alarm, Uncle Jay," Colly said. "That was starting to be fun."

Guilt tore at his heart. He thought *he* had problems? "Me too, honey," he said softly, tightening his grip on her small hand. "Me too."

What the hell am I going to do with her?

"Sergei?" he tried.

Personal AIs were back on-line. "Yes, Jay?" Diaghilev said.

"Excuse me, Colly, I have to check on something with Andrew. Sergei, hush-field, please." The sounds of the crowd around him went away. "Phone Rand."

"Not accepting calls, Jay."

"God dammit, emergency override 'P-Town'!"

Rhea answered. *"What?"*

"What do I do with your daughter?" Jay asked brutally.

There was a short silence. "Can . . . can you take her? For a while, anyway?"

"What do I tell her?"

He heard Rand say something angry in the background. " . . . something good, okay?" she said. "Please, brother? I'll call you when . . . when we're ready for her."

It was the word "brother" that made up his mind. Rhea had never called him that before. She was begging. "Okay." He was prepared to end the conversation, but could not decide how. Did he say "Good luck"? Instead he said, "I'll wait for your call. Off."

Something good, okay?

"Colly, you're coming home with me. The cronkites want to interview your mom and dad about the flare—you know, celebrity on the spot stuff."

It was weak; no one had interviewed them after

the previous, genuine emergency. But Colly bought it. "Neat! Maybe we can watch it at your house—they'll probably rush it onto the Net—"

Jay winced. "Well, maybe not right away. It'll take time to edit, you know—"

"Phone, Jay," Diaghilev said. "Two calls waiting: Andrew and Francine."

Jay wished someone would solve brain-cloning. "Colly, excuse me; Sergei, give me both of them; Andrew, Francine, I can't talk for long right now, but . . ." His mind raced. " . . . uh, today's a wrap. We'll do the tech rehearsal tomorrow at noon; first dress after supper; final run-through will have to be the afternoon of the performance."

"Are you sure, Boss?" Francine asked. "We could do the tech tonight—cancel the pony show."

"No," Jay said. "After something like this, the cabaret show is *essential*. I won't be there, but trust me: you'll never have a better house. They'll cheer themselves hoarse, and tip like Shriners. Everybody needs to celebrate still being alive"—*well, almost everybody . . .* —"and not being trapped in a swimming pool for three days. I've got to go; I'll leave my notes from this afternoon with your AIs later and talk with you tomorrow. Off."

"Calls waiting, Jay: Katherine Tokugawa, Evelyn Martin, Eva Hoffman . . . and another just coming in, Duncan Iowa."

"Suffering Jesus! Flush Iowa and Martin, tell Eva I'll call her back, refuse all further calls, and give me Kate. Greetings, Tokugawa-*sama*—some excitement, eh? I know why you're calling, and don't worry: we'll be ready when the bell rings—"

By the time he had given his boss every reassurance he could counterfeit and gotten her off the phone, he was back home. Once inside, he turned Colly over to the White Rabbit; it checked, learned that Room Service was not yet back on-line, and led her off to Jay's personal pantry, glancing irritably at its pocket watch, for the stiff peanut-butter and jelly it knew she required. Jay took a deep breath—

—let it out; took another—

—thought longingly of a drink, and retracted all the furniture in his living room, and began to dance. And kept on dancing, ricocheting around the room in great energy-wasting leaps and landings and spins and recoveries, until his body was as exhausted as his brain. He poured all his fear and confusion and guilt and anger into the dance . . . his irritation with his beloved brother, for picking now to be betrayed . . . his sneaking sympathy for the bitch who had picked now to put the horns on his brother . . . his heartbreak for the small child who was about to become a helpless leaf in a storm she would not understand for years . . .

When he finally stopped, Colly's applause startled him. He had not been aware of her watching, hadn't thought to censor what his body was saying. But she was not disturbed by his dance, only impressed; her applause was sincere. She was oblivious to her doom.

They ended up napping in each other's arms.

17

Nova Dance Theatre
The Shimizu Hotel
22 January 2065

Early on in the dance, Eva knew she was in good
hands, and relaxed.

You couldn't always tell, that early. Sometimes
a serious dance was over before you had decided
whether you liked it or not. Every piece must,
along with what it actually conveys, explain to you
the rules by which it is meant to be judged, and
sometimes that subtext can take as long to grasp
and evaluate as the work itself. For that very
reason, Eva had avoided seeing any rehearsals, so
she could assess the finished work fairly. But a
minute or so into *Kinergy,* she stopped praying
that her friend's work wouldn't bomb, and became
lost in it. Jay and his brother had meshed well,
for the second time: this piece, despite its origins

in the turgid head of Pribhara, was even better than *Spatial Delivery* had been.

It was not as cerebral as that piece, nor as simple. For one thing, it was staged in the sphere rather than in proscenium, so it had to work in any direction. The stage was bare: apparently none of the standard vector-changing hardware of free-fall dance was going to be used tonight . . . which meant the dancers were going to work harder. The piece's title was another clue. *Spatial Delivery* had been a single pun, based on a long-obsolete term—but *Kinergy* was a cascade of overlapping ones—synergy/kinetic energy/kinship energy/kin urge—all primal concepts of the human universe, as old as DNA and as unlikely to ever become dated. It had opened, in fact, with two chains of six dancers unwinding from a double helix in a sudden burst of illumination. The musical accompaniment that appeared as they separated was likewise timeless: the tones of its individual voices did not precisely match any classical instrument, but neither did they sound electronic. The music they made together was difficult to categorize; one could have imagined such music being played at just about any time in history. The dancers were costumed as neutrally as possible, in unitards that matched their complexions, with hoods that masked their diversity of hair styles and colors, and with oversized wings and disguised thrusters.

Nor did the ensuing choreography seem to contain any period or style "flags" in its movement vocabulary—not even those characteristic to its creator. Eva was familiar with most of Jay's work, and might not have identified this as his if she hadn't been told: he had managed to transcend his own limitations.

Ordinarily, for instance, he hated unisons, referred to them as "redundancies," and tended to use them as little as possible—but once his two chains of dancers had separated into twelve individuals, they spent several minutes dancing in unison, changing only in their dynamic relation to one another, like birds altering their formation in flight.

Eva slowly realized that the piece *did* have an unavoidable period flag: since the dancers were weightless, the dance had to belong to the twenty-first century. Few of its sweeping movements could have been performed any earlier in history, on Terra, without the help of special effects. But as that realization came to her, Rand's shaping began, and cut the piece adrift in time again. The audience facing her on the far side of the theater went away; the dancers were now flying in a blue Terran sky that went on forever, peppered with slow-moving clouds. The sun, its brilliance tempered to a tolerable level by an intervening cloud, was directly opposite Eva, so her subconscious decided that she was lying on her back, *mere thousands of meters above Terra,* about to fall, an effect so unsettling that she grabbed for her seatmate. (Glancing briefly around, she noticed that many others were doing the same—but not those who were spaceborn.) But the clouds and dancers did not recede, she did not "fall"; before long she relaxed and accepted the fact that she could float in a gravity field, that she was simply lying on a cloud. She resumed watching the dance.

How old is the concept of fairies? Of winged

humans who play among the clouds? These dancers played *with* the clouds, buzzing them, bursting
through them, batting them to and fro like fluffy
beachballs. A sextet formed, grabbed each other's
ankles and made a great circle just in time for a
cloud to thread it in stately slow motion. Another
group at the opposite end of the theater seemed to
echo the phrase, but contracted as the cloud was
passing through their circle and pinched it into two
clouds; the sextet broke into two trios, and each took
one of the cloudlets to play with. The remaining six
formed a puffball, like fish in the pool, with a cloud
at their center; it slowly expanded outward through
them, moving up their torsos, and became a translucent wispy sphere around them, then a globe of
water, swirling with surface tension. All six came apart
from each other and burst the bubble: it popped with
a comical moist sound and sent droplets cascading
in all directions like a cool firework blossoming. The
ones coming toward Eva vanished just before
arriving.

She was delighted. The simple beauty of weightlessness, which became prosaic for every Shimizu
resident through daily familiarity, was made magical again by the setting. In this context, the dancers seemed somehow *more than* (or was it less than?)
weightless; they seemed to be nearly massless as well,
ethereal. They could meet at high speed without
apparent impact, change vector so that it seemed to
be their will rather than thrusters which caused the
change, bounce from a cloud as easily as penetrate
it, pivot on a passing breeze.

Fetch a Sumerian shepherd with a time machine,

give him an hour or two to get used to zero gee, and show him this piece: it would communicate to him instantly. The same for a Cretan stonecutter or a medieval alchemist or, Eva imagined, a hypothetical twenty-third century energy creature. There were probably *apes* who would appreciate this dance. The creative audacity of trying to rekindle the ancient wonder of flying, for people in an environment where one had to fly to get to the bathroom, people who had been striving since their arrival inboard to become blasé about that very miracle, was inspired. Eva had been in space for a long time, and this was the first time in years that she had reflected on how *lucky* she was: that mankind's oldest dream—to fly like a bird, and never fear hitting the ground—was for her a commonplace.

During the brief interval between movements, Eva reached up and tapped the program-button in her ear; she had deliberately not audited the program notes before the piece began, but now she wanted to know what the creators had had to say about it. She heard the recorded voice of the immortal Murray Louis, reading from one of his own books:

> *Performance is not mired, it floats. It exists upward, it hovers. It is immediate. It happens. It has no roots, it feeds from the air. It floats above all the tangibles that create it. From its loftiness, its aura descends and permeates all, lifting everything to its height as well as its depth. Performance is the revelation that speaks for itself.*

She switched off as the credits began; the second movement had begun. During the interval the dancers had all exited—seeming to shimmer out of existence, one by one—and the clouds had thickened into banks of rolling thunderheads that blotted the sun and darkened the sky. Now the darkness was nearly complete; one could just make out individual billowings in the roiling storm. The temperature seemed to drop slightly, and the air pressure to rise.

Suddenly, with an earsplitting crash, a fractal fork of lightning arced between two prominences. It came *toward* Eva, ended only meters from her; for the second time she clutched her seatmate tightly. The audience gasped, then muttered and tittered nervously. Five or ten seconds later a second bolt, shorter and with a different vector, again gave a snapshot of the interior of the storm. The music began to sound like mountain horns in the far distance, great deep bass tones punching through intervening winds. Another bolt, more crooked than the last, flared and died . . . then another, and another. Their randomness was convincing; they came anywhere from two to twenty seconds apart, lingering in the eye for nearly a second.

Then all at once all twelve dancers were there, caught in the sudden glare of God's flashbulb, frozen in tableau. Again the audience murmured. The next flash found them in a different tableau, and the next. Sometimes they were arrayed as two sextets, sometimes as four trios, or three quartets, or a septet and quintet, or six pairs; sometimes they were simply twelve lost individuals. No matter how close together the flashes came, the dancers were never

caught in motion. Eva wondered how they managed
to navigate to each new position in the dark without colliding, but refused to let herself speculate on
how the trick was being done, preferring to simply
enjoy it. Soon she was noting patterns in the pro-
gression of patterns itself. The whole thing began to
remind her of the ancient computer game called
"Life," in which a collection of cells changes shape
and structure in successive frames, "evolving" and
"growing" according to simple rules. This was like
a three-dimensional Life sequence run at a very slow
frame rate, had the same weird but intuitively
appealing beauty, constantly changing yet remaining
stable over time.

Just as seeming chance brought the dancers fairly
close together in a cluster, an especially bright bolt
of lightning lingered longer than usual, split again
and again, fractured into a hundred snake-tongues
of fire that raced around the entire storm—and in
their flickering light, the cluster of dancers began to
move in space, turning end over end like a Catherine
wheel. As the actinic sparkles faded slowly away, the
dancers themselves began to glow softly, somehow
emitting their own light, shining from within like fireflies. They began to move bodily too, without losing their place in formation, first in unison and then
individually, and before long the tension of their solos
tore the cluster apart into smaller groups.

Two of the groups, asymmetrically opposed, began
to leave trails of light behind them as they moved.
Short at first, mere afterimages, the trails slowly
lengthened until they were winding tails, as though
the invisible eraser that chased them was falling

farther and farther behind—then they vanished, and three other groups began to leave trails of their own. Soon dancers were making light sculptures all over the sky, like particle tracks in a cyclotron, occasionally mirroring one another for a time and then diverging. Again Eva was reminded of something from the dawn of the Age of Silicon: a screen-saver program called Electric Fire. The effect was hypnotic—but a kind of hypnosis that made the pulse race and the breath come faster, a *heightening* of alertness. Forks of lightning still flared here and there among the clouds, imbuing the whole scene with a sense of energy, largeness, danger. Perhaps there were subsonics buried in the score as well. One sensed that something awful, cataclysmic, might happen if one of the dancers missed a movement, distorted the weave of the incomprehensible pattern they were shaping together. Something on the scale of Ragnarok. The speed and intensity of the dance increased, until all twelve were racing to and fro at the highest speeds they could reach without crashing into the unseen audience, threatening to lose control and do so. The very clouds seemed to back away from them. In their boiling frenzy, they came to resemble the classic historical footage of the Fireflies confronting Shara Drummond . . . save that they were not red. Each glowed a *different* color now, twelve distinct shades; together they seemed the shards of a proto-rainbow struggling to form.

As the music swelled and steadied, they succeeded: seemingly by chance, they settled one after another into the same stable orbit, a great ring whose axis kept changing, like the "orange-slice" orbit of

Peace Monitor satellites around Terra, like a primitive model of an atom with twelve electrons. Their trails became one orbit in length: a coruscating rainbow chased itself around the globe.

A short blast of trumpets, and the rainbow flared, doubling in brightness. Each and every cloud dissolved into a trillion spherically expanding droplets of water, a trillion seeds, each carrying with it a tiny reflection of the rainbow. As they dispersed and vanished, the stormclouds lightened in color and mass, thinned out, became wispy, melted away save for a handful of benign white clouds. The storm was broken; the sun returned, and the achingly familiar blue of the Terran sky. (Even spaceborns, studies had long shown, resonated emotionally to that color; it seemed to be in the DNA somewhere, though none could say how.) The music moved gradually up the scale, from deep baritone horn sounds to medium frequencies that sounded eerily like human voices, yet moved in ways no human culture sang. The dancers glowed so fiercely now that they seemed to have enlarged, and their features were indistinct.

Then the rainbow-ring came apart, and they were again the playful, independent sprites they had been in the first movement—but shining, gleaming. The voices became a vast choir, hundreds of voices singing their hearts out in a language Eva had never heard before. The net effect was dysharmonic, but occasionally little resolutions came and went, as if the choir were singing a dozen songs in a dozen keys simultaneously.

The blue sky turned suddenly to gold. Groups of dancers formed, interacted and broke up with dizzying speed. A quartet would come together, agree on a movement phrase, split apart and bring the phrase to other groups, which made up new phrases to combine with them, then split apart in their turn. Choreographic ideas appeared spontaneously and spread around the stage like heat lightning or rumor. A unison formed by apparent accident among the twelve dissolved, then returned—while in the score, more and more singers reached agreement on a key and rules of harmony, until they too were working together to build something. Dance and music together established a stable base and began to climb higher.

Literally! Clouds came toward Eva, and wind into her face: she and the dancers were rising, leaving unseen Terra behind them. The illusion was utterly convincing, and quite breath-taking. The wind fell away, and they left the clouds below; the golden sky began to darken again—not the turgid dark of the storm, but the pure star-spattered blackness of space.

No, not pure. They traveled through a fine mist of some kind of dust. Red dust. It began to accumulate on the bodies of the dancers, until they were caked with it, coated by it, covered in it, each of them glowing a shade of red: ochre, umber, amber, crimson, scarlet, ruby. It was Symbiote, and they a dozen newborn Stardancers, spreading their wings now, spinning them out into lightsails, joyously learning a new way to dance together, rubbing together like blobs in a lava lamp.

Eva put all of her attention on keeping perfectly still and calm. It was difficult—but Reb had trusted her. Many decades of lucrative poker came to her aid.

Briefly the twelve boiled together at the center
of the stage like swarming bees, a "quotation" of the
Fireflies who had given mankind the Symbiote—then
they opened out again, formed a spherical
matrix . . . and folded gracefully together into the
kukanzen posture of those who meditate in space,
each facing out from the center, away from all the
others. Together they bowed, to the Universe; the
music resolved at last into a major chord spanning
the entire audible range; dancers and music began
to fade away, like Cheshire cats, until there was only
silence and infinite space and the burning stars; then
they too dwindled and were gone.

Five full seconds of total silence. Then, pan-
demonium—

One of the many reasons art in space is performed
in spherical theaters is acoustics. Applause reinforces
itself, just as a person standing in a hemispherical
building on Earth can hear with total clarity a whis-
per from someone standing precisely opposite him.
Any ovation in space sounds like a Terran audience
going mad; it makes up for the fact that they cannot stand to deliver it. But *this* ovation would have
shaken the walls of the Bolshoi.

Eva let herself glance at Jay and Rand, now, as
the house lights came up. They were together at the
opposite end of the vip section, unbuckling their belts
to join the dancers for the bow. Her eyes were not
what they had once been, but she had a century of
experience in intrigue: one glance at Jay's face and
she was intuitively certain *he* didn't know Reb's
secret. Rand was much harder to read. Ev Martin—
hearing that Rand's wife had left him yesterday,

taking his daughter back to Provincetown with her—had spoken with the house physician. The shaper was stoned to his cheeks, smiling beatifically. His eyes were wounds, and he was jaunting like a tourist, but he would pass muster for the media.

Could *Rand* know something? Unlikely . . . but then, it was a visual that had shocked her, rather than choreography. Still, perhaps it was just coincidence . . .

The crowd was merciless in its admiration, demanding eight curtain calls before the exhausted dancers were allowed to go backstage and peel off their soaked costumes. Eva stopped clapping much sooner; her aged hands gave out. Finally the ovation was over, and her companion, Chen Ling Ho, was murmuring, "I liked it very much . . . despite the ending."

Again she had recourse to her poker experience. "Wasn't that blackout section terrific? Where they did the tableaux in the lightning flashes? How do you suppose they got around in the dark without a train wreck?"

" 'How do I get to Carnegie Hall?' " the trillionaire replied.

"You can't possibly be old enough to remember that joke—Carnegie Hall was torn down before you were born!"

His eyes twinkled. "I like to think of myself as a student of classical humor."

She blinked. " 'Your money or your life?' " she asked, quoting an ancient radio joke.

Chen gave the correct response: dead silence.

She rewarded him with a smile, unbuckled herself

with one hand and took his arm with the other. "Let's head for the reception—I want to congratulate the boys before the crowd beats them stupid."

Rand and Jay were already glazing over by the time Eva elbowed her way into the receiving line with Chen, but she caught their attention—and managed to fluster them both—when she said, "Lads, somewhere Willem Ngani is smiling tonight."

"He'd have loved that piece," Chen agreed, and the two thanked them, both stammering. Then Eva let herself be chivvied away by assistant cronkites— this was the worst possible time and place to probe Rand's secret thoughts.

She and Chen returned to her suite. He accepted a drink, and they moved to the window. Terra was about a quarter full. The illuminated crescent contained China; twilight in Beijing. They shared silence for a few minutes. Then he said, "You did not respond to my criticism of the ending of *Kinergy*. Did you like it?"

She felt like she was juggling eggs in a gravity field. "Yes, I did. It resonated for me. What didn't you like about it?"

"The Stardancer motif."

"Too obvious?"

He hesitated. "Yes, that."

"Something else?"

Again he hesitated. "You know my true feelings toward the ones in red."

"Not really," she said. "I'm aware that you're not a major fan—and that you don't want that publicly known. Given your father's history with the Starmind, I understand that. But do they really bother you so much that a reference to them spoils a work of art for you?"

"Yes."

"For heaven's sake, Ling, why? Personal feelings aside, you of all people must know how much the human race owes them—"

"Precisely. How then can I not resent them?"

"Oh, that's silly!"

There might not be another person alive privileged to say that to Chen Ling Ho; from Eva he took it. "Gratitude implies obligation. The scale of the obligation is, in this case, horrifying."

"But there's almost nothing they want that we have—just trace elements we'll never miss. The bill will never come due."

He nodded, and again said, "Precisely. That makes the obligation even more intolerable. It is, on both sides, literally unforgivable."

She frowned. "There's more to it than that."

"What do you mean?" he asked.

"You're not mankind. Your personal share of the debt . . . well, with your resources you could probably pay cash. At most, it's a philosophical abstraction. To spoil a dance, something has to have its roots in your gut, not your head. What really bothers you about the Starmind?"

"Their virtue," he said.

"Come again?"

For the first time, emotion came into his voice. "They are so damned virtuous! So relentlessly admirable. My instincts tell me to despise and fear anyone who appears above reproach. Their harmlessness disarms us. Again, literally! We allowed them to abolish war for us, allowed them to strengthen the United Nations into a true world government. Perhaps war is not, after all, a truly necessary evil—there are more efficient ways of getting rich now—but we may find one day that it was necessary in ways we do not yet grasp."

"Jesus, Ling—you want *war* back? Even I'm not that nostalgic."

"I feel in my heart that in the old days, when we were a brawling, clawing, struggling world, we were more human. Now we grow fat and soft on the riches flung down to us from on high—and because our short-term wealth has *temporarily* overtaken population growth, *we have stopped fearing population growth*. One day we will reach a point where no input of new wealth can help us . . . and then civilization will fall, and millions, billions, will die. Conceivably *all*. All humans. But not the Stardancers. They may *never* die." He heard emotion creeping into his voice and caught himself. "You understand, I do not discuss these matters publicly. Stardancers are much beloved. In this age, no man can hold real wealth or power save he treat with them. Humanity is drunk, today, happily drunk, and in no mood for grim warnings. But how can the Neanderthal not hate the Cro-Magnon, Eva?"

She nodded. Time to change the subject. "Well, I can't say I share your feelings, but at least I think I understand them now. Thanks for explaining. I'll remember not to buy you the new Drummonds holo for your birthday."

"Oh, no," he said. "Please do, if you like. One may admire the exquisite gyrations of cancer cells in the microscope. The choreography of the Stardancers themselves I find very interesting; it's only their existence that offends me."

That made her smile. "It's a shame your country gave up emperors, Ling. You'd have been one of the great ones."

"One hates to be a merely good emperor," he agreed, and finished his drink.

She followed suit. "Are you sleepy?"

"No."

"Shall we go to bed?"

He bowed and took her hand. "All my life I have wondered why other men prize young women."

"Perhaps," she suggested, "they do not feel they deserve the best."

He smiled, and came closer.

18

The assistant director of the United States Internal
Revenue Service knew that her office was as snoop-
proof as human ingenuity could make it. Nonetheless she got up from her desk and personally made
sure her office door was locked. Then she told her
AI to cancel all appointments for the day and hold
all calls, and opened a "Most Secure" phone circuit
to Brussels.

Her global counterpart, the Right Honorable
Undersecretary of Revenue for the United Nations,
and Assistant Chairman of the Committee on Fiscal Anomalies, answered promptly. "Hello, LaToya.
This is early in the day for you to call. What is it,
8 AM in Washington?" He looked closer. "My God—
are you ill?"

"I've been up all night, George."

The Undersecretary sighed. "Something serious, then. All right, which hat shall I wear?"

"Both of them, I think. And hold on to both. You may have to invent a third hat: I don't think there's any precedent for this."

A sigh. "Go ahead."

"George, I've run the integrations through again and again. I used three methods, different machines, I even had the software triplechecked."

"And—"

"You'll be receiving more than you're expecting from us this year."

The Undersecretary lifted an eyebrow. "How much more?"

"On the order of ten percent."

The other eyebrow rose to join the first. "You are telling me the gross national product of the United States has taken a ten percent jump. *Up.*"

"That is part of what I'm telling you. I talked with Jacques and Rogelio last night . . . and they report nearly identical bulges. Jacques puts his at nine percent; Rogelio is running behind, but says Mexico will probably run eleven and a half."

The Undersecretary was frowning. "So someone is pumping serious money into North America. Is it real, or just pixels?"

"As far as I can learn, it's genuine money."

"Where is it coming from?"

"It falleth as the gentle rain from heaven. Drop by drop—all over."

A grunt. "Stonewalled, eh? Very well—where is it *going*? Who's paying taxes on it? What categories?"

"Take a tranquilizer."

The Undersecretary frowned, then did as he was bid. At once the frown smoothed over. "Go ahead."

"One category: self-employed income."

"Self-employed?" That was the last sector in which he would have expected such a surge in earnings. "Any breakdowns as to subcategories yet?"

The assistant director nodded. "Again, one. Self-employed artists."

The Undersecretary stared. After a full ten seconds of silence, he said, "What kind of artists?"

"All kinds of artists. Live theater, dance, film, music, literature, sculpture, painting . . . what it comes down to is, in every genre and subgenre there is, from grand opera to street theater, roughly ten percent of the working professionals have had a very good year."

"And all from the same source?"

"No. Maybe. I don't know. I suspect it, because it all seems to be coming in the same way: anonymous donations, rather than grants or box office. One donation per artist or arts group. Substantial ones."

"But then it's simple!" the Undersecretary said. "Who's declaring the increased donations on their taxes?"

"That's the problem. Nobody. Not in North America anyway. But why the hell would someone overseas want to take such a huge flyer in North American art?"

"Confusing," the Undersecretary agreed.

"Confusing, hell. It *worries* me, George. Good news on this scale is ominous. I smell a swindle of some kind."

"I don't suppose there's any chance these

benefactors are North Americans who elected for some reason not to claim . . ." He trailed off.

She politely pretended she hadn't heard him. "Will you look into it, George? *Quietly?*"

"I'll get back to you," he said, and broke the connection.

For the rest of the day work devoured her attention, but she fretted most of the night. The next morning at the office she flinched when her AI said, "The Undersecretary of Revenue."

"Accept!" she said at once.

"He is not on the phone, ma'am. He is in your outer office."

"Jesus." She took a deep breath, and rose to her feet. "Admit him."

Two bodyguards entered first, scanned the room carefully, and nodded through the door. The Undersecretary came in, and dismissed them with some unseen signal. She started to come around her desk to greet him, but he waved her off. They sat together; he came to the point without formalities. "This room is secure?"

The assistant director checked a telltale. "Yes."

"It's happening all over the globe. And in space. High Orbit, Luna City, everywhere. Has been for over six months now."

"Everywhere? The same way?"

"Not everywhere. Just the places where people make art for money. But all of those."

She looked surprised. "All? You don't have up-to-date data from all, do you? I thought there were several nations still refusing to switch over to a December 31 tax deadline."

"True; there are nonconforming nations. But almost *all* nations require self-employed artists to report quarterly. I can't prove there are no exceptions, yet, but I'd bet money. The pattern is clear."

She powered her chair back away from her desk until it hit the wall. "Isn't this the *damndest* thing?"

"Have you anything new to report?"

It took her a few moments to respond. "Null results, mostly. I tried to do further breakdowns and correlations, to see if I could get a clue regarding motive. *Which* artists are getting money? Why them? How much? That sort of thing."

"And?"

"Nothing helpful. Some of them are starving-in-a-garret types, but some are major stars or companies, and some are in between. No geographical, financial, political, religious or even aesthetic connections I can find. Competing schools of theory, some of them. The one steady correlation I've identified tells me nothing useful."

"And that is—?"

"The amount. Apparently, each lucky beneficiary—from the poorest poet to the richest director, from barbershop quartet to symphony orchestra—had his or her or its annual budget approximately quadrupled. In a few cases, that comes to megabucks."

The Undersecretary nodded grimly. "That accords with what I've been able to learn."

The assistant director paled. "Good God, George—there are less than a half dozen fiscal entities on or off Terra who are in a position to disburse *that* kind of money—"

"I know."

She got a grip on herself. "So you went to the Secretary."

"I deemed it necessary, yes. This is too big for a bureaucrat like me; I needed a statesman."

"And he said—?"

"He said that an anonymous donation is an anonymous donation, regardless of size. He said no law requires a philanthropist to take a tax deduction. He said support for the arts is not a crime. He said it is the policy of the United Nations to respect the right of privacy. He said, with emphasis, that anyone who violates privacy with respect to support for the arts will be broken back to a G-7 clerk."

She was staring at him in growing disbelief. "He said to forget it. That's what you're telling me."

"He said nothing of the sort. Forget what?"

She opened her mouth. Thirty seconds later, words came out. In the interval, she examined her life, for the first time in decades. "I forget," she said at last.

He nodded. "Elephants never look happy."

She powered her chair back to her desk, looked at it, drummed her fingers on it. "The story *will* come out," she said finally. "Artists always talk to cronkites. Sooner or later one will listen, and realize he has actual news on his hands. The data are public information."

"They will be when we release them," the Undersecretary agreed carefully.

She did mental arithmetic, checking a few figures with her desk. "George, this is scary. *Whoever* is doing this, they're spending themselves broke. At the present rate of outlay, any conceivable candidate donor will be bankrupt in about five years."

George nodded. "That's the figure I arrived at. But there are signs that the rate is increasing."

"My God! George, you know better than I: a fluctuation of this magnitude in the global economy simply has to translate into suffering and misery, sooner or later. Doesn't the Secretary *see*—?"

"I'll tell you what I wish," he said.

"What?"

His voice was wistful. "I wish I had kept up the guitar."

PART SEVEN

19

Provincetown, Massachusetts
24 February 2065

Rhea opened the front door wide. "Goodnight, Tommy," she said politely, and hurled him through the door and clear off the front porch. Tom Cunha landed well, and turned back to her with a baffled expression. She tossed the plastic bag of fresh codfish he had brought her after him, scoring a direct hit on his head. "Not tonight," she said. "I have a haddock." She cackled with laughter and slammed the door on him.

The laugh didn't last long; she was too angry. And then the anger too failed her, and she was back to sad. Her shoulders slumped; she turned and headed wearily for the kitchen.

Two weeks to the day since Rand had gone back up to the Shimizu—for good, he said, and she believed him. Fourteen days since her marriage had officially ended. Half a moon of loneliness and celibacy. Provincetown was a small town, its jungle drums especially efficient in winter; the unaffiliated were already beginning to sniff around. P-town being P-town, no more than half of them were male, Rhea's own preference. But God dammit, couldn't *one* of the oafs approach the business with any *class*? She wasn't asking for love, or even strong affection. Given the least salve for her pride, she might have relished a chance to lose herself in simple sweaty exercise. Instead she got fresh codfish and jovial offers to "take her off the hook."

Soon the global literary grapevine would catch up . . . and then the offers would be even more offensive.

A whole planet of men to choose from, and she didn't know one she'd swap for another night with Rand.

Or Duncan, for that matter. As she passed through the living room on her way to the kitchen, her eye fell on Driftglass, tumbling slowly end over end beside the bay window, balanced on an air-jet at head height. She had placed the vacuum sculpture there, defiantly, the day after Rand had gone back to orbit—right beside the spot where the family-portrait holo of the three of them stood. She stopped and contemplated it now. It seemed to belong there, next to the bay view, among all the old photos and mementos of Paixao history, looked to be a true part of Provincetown.

And all at once that irritated her. It was *not* of Provincetown. It was of space. It did not belong in that living room. The symbolism was wrong, it clashed. Things in Provincetown did not turn end over end in mid-air, defying gravity. Nothing in Provincetown was formed by vacuum except the town government. Space had not only taken her husband and her marriage, it had sent a tentacle down into her very own living room here on Earth. And made her like it. It had seduced her the same way it had Rand . . . with beauty. She could never, would never, go back . . . but she would never again fully leave space behind. A piece of her heart was caught there.

All right: if even her childhood home wasn't safe, there was always the shore. There was nothing of space there. She reversed direction and headed for the door. No sense going to the kitchen anyway; she hadn't been able to choke down a bite in days.

She paused on the porch, to make sure both that Tommy was gone and that she had smart clothes on, and then summoned the car. The bayside beach was less than a block away by foot . . . but the ocean beach on the north side of town would be windier, and thus less populated now that the sunset was long over.

As the seat harness enfolded her, she noticed that the passenger seat beside her was still set to Rand's dimensions. With a sharp gesture, she randomized it again. On second thought, she adjusted it to Colly's shape, and randomized the back seat. Time for the kid to start sitting up front. "Herring Cove, public lot, via Commercial Street," she said, and the car moved forward at the local maximum of 20 KPH.

The four days of Rand's visit had been agony. The first day was Colly's birthday, and both parents were invincibly cheerful, maintaining the truce even when

Colly wasn't around for fear of shattering it. That was bad, but it was worse when they began talking on the second day. It took them two more days, progressively worse through exhaustion, before both were willing to concede that there was nothing to say, nothing to be done. Rand was staying in space; she was staying on Terra; no compromise existed. Once they had admitted that, they'd made love one last time, ceremonially. Rhea had never made love in despair before. She did not quite regret it in retrospect . . . but she wished she could stop remembering it for a while.

Perhaps oddly, Duncan's name had not come up even once. She would always remember him fondly, had interceded with the Shimizu to save his job—but she and Rand both knew he had only been a symptom, an excuse, a way out of a dilemma she had not been consciously willing to resolve. And in any case, that relationship was over: Duncan was, by birth, just as committed to space as Rand intended to become.

She phoned Tia Marguerite on her way to the ocean, and was told that Colly was fine, Tia Marion was just giving her a bath, don't you worry about a thing, dear. She cut the connection, and worried.

It had been two weeks. She could not stall forever. Sooner or later she was going to have to have a long talk with Colly, and try to explain the change that had come into both of their lives. Colly knew that she and Mommy were going to be living on Earth again for a while—but had not been explicitly told why, or for how long. She did not yet know that Daddy's visit earthside had been his last. The longer Rhea waited, the harder it would be. But the wordsmith had not yet found the words she needed. Or perhaps it was courage that eluded her.

Commercial Street was a single one-way lane along the waterfront, not much wider than her car. Her progress was sporadic: in compliance with local statute, her car braked for all pedestrians and pets. On either side of her as she drove were a parade of temptations, bar after lounge after club after bistro, each as inviting as human ingenuity could make it, overflowing with the light and warmth and sounds of convivial merriment. She shuddered at the thought of entering one. She began to regret choosing this route—but it did keep her within smelling distance of the shore the whole way, and that was worth the aggravation of being surrounded by people and their damned gaiety. She was glad when she passed the rotary and breakwater by the Provincetown Inn, and left town behind. The car speeded up, and soon her headlights showed only dunes and marshgrass and rosehip and blueberry bushes.

She switched on her clothes, and by the time the car parked itself at Herring Cove they had warmed up. She set out at once into the teeth of the wind, leaving her face unlit to indicate that she did not welcome company. She walked along the shore, feeling her way in almost total darkness, until she found a private semicircle of dune, and crept deep into its pool of shadow. It was too overcast to really see the ocean, but the sound of the surf overpowered and calmed her thoughts, and the shore-smell sank into her bones. She lay on her back in the sand, and

dialed down her clothes until she could feel some
of its coolness.

She was very near to something like peace when,
an hour later, the overcast blew away—and the stars
came out.

Even here, half of the entire world was space. The
only difference between the view here and that from
any window in the upper hemisphere of the Shimizu
was that here she was under one gravity of acceleration—and here there was not even a layer of
glassite between her and all that emptiness. . . .

No, there was another difference. Rhea had *always*
loved the stars. And this beach had always been one
of her favorite places from which to view them. Now,
as the wind whipped over her, she was forced to
admit that they were prettier without atmosphere in
the way. In space the stars did not twinkle or shimmer, just burned steadily down forever. There was
a better perception of depth, of scale, there. And the
distinctions astronomers made—blue star, yellow star,
red giant—in space you could actually see them.

Oh, if only the stars could be seen that way without sealing yourself up in a claustrophobic little can!

Or hiring a good shaper . . .

She found herself clutching at the sand on either
side of her, and sat up abruptly. As soon as she did,
she realized she would not have this stretch of beach
to herself much longer. Something over a dozen
people were coming her way along the shoreline,
faces glowing softly like jack-o'-lanterns. Unusually,
they did not seem to be chattering, did not seem to
have fetched any kegs or food or instruments or col-
lected any driftwood for a fire. For a moment,

instinct made the hairs rise on the back of her neck—but there had not been any serious crime in Provincetown in decades. She watched them approach, hoping they would pass by and keep going.

To her disappointment, they stopped not far away. She stiffened when she saw them form a circle. Trancers! Just what she needed now: dance imagery against the backdrop of the stars. Worse: trance-dance—as close to zero-gee dance as you could find on Earth, in spirit and in phrasing. She got up, had her clothes repel the moist sand that wanted to cling to her back, and headed back to her car, giving the Trancers as wide a berth as the terrain permitted.

Nonetheless, one of them left the group and approached her, just as the first dancer was getting under way in the center of the circle. She started to speed up to avoid him—but slowed and then stopped as she recognized him: Manuel Brava.

He pronounced his name in the old Portagee way, "M'nal." He was a local character, even in a region rich with colorful eccentrics. There was no telling his age; Rhea did not know anyone in town of any age who didn't have childhood memories of him. Nor did anyone know how he made his living. One saw him from time to time, usually in stillness: sitting motionless by the shore of the ocean beach, or on a pier on the bay side, staring out to sea and smiling faintly. He was sort of the Cape Cod equivalent of the wandering Hindu holy man, who lived simply and said little and was fed by all he passed. In return he would give single, short sentences, which were never overheard by anyone but the recipient. People were reluctant to discuss whatever it was

Manuel had told them, but the consensus was that he was a smart old bird.

In Rhea's own case, she had wandered past him one day in her sixteenth year with an extra cheese sandwich . . . and in return for it had been told, "When you're alone . . . you're in pretty good company." It had meant little to her at the time, but she had never forgotten the comment, and over the ensuing years it had come to seem wiser and wiser.

At sixteen, being alone had been her greatest fear, and the root of it was exactly as Manuel had diagnosed: a failure to treasure herself. Manuel's casual, offhand comment might as well have been the final sentence of a full day's conversation between them. He had known her, without her knowledge, before she'd ever said a word to him. He seemed to know everyone in town that well; at least, he never seemed to need a second sentence.

Why that wasn't creepy was that what he had said, after studying her that well, was something kind. Good return on a cheese sandwich.

As he approached, now, there was no doubt in her mind that he knew all about the recent upheaval in her life; she waited for her nugget, wishing she had a sandwich on her. God knew she could use a little insight just now.

He stopped beside her and turned so that they both faced the sea and the Trancers. They watched them together for a timeless time. Shortly she forgot that she was waiting for him to speak. Trance-dance lived up to its name: there was something elementally hypnotic about it. There was something otherworldly about it too: in some subtle way she could not pin down, the Trancers reminded her of Stardancers. Perhaps it was only the rosy glow of their illuminated faces against the black sea and sky. Their dance did not seem to require any great skill, yet it held her spellbound. For the first time she began to understand why one would want to spend so many hours doing that.

"Be ready," Manuel said. "It's gonna be good."

She turned to look at him, and he was smiling. Her first reaction was to ask, what is going to be good? And when? But Manuel never explained, never amplified. So she was surprised when she heard herself ask, "Will I know when it's coming?"

His smile broadened. "You won't miss it."

Two sentences was a record. She decided to go for broke, and ask him *how* to be ready—but he was already shuffling back through the sand toward the Trancers. She watched in silence until he joined in the dance. Then she turned and trudged away toward her car.

Halfway there she stopped . . . stood for a moment . . . then turned and retraced her steps. She stood at the fringe of the dance for perhaps half an hour before joining it. When she did, it welcomed her.

She returned to linear consciousness in the car, on the way home. Her watchfinger said it was a little after four in the morning. She did not feel as tired as she should have; somehow the dance had given more energy than it had taken. She felt as though if she were to unseal her seat harness, she might float up to the ceiling.

In addition, there was an odd, almost forgotten sensation deep within her. She was hungry . . .

She entered the house at a dead run, and ate nearly half a loaf of *massa cevada,* Portuguese sweet bread, slathered with butter, washing it down with pirate-strength black tea. When she was done, she made and kneaded a vast batch of bread dough for *malassadas.* The fried sugarcoated treats—a Portuguese version of beignets, known locally as "flippers"—were Colly's favorite breakfast.

While the dough was rising, she went upstairs and outside onto the roof, to watch the sun rise from the widow's walk. It was one of the few authentic widow's walks left in Provincetown; five generations of Paixao women had paced these very boards, scanning the horizon for signs of their returning husbands. Every time they had been successful too, eventually; none of the Paixao men had been lost at sea—which probably made this the luckiest widow's walk anywhere. Rhea was conscious that she was breaking the string of good luck, and it brought a pang—but as the colors began to take form on the horizon, she decided it was one she could endure.

Most of the boats had gone out long since, but one unfortunate captain with a cranky engine was just putting out from MacMillan Wharf, warping around the breakwater. A delivery truck was clattering down Commercial Street, and gulls were harassing the garbage collectors. From her high eyrie, Rhea could see the silhouette of a lone figure walking along the shore, beachcombing.

That trance-dance had been her first extended break from pain in many weeks. No, not from pain, but from the suffering of it. At no time had she lost a preconscious awareness of her emotionally damaged condition . . . but she had relaxed to it, ceased to fear it. She believed now that she was healing—even if she had no idea how long the process would take. And she knew she would be returning to the ocean shore to join more trance-dances. Perhaps Colly might enjoy it too; Rhea had seen children at daytime trance-dances, and it was something they could share. . . .

Just as there was enough light for her to make out Tia Marguerite and Tia Marion's house, a few blocks distant, she saw a light go on in the room where Colly would have slept. She went back downstairs and punched down the *malassada* dough. She cut it into pieces, stretched them a little, and set them aside. Then she called Colly, making sure to tell Maxwell not to wake Colly's guardians if she failed to answer.

But she did answer, at once. "Hi, Mom!"

"Hi, honey. Are you having a good time?"

"Sure!"

The enthusiasm was plainly counterfeit; Rhea was recovered enough to hear that now. Colly loved her great aunts—but knew perfectly well that she only slept under their roof when she was being left out of something. "Well, I don't want to spoil any big plans or anything . . . but if you're not here in ten minutes, the flippers won't be hot when you eat them."

"Flippers? Homemade? Wow! Quick: open the

door so I don't break it." She hung up—and was in the kitchen before the oil was hot. They made the *malassadas* together, giggling, and gorged themselves until they creaked.

And then they had a long, long talk.

20

Top Step
25 February 2064

Rand hung suspended like a fly in black amber at the precise center of the universe, tethered to a mountain. The only sounds were the oceanic ebb and flow of his own breath, and the persistent slow drumming of his pulse. All of creation was arrayed around him. He felt an impulse to put himself into a spin, so that he could see all of it, but knew that he would foul his umbilical if he did. Probably just as well; even half of infinity was a lot to take in at once.

He found himself thinking of a poem Salieri had retrieved for him last night. He had asked for "something with Fireflies in it," and the AI's search engine had yielded up a *hauta,* a species of Japanese folk song more elaborate than the more common *dodoitsu:*

Kaäi, kaäi to
Naku mushi yori mo
Nakanu hotaru ga
Mi wo kogasu.
Nanno in gwa dé
Jitsu naki hito ni
Shin wo akashité—
Aa kuyashi!

(Numberless insects there are that
call from dawn to evening,
Crying, "I love! I love!"—but the
Firefly's silent passion,
Making its body burn, is deeper
than all their longing.
Even such is my love . . . yet I
cannot think through what Karma
I opened my heart—alas!—to
a being not sincere.)

The truly remarkable thing was that the *hauta* had
been transcribed and translated into English by
Lafcadio Hearn in 1927—seventy years before "Firefly" meant anything but a species of insect. Yet it
seemed to fit Rand's situation with eerie accuracy.

The Fireflies had *created* humanity, seeding Terra
with life millions of years ago and moving on. The
Fireflies were of space. They had returned here the
instant man began making art in space. Surely, then,
space was where a human artist should go—even if
love called him back to Earth.

Space didn't solve your problems . . . but it sure
put them into a larger perspective.

"All right, people," Thecla said in his earphones. "Time's up. Precess."

Rand turned with the rest of the class, until they all faced the mountain they had come from: Top Step, the place where humans came to become Stardancers. He was a little self-conscious; he knew he did not really belong here, with these Novices. They were second-month students, only another month away from renouncing their former lives forever and accepting Symbiosis. Being among them made him feel a little like a tourist on Death Row, or an infidel smuggled into Mecca. But Reb Hawkins himself had suggested that he join this class.

Rand already had his "space legs," could handle himself in free-fall—but all his experience was indoors, inside pressurized cubics. Everyone said that to really *feel* space, it was necessary to spend a lot of hours EVA. The Shimizu was equipped to take guests EVA if they wished—but strictly as tourists, carefully shepherded and pampered, in permanently tethered suits with no thrusters at all and so much radiation shielding that mobility was severely limited, for a maximum of half an hour. Groundhogs were just too good at getting themselves killed outdoors. Spacers all laughed at anyone whose only EVA hours were in Hotel Suits—but more advanced training was not offered in-house.

When he'd met Reb Hawkins, he'd found himself telling Reb his problem, and the monk had invited him to visit Top Step and join a Suit Class. "But won't your students resent an outsider?" he'd asked.

"There'll be no reason for them to know you are

one," Reb said. "Top Step is a big place now, and we have a strong custom of privacy going back half a century. If you show up in a class one day, people will just assume you've transferred in for some reason, and leave you alone. Most of them will be in the middle of life-reviews of their own."

Rand had thanked him—but still felt uneasy about the idea, and put it out of his mind.

Until his marriage had self-destructed.

When both Jay and Eva had suggested, within hours of each other, that he take Reb up on his invitation to visit Top Step, Rand had shrugged and acquiesced. He and Rhea had agreed that there was nothing a counselor could do to help them—but now that the plug had been pulled, he found that he needed to talk to *someone*. A legendary holy man who made his home in space didn't sound like a bad choice. Rand had liked Reb at once when they'd met, and Jay and Eva vouched for him, "punched his ticket," as Eva called it.

And now, as he rotated in space and faced Top Step—an immense stone cigar, glowing softly at the tip—he had to admit that coming here had been a good idea. Talking with Reb had helped: Reb's end of the conversation had consisted entirely of questions, just the right questions. Taking class had helped: it was hard to sustain self-pity out in naked space. And being around Postulants and Novices and Symbiotics had helped too: all these people were in the process of saying goodbye to their lives, and their company helped reconcile Rand to living his own.

"All right," Thecla said, "we're going to try

something new, today: you're all going back in on your own power."

There was a buzz of excitement, but it cut off quickly. Nobody wanted to louse this up.

"One at a time," she added. "I don't want you unsnapping until the person before you has made it all the way inboard. Abadhi, you're first."

One of the two dozen-odd p-suited figures in Rand's field of vision tapped his umbilical join. The tether separated, and Top Step began reeling it in. He oriented himself, starfished, and waited.

"Go ahead."

There was no visible exhaust from Abadhi's thrusters, but slowly he began to move toward Top Step. Very slowly. The trick in EVA maneuvering was to go about half as fast as you thought you should—then you only arrived about twice as hard and fast as you wanted.

At such speeds, covering ten thousand meters takes some time. Porter came far down the alphabet. Rand had plenty of time to study his classmates as he waited for his turn.

He had lost a marriage: these people were surrendering *everything*. They were more committed to space than he would ever be, and they were giving up more to be there.

And in return they would gain so much that part of him envied them. Centuries of life, life free of fear or hunger or loneliness, in the bosom of the largest and closest family that had ever been, working and playing among the stars. Those of them who were artists could spend the next century or two pursuing their art, twenty-four hours a day if they chose, with no need to seek commercial or popular or critical success. Or to look for love.

Maybe someday, he thought. *Maybe in another ten or twenty years, I'll come back here for real.*

The thought came back, *why not now?*

He was not done yet, that was all. Married or not, he was still a parent, and would be for at least another decade. He had not used up his visions yet; he still had shapings to create which would not have worked in a Stardancer context. He had still not outgrown his need for applause, his need to achieve. He had fought for his present position so long and so hard that he could not abandon the cup until he had drained it dry. It had, after all, cost him a good wife.

"Porter—get ready!"

He snapped out of his reverie and ran through the procedure in his mind. *This* sequence of commands tells the tether to go home; *that* combination of taps on the palm keypads will deliver matched bursts from all five thrusters; move my chin like *this* for the heads-up targeting display . . .

"Ready, Thecla."

His tether wiggled away toward Top Step. He centered the target ring in his display, stiffened his limbs, and triggered the thrusters. Aside from a mild pressure at wrists and ankles, nothing seemed to happen. The thruster at the base of his spine produced no sensation at all. Could it be broken? No, his display claimed he was jaunting, just as planned. He glanced around, and saw that the others were indeed receding, just quickly enough to perceive. He waited—and after a while, Top Step suddenly began to visibly approach. He checked his position carefully, decided he needed a course correction, and made it.

His aim was good: if the vast open window of the Solarium had had a bull's-eye, he would have hit it on his way through. His deceleration was equally perfect: he ended up motionless within arm's reach of the handgrip he had been aiming for. He saw admiring glances from other returnees, and preened. "Very nice," Thecla said. "Okay, Pribram: get ready!"

His AI, Salieri, whispered in his ear. "Phone, Rand. Reb Hawkins."

He cut off his suit radio and took the call. "Hi, Reb."

"Hello, Rand. Are you enjoying EVA?"

"A lot!" he said. "Thanks for letting me sit in. It's *different* outside . . ."

"It certainly is. Listen, I just wanted to tell you I'm not going to be around for the next couple of days. I have to shuttle over to the Shimizu."

"Really? What's up?"

"A party, of sorts. You're invited if you want, actually—if you don't mind taking a couple of days off from EVA classes, you could hop over and back with me. It should be a memorable event."

"What's the occasion?"

"You know Fat Humphrey?"

"Who doesn't?" The round restaurateur had been famous ever since the release of Armstead's Starseed Transmission at the turn of the century; it was said that his Le Puis rivalled the Hall of Lucullus as a gourmet's and gourmand's paradise. Armstead claimed you never had to tell Humphrey what you wanted to eat, how you wanted it done, or how much you felt like eating. Over the past week, Rand had found that to be literal truth.

"Well, he just turned one hundred . . . and he's retiring to the Shimizu to enjoy his golden years."

"Wow. That's going to disappoint a lot of folks."

"Yes, it will. He's been swearing for decades that he was going to retire the day his odometer showed three figures, and it seems he meant it. Last night after dinner he took off his tux and spaced the thing. The chefs are all people he trained, of course—but it just won't be the same without him sizing up the customers and serving the orders. Fat sweetens the air where he is. Anyway, he won't let us have a farewell party for him here, prefers to just leave like a cat—so Meiya and I are bringing him over to the Shimizu tonight in a special shuttle. There's room for you if you want to come along."

"Sounds good," he said. "I'd like a chance to get to know Fat half as well as he knows me. Every time he pulls that magic act of his, I can't help wondering what *he* likes to eat."

Reb's answer was a moment in coming. "Do you know . . . in almost fifty years, I don't believe I've ever *seen* Fat eat?"

"He must do it some time," Rand said dryly. Fat Humphrey massed well over a hundred and forty kilos; in repose he resembled a Jell-O model of the Shimizu.

"True enough. Well, maybe we'll get to see him in action when we get him to the hotel."

"I'll take him to Lucullus's tomorrow," Rand said.

"It would be an honor to buy Fat Humphrey a meal. And you and Meiya."

"Done," Reb said. "Meet us at the dock at 17:00." He broke the connection. Reb never seemed to be in a hurry—but he never wasted time or words either.

The last of the students had returned inboard; Rand turned his radio back on in time to hear Thecla dismiss the class. He left the Solarium and with Salieri's help found his way through the maze of tunnels that honeycombed Top Step to the room he'd been assigned. There he took off his airtanks and thrusters and set both to recharging, and packed a small overnight bag. He was not yet ready to return to the Shimizu full time, but a day or two couldn't hurt. It might be instructive to test the strength of the scab Top Step had begun to form over the deep wound in his heart.

And he could check in with Jay, see how the new piece was going. He hadn't produced a note of music yet, hadn't even viewed the working tapes Jay sent every day . . . but Jay would understand. Rand had left him a perfectly good shaping to use—the New Mexico desert setting he'd already had in the can— and Jay knew his brother was perfectly capable of showing up a week or two before curtain and producing an acceptable score for whatever choreography he came up with. This retreat had been Jay's idea as much as anybody's.

A thought struck him as he packed. "Salieri—can you determine relative locations for Colly and Rhea?"

"Maxwell indicates they are approximately fifty meters apart, Rand."

"Good. Get me Colly on a hush-circuit."

"Hi, Daddy! What's up?" Colly's cheerful voice asked a few seconds later.

"Hi, princess. I just wanted to let you know I'm going back to the Shimizu for a couple of days. I know we were scheduled for a long chat tonight, but it looks like I'm going to be too busy. Can we reschedule for Thursday?"

"Sure. I guess . . ."

"Problem?"

The answer was a while in coming. "Dad?"

"Yes?"

"I . . . uh . . . Mom and I had a talk this morning."

"Oh." The first sensation he was conscious of was of a large weight leaving his shoulders. He had not relished the prospect of explaining things to Colly— but it hadn't looked as if Rhea was ever going to get off the dime. He was enormously relieved to learn that she had.

Then he realized that only half the weight was gone. "Are you . . . okay with that?"

Again the answer was agonizingly slow in arriving. "Can I ask you something? I asked Mom, but she said she didn't know, and I should ask you."

He took a deep breath, and held it. "Go ahead, honey."

"What's the most time I can spend up there with you?"

He exhaled noisily. There was a sound in his ears like bad reception on a suit radio, a sort of vast echoing hum. "Without adapting, you mean."

"No, I found that out from the White Rabbit," she said. "I mean, without being a pain in the butt."

His heart turned over in his chest. "The max, baby. The max. And if that isn't enough to suit us both, I'll come down there and see you sometimes. Until I adapt, anyway."

"That's good," she said firmly. "Uh . . . can I ask you one more thing?"

"Sure."

"Are you still mad at Duncan, Daddy?"

The question was like a surprise punch in the stomach. He took it, and shook his head, and answered honestly. "No, Colly. I'm not mad at Duncan."

"I'm glad. Tell him I said hi. Bye, Daddy—I love you!"

"What an extraordinary coincidence: *I* love *you*."

"What are the odds of that, huh?" She hung up smiling.

Rand finished packing. Then, with time to kill before he was due at the dock, he played some of Jay's tapes, and tinkered with ideas for musical accompaniment. Hell, maybe he should stay at the Shimizu when he got there, and get back to work. Maybe it was time to resume his life. He could play around with EVA another time, when there wasn't so much to do. He thought of calling Jay, to tell him he was coming. But the timing was bad: Jay would be in the studio now. He decided to call when he got in.

The trip to the Shimizu was thoroughly enjoyable, despite the spartan furnishings aboard the small shuttle. Fat Humphrey in a p-suit was an unforgettable sight, for one thing. And as a traveling companion, he was the original barrel of monkeys; while they were all unstrapped between acceleration and deceleration he even managed to produce a recognizable parody of *Kinergy* that reduced Rand and everyone else aboard to tears of laughter.

Rand was honored to be included in the merriment. It was apparent to him that this trip was a sentimental journey for Reb—and for Meiya, Reb's successor as Head Teacher at Top Step. While they had been training and graduating a quarter of a million Stardancers together over the past half century, Fat Humphrey had been one of the very few constants in their lives. Meiya, a quiet, solemn woman, wore an expression that reminded Rand of old pictures he had seen of mothers sending their sons off to war.

As he watched Fat Humphrey mock the moves of a Stardancer, he suddenly wondered why Fat had not accepted Symbiosis on retirement. But he knew he would not ask, not today anyway. The question was in an area of privacy you learned not to violate if you spent any time at Top Step: he didn't know Fat well enough yet.

And the man read his mind. The moment the laughter for his performance had died away, he looked at Rand and said, "You wonderin' how come I didn't eat the red Jell-O for my dessert, huh?"

"Well . . . yes, Fat, I was, as a matter of fact."

Fat Humphrey grinned. "You ever hear about the time them assholes blew up about a cubic kilometer of Sym?"

"Sure." Almost a decade before Rand's birth, a fanatic antiStardancer terrorist group, headed by Chen Ling Ho's father, had somehow managed to destroy a large mass of Symbiote on its way from its source in the upper atmosphere of Titan to Earth orbit, where it was supposed to serve the needs of the next generation of Top Step graduates. Several Stardancers riding herd on the load had been killed.

"Well, most o' that was suppose' be for me. They been tryin' to catch up ever since, but it's gonna be another twenty year or so before they ready to handle me again." Rand cracked up; so did Reb and Meiya. "I figure in the meantime I watch a little TV, go for a swim, catch a show. You get me a good seat?"

"Well, I'll tell you, Fat," he said thoughtfully, "in terms of sightlines and vectors, maybe what we should do is mount a special show just for you."

"How you mean?"

"Put you in the center of the theater, and work around you."

Fat roared with glee and slapped him on the back; fortunately his seat belt held. "You're all right, kid."

They reached the Shimizu by 19:30. The deceleration was as mild as the acceleration had been, no more than half a gee, and for only a few minutes. Rand could have taken more easily, but the others were all spacers, intolerant of gees.

Fat Humphrey had specifically requested that there be no reception on his arrival. Of course Evelyn Martin had double-crossed him, and was waiting at dockside to drag him off to a press conference. But Rand had halfway expected that: he debarked first, took Martin aside, and threatened to take him by the testicles and fling him through the nearest bulkhead into hard vacuum if he didn't change orbits, now. Grumbling and muttering, the little PR man complied. It is difficult to slink in free-fall, but he managed it. "Don't bother with check-in," he snarled over his shoulder as he went. "It's covered. Just take him right to P-427."

Rand rapped on the hatch to signal that it was safe, and the others emerged. As nanobots scurried away with luggage, he tried to show Fat Humphrey where to insert the wafer that would install his AI in the Shimizu's data crystals . . . and was startled and a little nonplussed to learn that Fat did not have one.

"How about you, Meiya?" he tried.

But she shook her head too. "I won't be inboard long enough to bother. We'll all use Reb's to get around."

"Well, okay," he said. "But stick close to him. This place can be a rabbit warren if you don't have an AI."

"There are public terminals all over, left over from the old days," she pointed out. "If I get lost, I can just ask for you."

"Sure. I'm not listed, but my AI is: Antonio Salieri. How about if I go get my brother and meet you all at Fat's new suite in about an hour? I'd like to grab a shower too; I've been in this p-suit all day."

"Good with me," Fat Humphrey said.

"We'll meet you there in an hour," Reb said, and installed his own AI. "Rild—direct us to Suite Prime 427, please."

One of several exits began to blink softly. "This way, *Tenshin*."

Rand jaunted to his own room, checked the time, and decided to phone Jay before showering. He would have just finished dinner by now.

"Hey, bro, what's shapin'? When are you coming back?"

"About five minutes ago. Want to meet the happiest fat man in human space?"

Jay blinked. " ' . . . the happiest fat man . . .' Hey, you mean Fat Humphrey? Is *he* here?"

"To stay. He's just retired; it's his centennial. I came along for the ride; I'm going back with Reb tomorrow. Little gathering at his new digs in about an hour; just him, you, me, Reb and Meiya, as far as I know. You know Meiya, right?"

"Sure. Hey, this is great! I've always wanted a chance to kick back and talk with Fat for a few hours. Where's he at?"

"Prime 427. Meet me at the nearest corner at 20:25 and we'll go in together."

"See you there."

Fifty minutes later he was waiting at the appointed spot. Almost at once, Jay arrived from another direction, grinning. They hugged, and pounded each other's shoulder blades.

"How are you, bro?"

"Fine," Rand said. "I've gotten a *little* work done— I'll show you later."

"The hell with that—how *are* you?"

"Okay," he said. "Not well, yet, but I can see daylight, you know?"

"That's good. I told you that place'd be good for you. Hey, Eva's gonna be here too: Reb called her. Probably in the suite already, in fact; I spoke with her half an hour ago and she said she was leaving right away. I get the idea she and Fat are old friends."

"It wouldn't surprise me in the—"

The lights went out.

"What the *fuck*—" Jay said. "Diaghilev!"

No answer.

"Diaghilev, God dammit!"

"Salieri?" Rand tried.

Silence.

There was a public terminal nearby, but it was unlit, presumed dead. "Jesus," Jay said softly, clearly controlling his voice with an obvious effort. "I think the whole fucking system is down. That's never happened. I'd have bet a billion dollars it couldn't possibly happen."

They heard a scream somewhere in the far distance; no telling even the direction. The Shimizu corridors had some funny acoustics.

Rand's heart hammered. "Oh my God . . ." If they had no lights, no AIs, no phones—how long before they had no *air*? He fought for calm in the claustrophobic darkness. "All right, what's our move?"

Just then lights came on. Small red emergency lights, every hundred meters along the corridor, with larger blinking ones marking intersections. Rand found them an immense relief, a sign of recovery, but he saw Jay frowning. "They should have kicked on a *lot* sooner, even if this is a total system collapse," Jay said. "Something really weird is going on."

"Have we got air?"

Jay spotted the nearest grille, jaunted to it, and put his face near it. "Yeah. Reduced flow, but it's air."

"What do you think: is this just local, or is the whole damn hotel really dark right now?"

"Beats me. They're supposed to be equally impossible. I pray to God it's local."

A suite door opened not far from them, and someone stuck his head out. "Hey, mate," he called in an Aussie accent, "any idea what the bloody hell is goin' on?"

"Look at it this way," Jay called back. "You're getting tonight's rent free."

"Too right," he said, and closed his door again.

"God," Rand said, "Fat and the others must be freaking out in there. If they had the window closed when the power failed, they're in minimal emergency lighting: it could take them an hour to find the manual door release, let alone figure out how to use it."

"Hell of a welcome to the Shimizu," Jay agreed. "Come on, let's go try and calm them down."

They jaunted in the eerie pale red light to Suite 427. "We'll never convince Fat the place is safe now," Jay complained as they neared it. "Shit, I just don't *believe* this. The only thing I can imagine taking out the Shimizu system is a comet right through the core crystals—and we didn't feel any impact. It just doesn't . . . oh, you asshole." Automatically, he had stopped in front of the door and waited for an AI to ask his business. "Hit that release for me, will you, bro?" he said, pointing.

Rand pulled open the access hatch indicated and pulled the handle inside. It moved easily—but the door did not move. "Seems to be broken," he reported.

Jay grimaced. "Naturally. Things never go wrong one at a time." He put his hands on his hips. "Christ, the door's soundproof—we can't even bang out 'Calm down' in Morse code."

"What's Morse code?" Rand asked.

"Eva would know, but it doesn't—wait a god damn minute! What do you mean, 'broken'? That's a mechanical latch: it *can't* be broken."

"Okay," Rand said agreeably. "Then what *does* nonfunction and a blinking red light mean?"

"A blinking—"

In free-fall one almost never pales visibly; blood does not drain from the head as pressure drops. But even in the poor light, Rand could see his brother's expression come apart. He jaunted quickly to Rand's side and stared at the little flashing pilot bulb. After a few seconds, he began to shake his head slowly back and forth, the picture of denial.

Rand grabbed his shoulder, *hard,* and shook him. "What does it mean?" he cried.

Jay turned to him. There was horror in his eyes. He needed three tries to get the words out, and when he did, they were barely audible. "There is no pressure on the other side of that door."

21

High Earth Orbit
25 February 2065

Sulke Drager had always hated it when everybody talked at once. Thirty years as a member of a telepathic community had taught her a great deal about handling multiple inputs—more than any human being had ever known—but never before in history had so much of the Starmind all been sending at the same time. And underlying it all, pervading the whole Solar System like a taste of metal in the back of the mouth, was the wordless shriek from Saturn.

And naturally, the "voices" she most needed to "hear" were the weakest. They were also the closest, but distance means nothing to a telepath; signal strength and bandwidth were all that counted.

So she borrowed energy from every Stardancer in the heavens who was *not* shouting something, and used it to drive a message that had never before been sent across the matrix.

Shut the fuck up!

The System seemed to echo in the sudden relative quiet. Even the wordless wail from the Ring halved its "volume" and "pitch" and dropped back down into the region of speech. The words—*Save him, Sulke!*—repeated endlessly, like a mantra.

And now Sulke could clearly hear the gentle voice she most needed to hear. *All right so far, cousins,* Reb said. *We are all unharmed so far, which means they intend to parley. Be calm.*

She knew his location precisely now. The vessel in which he was imprisoned was superbly stealthed—the combined power of the United Nations could not have found it—but she had detection gear no battle cruiser could match, if the target was another telepath. Reb had been one years before he'd met his first Stardancer; a natural adept. So were Fat Humphrey and Meiya.

So were four other humans currently in space, and fourteen on Terra. About average for humanity. All of them had been kidnapped too, at the same time as Reb, Fat and Meiya—every one was now a prisoner—but *this* vessel was Sulke's pidgin: the one she personally happened to be close enough to do something about. She instructed her subconscious to monitor the other ongoing rescue operations for data relevant to her own problem, and consciously ignored them.

She fed Reb's location to those who were good at orbital ballistics, grabbed the report that echoed back and swore. *You're going nowhere fast! Your trajectory is taking you up out of the ecliptic, and there's nothing there!*

He was still calm. *Naturally. We knew they must have a covert base in space; now they're leading us to it. We already know where the ones dirtside are being taken.*

Yeah, and we can't touch the place. What if where you're going is just as well defended?

Then we will have to be very clever. And very lucky.

She went briefly into rapport with those who had had military training back in their human lives, and swore again. *We have Stardancers vectoring to intercept your projected path at multiple points . . . but there's no way to know where you're going until they decelerate. And if they maneuver in the meantime, we could lose you completely.*

They probably will. They're paranoid; they'll assume their stealthing may not be good enough, and try every trick there is.

I can match orbits with you right now, she said. *You're coming right at me, near enough.*

What about relative speeds?

She was already adjusting her lightsail, spinning out Symbiote like pizza dough. *You're a bat out of hell—but if I can grab hold, and it doesn't kill me . . .* She had an unusually powerful thruster on her belt she had never expected to use; she poked it carefully through the Symbiote membrane, borrowed a hundred brains to help her aim it, and fired it to exhaustion.

What can you accomplish? Meiya asked.

Tear off antennas, bugger up their communications,

*bang on the hull and distract them while you jump
'em . . . if I have to, I'll unscrew the fucking drive
with my fingernails.*

There was a hint of a chuckle in Reb's voice. *I
love you too, Sulke. Whoops—they're about to drug
me . . .*

Me too, Fat Humphrey said. *Watch your ass,
Sulke.*

She could see them now, by eyeball, and they were
indeed coming on fast. But she was confident; she
had learned to board a moving freight when she was
eight years old, leaving a place then called East
Germany. *Yeah?* she sent back. *I'll give you a two-
kilo gold asteroid if you can pull off that trick, pal.*

His answering giggle was the last thing she ever
heard. She never saw the white-winged figure who
came up behind her and put a laser bolt through her
brain.

PART EIGHT

22

The Shimizu Hotel
25 February 2065

Jay remembered an old story from the dawn of spaceflight: a Skylab astronaut had awakened to a lighting failure, and had taken nearly twenty minutes to find the backup switch—in a sleeping compartment the size of a phone booth. Darkness and free-fall were a disorienting combination.

He knew his way around the Shimizu about as well as anyone alive—but in the eerie, feeble glow of emergency lighting, everything looked *different*. In places even the emergency lights had failed, and almost everywhere he and Rand encountered adherents of the ancient philosophy, "When in danger, when in doubt, run in circles, scream and shout." There was absolutely no doubt in Jay's mind that somewhere Evelyn Martin was hemorrhaging and tearing his hair out in clumps.

For the first time in his life, Jay did not give a damn about offending guests; he and Rand went through them like buckshot, leaving a trail of outrage and broken bones that was sure to give birth to expensive litigation.

The destination that would most efficiently allow them to find out what was going on, report what had happened, and do something effective about it, was Kate Tokugawa's office. There were other nerve centers, but that was the only one Jay was confident he could find in his sleep without AI assistance. It was startling to realize how much you depended on the damn things. *God help me if I suddenly need a cube root or something,* he thought wildly, bouncing a fat bald groundhog off a bulkhead.

Rand deked expertly around the ricocheting guest and pulled up alongside him. "They couldn't have started losing pressure before the blackout, or we'd have heard alarms. To reach zero by the time we tried that latch, they must have blown out *fast.*"

"The whole window must have gone," Jay said. "Is that possible?"

"No. Not without help."

"So they're dead?" He clotheslined an employee who was, quite properly, trying to prevent them from speeding recklessly through a developing riot—and, since it was the quickest way to explain, regretfully sucker-punched the woman as he went by.

"Probably. But maybe not."

"How do you figure?"

"I ask myself, what could take out a whole window? I come up with a ship designed for the purpose. I think they've been snatched. I think when they jaunted into that room, the window was already gone: *they saw a holo of one.* And at some point they all got sleepy . . ."

"And somebody came through the holo and towed them away . . . wouldn't somebody *notice* a fucking barnacle attached to the Shimizu?"

"Remora," Jay corrected. "It moves. Not if it was stealthed well enough. Fat's room is all the way around from the docks. And by now it's gone—and the sphere of space within which it could possibly lie is expanding every second. You can spot even the best-stealthed ship by eyeball, by occultation of background stars—but you have to know just where to look."

"Maybe we should quit dawdling, then." They were into the final corridor now, a straight run of perhaps two thousand meters; perhaps a dozen flailing figures cluttering the way between them and the door to Management country. He lifted his head, bellowed "FORE!" at the top of his lungs, tucked his chin and triggered all his thrusters at max.

Jay did likewise. Miraculously, everyone managed to scatter out of their way. Halfway to the door, they shut down, flipped over, and began to decelerate—and discovered that they had both burned themselves dry. They impacted with bone-jarring crashes, desperately grabbed handholds, and nearly had their arms pulled out of their sockets by the rebound. Jay's first thought was for Rand, but his brother threw him a shaky grin and a circled thumb and forefinger.

Jay found the manual doorlatch and released it. He was greatly relieved when this one worked; he had not been sure he would find pressure in Management—

and had had no idea what to do if he didn't. They scrambled in together, then resealed the door to keep out guests who wanted a refund. There was nobody at the front desk, nor in the outer offices beyond it. "Where the hell *is* everybody?" Rand snarled.

"I don't know," Jay snapped, even more nervous than his brother. This was wrong, wrong—"Wait a minute." He doubled back, went to the front desk. "I filled in for a guy once or twice," he said as he got there, and began tapping code on a drawer under the counter. "Let's see if they still . . . ah!" He got the drawer open—and took from it a totally illegal police-issue GE hand-laser. "Sometimes Security doesn't show up fast enough when you call them," he said, checking the charge and clicking off the safety. "*Now* let's go see what's in back."

"I'll go first and draw fire," Rand said. He and Jay exchanged a glance. It became a grin. "The Hardy Boys in High Orbit," Rand said.

"And in a big-ass hurry."

They worked their way back through the outer offices to Kate's door cautiously but quickly, Rand preceding his brother through every doorway. Finally they floated outside her office.

"No point in listening at a soundproof door," Jay said.

"No point in knocking, either," Rand agreed, and opened the manual release compartment. "I'll go first, again."

"No need. I'll *know* where the target is, if there is one."

"Okay. If there's trouble in there, you go right and I'll go left."

"Which way is that?" They happened to be upside down with respect to each other.

"You go away from me and I'll go away from you." Rand unlatched the door. It let go with a pop, and opened a few centimeters. He gripped the release latch to brace himself, and slid the door the rest of the way open. He and Jay entered together, and stopped.

And then both began to laugh.

They knew it was inappropriate; that only made it worse. Facing them was one of the most ridiculous sights they had ever seen: Evelyn Martin, holding a gun.

Laughing, Jay tried to move away from Rand as agreed—and remembered that his thrusters were dry. He still was not worried; he and his brother could outjaunt a spastic like Martin with muscles alone.

Then he saw Katherine Tokugawa well to his left, also armed. His laughter died away. They were outgunned. He shook Rand's shoulder and pointed her out. After a microsecond's thought, his own gun steadied on Martin. If he were going to be killed by one of these two, he preferred Kate. More dignity.

"Drop it," Martin yapped.

Jay thought hard for a whole second, then opened his fingers. The gun, of course, stayed where it was.

"*Lose* it," Martin corrected, expressing his exasperation by putting a bolt into the wall beside the doorway. The smell of burning bulkhead plastic filled the room faster than the air-conditioning could suck it away. Jay gave his own gun a finger-snap, like a child shooting marbles; it drifted away toward Martin. Ignoring the man, he turned and addressed Kate.

"I should have figured you'd have to be in on this," he said. "But I'm damned if I can see how you expect to come out of it with your job."

"Oh, I'll probably lose that eventually," she agreed. "But by then I'll have a better job."

"A better job than *this*?"

"Much better. I'll be running something a little more prestigious than a hotel."

"What's that?"

"High Orbit," Martin said, and snickered.

"Shut up, Ev," Tokugawa snapped.

He stared. "What the *hell* are you talking about? Nobody runs High Orbit."

"No," Martin said. "The UN wouldn't let them. But the UN isn't going to be around much longer." He giggled nervously.

"Shut *up*, Ev," Tokugawa barked. "You can tell them things like that after they're dead. Not before."

Jay tried to restart his laughter; it didn't catch. "You seriously think you can take on the UN—and the Starmind—and win?"

Kate couldn't resist answering. "Not me," she said. "But I know people who can. I've been working for them all my life."

"You artists are always yapping about your 'vision,'" Martin said, and brandished his gun. "Ha! You assholes don't know what vision is! We're gonna reshape the future."

Jay felt the universe shifting in his head, crushing his brains beneath it. Surely this was lunacy. Even the UN itself could not have defeated the Starmind. He could conceive of nothing human that could.

"Come in, gentlemen," Tokugawa said then. Jay

glanced over his shoulder, and saw two Security men enter with guns drawn. Each, he noticed, wore an unfamiliar earplug and an unobtrusive throat-mike. Communications gear that did not use the house system. Turning back, he saw that Tokugawa and Martin both had them too.

"So," he said to Kate, "you already know more about what happened in Fat Humphrey's room than we do."

She nodded. "Oh, yes. Much more."

"Of course. You assigned Fat his room. So this is where you gloat, and tell us what's going on, so we can be awed by your cleverness?"

"No," she said. "This is where you get taken away and killed. Goodbye, Sasaki." She sketched a *gassho* bow. "It has always been a pain in the ass to work with you. Martin, you go along with them—make sure it looks pretty; that's your line of work."

Jay opened his mouth to say something, but never got a chance to learn what it was going to be. Something touched the back of his neck, and he slept.

It was a very troubled sleep, full of unpredictable accelerations that triggered horror-dreams of falling from his terrestrial past, and unfamiliar voices shouting incomprehensible things in the near and far distance, and the nagging certainty that something he couldn't quite recall was terribly, terribly wrong.

You were *meant* to come out of the drug confused. But his surroundings when he finally did certainly enhanced the effect.

He was in a corridor. Not a public one, a . . . the term took awhile to surface. A service tunnel, that was it. The lighting was even lousier here. Things were floating in his vicinity—important ones, he sensed. First he counted them: four. Then he classified them: human beings. Next he laboriously identified them. Evelyn Martin. His third-grade gym teacher—no, that was . . . was . . . right, one of the security guards who was going to kill him. Sure, there was the other one. And the extra one . . . hell, know him anywhere: that's my bro. Like a brother to me.

So now he had them broken down into two groups. Friends: one. Foes: three. That didn't seem like a favorable ratio. On the other hand, one of the guards seemed to be lacking a face; that evened things up a little. And Ev Martin's head hung at a funny angle . . .

A few more foggy seconds of contemplation and he had a second breakdown he liked much better. Rand was breathing; the rest were not.

The example inspired him; he breathed deeply, stoked his brain with oxygen and felt the cobwebs begin to melt away. *This is great,* he told himself. *How did I do this?*

As Rand began to show signs of recovering consciousness too, a hatch opened nearby and Duncan Iowa appeared. "Good," he said. "You're awake. I ditched their comm gear on the assumption it's trackable, but we ought to move anyway. No telling which systems they have up and running." He moved to Rand, started to slap him awake . . . then thought better of it, and instead spun him, to centrifuge blood into his head. "Take this and keep lookout," he added.

Jay got his hands up in time to catch a laser

considerably more powerful than the police-issue job he'd liberated from the front desk. He blinked at it for a moment—then snapped out of his fugue. He checked charge and safety, assessed the tactical situation, and assigned himself a guard post. "You're something else, kid," he said wonderingly. Duncan ignored him, busy with Rand.

Rand spent less time in stupor than Jay had. Groundhogs and new spacers usually shook off drug effects faster; their blood pressure was higher. He looked around at the drifting bodies, shook his head like a horse shooing flies, glanced at Jay and turned back to Duncan.

"I punched you in the mouth," he said wonderingly. "And you let me live."

"I had it coming," Duncan said tightly. "Look, we've got to move. I don't need to know who we're running from or why just now, but if you know anything that would suggest where to, I'd love to hear it."

"Shit," Jay said. "I wish I knew more about riot-control procedures . . ."

"What do you need?" Duncan asked.

"For a start, a large tank of sleepy gas with a hose on it."

"Come on," Duncan said, jaunting away. "I'm an Orientator—I know this dump better than Kate Tokugawa."

I hope you're right, Jay thought. Rand jaunted after Duncan, and Jay took up the rear, gun at the ready.

In the discreetly unmarked riot-control compartment Duncan led them to, they found the tank Jay wanted, fresh thrusters, and a sonic rifle for Rand. While they swapped the new thrusters for their exhausted ones, they also exchanged information.

"I was heading for Deluxe country, I knew the panic would be worst there, and I took service corridors to make better time. Then I saw Martin and those two goons go by at an intersection ahead of me, guns out, towing you two. They didn't see me in the lousy light."

"What made you decide to butt in?" Rand asked. "And how did you know which side you were on?"

Duncan didn't duck the question. "I'm in love with your wife, and she's in love with you. I didn't want her hurt."

Rand didn't duck the answer. "I understand. How did you ever manage to take all three of them?"

Duncan shrugged. "All three were earthborn. Taking Martin's gun wasn't a major challenge. Actually the other two didn't do too badly; I was trying to keep one of them alive to question, but they hurried me. So tell me: who are the bad guys and what do we do about them?"

"Anybody could be a bad guy," Jay said. "But the one we know about is Kate Tokugawa herself." Duncan's eyebrows raised, but he made no comment. "And what we're going to do is take her alive for questioning. But I almost hope she hurries us. She's behind the system crash—she's using it to cover a kidnapping."

Duncan's eyes widened, then shut tight. "Jesus."

"You think they're alive, then?" Rand said.

"Have to be. There are much easier ways to kill somebody."

"Easier ways to kidnap people too. They could have snatched us off the shuttle without all this hooraw."

"The Space Command keeps a careful eye on moving objects in High Orbit," Jay said, "but they hardly ever look at the Shimizu. Doing it here cost the bastards, but it probably bought them enough lead to get away clean."

"Who got kidnapped?" Duncan asked.

"Fat Humphrey Pappadopoulos, Reb Hawkins, Meiya and Eva Hoffman. Possibly others, but I'm sure of those. They snatched them right out of a suite: right out the goddam window and into a stealthed ship, long gone by now. I don't know what the fuck is going on, but it has something to do with a coup against the UN."

"Jesus Christ!" Duncan said. "An honest-to-God old-time coup d'état?"

"I think *coup du monde* is more like it, from the way Ev was talking. I don't care what historians call it, as long as they put 'failed' in front of it. So we need Kate—alive, and with her vocal cords intact; everything else is optional. She's in her office . . . and I think I know how to get her out, if we can get there alive. But that might be a problem. I'm sure she has a private surveillance-and-defense system. She let us approach the last time because Martin didn't want to have to explain embarrassing laserburns on our corpses to the cronkites—but if she sees us coming again, I don't think she'll hesitate."

"So what's the plan?" Rand asked.

Jay sighed. "I was hoping one of you would come up with something. *I* don't know how you storm a castle with a slingshot when they know you're coming."

"I do," Duncan said. "You use the servant's entrance."

Twenty minutes later, they peered out through the grille of an air-circulation tunnel ten meters from Tokugawa's office door. They were all wearing stock p-suits scavenged from the riot-control locker, but maintaining radio silence. Jay unsealed his hood and sniffed the air; when he didn't pass out, the others did the same.

"I think we're inside her perimeter," Duncan said. "I don't see anything in that hallway that looks like the business end of a laser."

Jay wedged past him and looked. Bare walls. He clutched the tank of sleepy gas to his chest. "So one of us tries it and the other two avenge him if necessary."

"Let's not rush into this," Rand said.

Jay laughed mirthlessly. "Feel a little stuffy in here to you, bro?"

"Now that you mention it, I'm sweating like—oh!"

"When a groundhog starts to sweat, he smiles and reaches for a cold beer. When a spacer starts to sweat, he reaches for his p-suit." The hotel's backup system had power for air circulation and limited lighting—but none for cooling. The Shimizu was a shiny ball of metal in the sunshine, full of heat-producing people, and contrary to groundhog belief space is not cold at all. "Folks are going to start dying if the system doesn't come back up in the next hour or two: we're running out of time."

"How do you plan to get her to open the door for your gas?" Duncan asked.

Jay grinned wickedly. "I don't need to. Ev Martin drilled a neat little hose-sized hole for me about a meter earthward of the door." He started to push the grille free, but Rand stopped him.

"Let me," he said.

"I claim privilege," Jay protested. "I've known Eva and Reb a lot longer than you have."

"My point exactly. You said before you almost hope she hurries you. I don't. I have less need to find an excuse to kill her."

"That could get *you* killed."

Rand grinned. "Well, bro, just now the world doesn't need a first-class shaper as badly as it needs her."

"I'm faster than both of you put together," Duncan said.

Rand turned to him. "Yeah. But that's a massy tank: you haven't got the muscles to hump it. Some things, earthborns are better at. Besides, it's my turn to do something heroic. Okay?"

After a moment, Duncan nodded. "Good luck."

"Thanks."

After all that melodrama, the capture itself was ludicrously easy. Everything went like a good opening night, just enough adrenalin to keep you in top form and no surprises you couldn't cope with. There were hidden gas-jets in the hallway—but p-suits made them irrelevant. The laser-hole by Tokugawa's door was the perfect gauge for Rand's hose. She had a p-suit of her own stashed in her office, and managed to reach it—but passed out before she got its hood over her head. Once they had access to her terminal, Jay and Duncan were able between them to coax the system back up and on-line in a matter of minutes. As the main lights came on, they could almost feel the cheer reverberating around the Shimizu. Then, ignoring the hundreds of incoming calls, they put in an SOS to the Space Command, and soon found themselves talking to an Admiral Cox, an old warhorse who was most interested in—and totally unfazed by—an attempted overthrow of the planetary government. With a minimum of words, he extracted from them every scrap of useful information they could give him, then put them on hold.

Despite a mild sense of anticlimax, Jay felt himself grinning. "We did it, guys," he said.

"Hell of a note," Rand said. "I started the day a respectable artist—and now I'm running a goddam hotel."

Jay giggled. "You may be going out there just a star, kid . . . but you're coming back a waitress."

"You know," Duncan said, "I always *thought* I could run this dump better than that asshole." He gestured at the sleeping Tokugawa, and all three of them broke up. She did look silly. In the absence of gravity, simply binding a person's wrists and ankles does not immobilize her effectively enough; instead you tape each wrist to its related bicep, each ankle to its thigh, then tape elbows and knees together. The result looked remarkably like a Buddhist in the midst of prostrating herself.

But their laughter chopped off short when they noticed that she was no longer breathing.

❖   ❖   ❖

" . . . and about half an hour later, Commander Panter showed up with six Marines in full armor—and here we are," Jay finished. He glanced at his watchfinger. "I'd say she died about two hours ago. That's everything we know, Admiral."

He and Rand and Duncan were in a place any small boy would have killed to visit: the command center of the Citadel, the UN Space Command's principal fortress in space. It looked just like it did in the movies. The only person with them now was Admiral Cox himself, a grizzled old centenarian with a startlingly warm smile—but Jay knew perfectly well that every word he'd just said had been heard by literally hundreds of people on and off Earth. It was beginning to make him distinctly uneasy too. Cox was treating them as vip guests—but Jay was beginning to suspect how long it might be before he slept in his own bed again.

Cox sucked coffee from a battered military-issue bulb, and nodded sadly. "Post mortem shows a fatal allergy to sedation. Iatrogenic, of course. Her superiors didn't even give her an option. They wanted her interrogation-proof. Interesting people."

"I'm sorry, Admiral. We should have thought—should have given her antidote right away—"

Cox shook his head emphatically. "There was no other way to take her; you'd have thrown your lives away trying. And it was too late for antidote the moment she lost consciousness. More coffee, gentlemen?"

Jay had been too busy talking to consciously taste his; he queried his tongue and learned that the brew had come from the Atherton tablelands of Queensland. "Yes, please, Admiral." The others accepted as well, and a servobot much uglier and clumsier than anything in the Shimizu brought them fresh bulbs.

There was a short silence while they all drank. Rand broke it. "We screwed up," he said hollowly— and Jay felt himself nodding in agreement.

"On the contrary!" Cox said. "You walked among the lions today, son, and all your blood is still on the right side of your skin. Are you sure none of you has had military training?" All three shook their heads. "If you were my cadets, I'd be sewing stripes on all three of you right now."

"But we don't know *shit*," Rand insisted.

"We know a lot more than we would if you three had gotten yourselves dead trying to take her cowboy-style! I'd be sitting here right now, listening to Kate Tokugawa tell me the emergency was over and thanks, but they didn't need any assistance. Who knows how long it would have taken for someone at Top Step to try and call Humphrey, and get a no-such-guest-in-house? Now we've got everything you learned, *days* before they thought we would— and five low-level thugs we were able to take alive, we can sweat them—"

"—and it all adds up to doodah," Jay said. "If the Security goons know anything useful, they'll be allergic to interrogation. And what we know just doesn't make any goddam *sense*."

"Not by itself, no. But it may tie in with other things . . . tell me, would you gentlemen consent to hypnointerrogation? You may know things you don't know you know."

"On one condition," Rand said.

"State it."

"Admiral, this is high-level stuff. I'm a civilian. I want your personal word that when you put this all together, you'll share it with me. I'll take any kind of secrecy oath you want—trigger me up like a courier if you want, so I *can't* talk—but I have to know. Not what the cronkites get told, but the truth."

"The same goes for me," Jay said.

"Me too, Admiral," Duncan said.

Cox did not answer right away, and they did not hurry him. He met each of their eyes in turn. Finally he said, "I agree to that, whether you consent to hypno or not. You've earned it. For a start, I will tell you that yours wasn't the only kidnapping. Data are still coming in, but there have been at least two others in space, and more than a dozen dirtside— beautifully coordinated, assorted methods but one hundred percent success rate. I am not aware of any other military engagement in modern history accomplished with such elegance and efficiency. Billions were spent. Well spent."

"What kind of people were taken?" Jay asked.

"Saints."

"*What?*"

"Holy men and women. Spiritually enlightened people. Like Reb and Meiya—and Fat Humphrey too, in his way. Several different faiths, and two whose religion has no brand name at all, but they're all what Reb would call *bodhisattvas*. Mother Theresas, if you're old enough to get the reference. You know: saints."

"You mean like the Pope?" Duncan asked.

"I didn't say religious leaders. I said spiritually enlightened people. One of them seems to be an Aboriginal witch woman. Another is a Pakistani musician who only plays hospitals."

"Of course," Rand said, slapping his forehead. "What's wrong with me? You want to overthrow the UN, naturally you kidnap saints, musicians and fat maitre-d's."

"It just keeps getting worse," Duncan said. "More than a dozen perfect military operations, carried out by wealthy morons."

"Admiral, is there anything the captives have in common *besides* . . . well, besides holiness?" Jay asked.

Cox lifted one bald eyebrow respectfully. "You do keep surprising me, Sasaki-*sama*. Yes. One and only one overt connection between them. They are all known to be on especially intimate terms with the Starmind."

Rand's eyes showed a gleam of excitement. "Some sort of hostage deal—" he began.

"I've asked the Starmind for their evaluation of the known data," Cox said. "It can take a week to get an answer from them on a simple question, sometimes, but they've promised me at least a preliminary answer by 12:00 Greenwich, about . . ." He winked briefly; his own watch was inside his eyelid. " . . . twelve hours from now. You'll have slept off the hypno by then. Meet me here at noon and you'll hear anything I do."

As far as Jay was concerned, he woke up with a click, totally refreshed and restored and in a comfortable bunk, one second later. He never managed to remember anything of leaving the command center, let alone the hypnointerrogation process itself. It did not trouble him, then or ever; he simply slid out of his sleepsack, confirmed that he had time to keep his appointment, stuck his head out the door and had the Marine stationed there cause breakfast to be fetched.

He did find himself wondering, as he ate, whether any alterations might have been made in his memories or motivations while he slept. But he reasoned, correctly, that the ability to form the question was a reassuring clue, and dismissed the matter. His generation had been the first in a century to grow up trusting its government. Instead he tried to imagine how possession of holy people gave anyone leverage over the Starmind and/or the UN. No rational answer suggested itself.

He reached the command center early, and was admitted by the Marines guarding it; Rand and Duncan arrived shortly thereafter. At noon exactly Admiral Cox jaunted in, looking exhausted. It was obvious he had not slept. "Good morning, gentlemen," he said. "I hope this won't prove to be—"

"*BILL.*"

The voice came from everywhere. Jay found it hauntingly familiar, but couldn't pin it down. Then he grasped what it had said, and was suddenly dizzy, a most unfamiliar sensation for a zero-gee dancer.

Cox was a common name. But this was Admiral *William* Cox. *The* William Cox—former commander of the *Siegfried*! Jay had assumed he was dead. He was used to the company of vips and uips—but he had been drinking coffee and chatting with a legend: the first human being to have set eyes on a Firefly . . .

"Yes, Charlie, I'm here," Admiral Cox said quietly.

Jay gasped aloud in shock. This could be no other than Charlie Armstead himself. Shara Drummond's video man, the man who had personally taped the Stardance; co-founder of the first zero-gee dance company in history; the second Stardancer who ever lived and the spiritual father of Jay's artform. He felt his dizziness turn to nausea.

But he felt infinitely worse when he heard Armstead say, *"I'M SORRY OLD FRIEND. I HAVE VERY SAD NEWS . . ."*

23

Somewhere North of the Ecliptic
26 February 2065

Eva woke hard, feeling every one of her hundred and sixteen years, tasting each one somewhere on her tongue. Her first coherent thought was that Jeeves must have been nipping at the cooking sherry. He had mutated into a Chinese gorilla and put on a white p-suit. But he still had that quality of shimmering self-effacement. "Good morning, gracious Lady," he said, and bowed. Even the bow was different.

"The hell it is," she replied—and realized they were conversing in Cantonese, a language she had not spoken in forty years. "Speak English."

"This one regrets that he cannot, Lady." There was something wrong with his p-suit speaker; it gave his voice too much treble.

She took several deep breaths, and felt the mists

begin to recede. That wasn't Jeeves—or any AI. It was a human being . . . sort of . . . and too dumb to be a servant. And why was he in a p-suit when there was plenty of air in here? Something was badly wrong.

She played back memory. The last thing she could recall was asking Fat Humphrey what he wanted from Room Service. She looked around. This was not part of Fat's suite—or anywhere in the Shimizu. It looked more like a construction barracks, unpainted metal and visible joins. She and this Cantonese thug were alone here. There didn't appear to be even any potential furniture—not so much as a sleepsack. No wonder her neck ached so badly: she had been nodding in time with her breathing for . . . God knew how long. Hours, at least. Her chest hurt too. In fact, her everything hurt.

Well, some phrases she knew in over a dozen languages. "Where am I? Where are my friends?"

"Lady, this one is too ignorant to be questioned. His instructions are to offer you nourishment, and then convey you to his master."

"Who is your master? You can't be *that* ignorant."

"That is not for this one to say, gracious Lady."

She decided asking him his name would be a waste of time. A tagline from an ancient comedy series flitted through her mind: *He's from Barcelona, you know.* "Skip the nourishment. Can you show me to the washroom?"

That turned out to be something he could handle, thank God. It was down a short corridor from what she was getting through her head was her cell. The Cantonese minder never took his eyes from her, and though he wore no visible weapons something about his bearing said he didn't really need any. She understood now that he wore a p-suit so that he could use sleepy gas on her if he felt he needed to.

As soon as the door sealed behind her, she tried to empty her mind of everything but the question, *Reb, are you alive? Are you here?*

Nothing came back. She thought she might have detected something like a carrier wave, a power hum, but there was no signal. And it might have been wishful thinking. Reb had only been tutoring her in this empathic sensitivity stuff for a couple of months, and her progress had been frustratingly slow. She tried "tuning in on" Meiya and then Humphrey, but was unsurprised to achieve no better results. She was on her own.

Well, she had a century and more of practice.

Bladder empty and face washed, she looked about the horrid little cubical for a useful weapon. The facecloth seemed to exhaust the possibilities. She gave up and left. Her self-effacing jailer was a discreet distance down the passageway, and quite alert.

"All right, Marmaduke: take me to your leader." She spoke in English, but he seemed to take her meaning. He led the way—but jaunted backwards, so that his eyes rarely left her.

She memorized the route, and kept her eyes open along the way. This pressure felt *bigger* than a ship, somehow. Indefinable subconscious clues told her it was something more like the Shimizu or Top Step: a massive habitat. More like Top Step in the old days: thrown together, rough carpentry, baldly functional. She also got the impression he was taking her by the back way. They passed few people, and once when they did, he and the others had bristled at each other like challenging cats in passing. She filed the observation away.

The room he led her to reminded her a little of her own suite in the Shimizu. Spartan simplicity— but expensive simplicity. She grew a chair and shaped it to suit her. "You may leave me," she said.

He grimaced. "This one regrets that he cannot, Lady. But he will cease to intrude." With that, he . . . became a piece of furniture. It was like a robot powering down; suddenly he wasn't there anymore, except in potential. She tried to catch him breathing, but to her wry amusement she found she could not keep her eyes on him for more than a few seconds; they slid off. She gave up, studied the right arm of her chair, and ordered strong black tea.

She was intrigued to notice that it appeared to arrive under its own power, herded not by microbots but by invisible nanobots. Rough carpentry, yes . . . but state of the art technology.

As she took the first sip, the door sighed open and Chen Ling Ho entered. The Cantonese powered back up and came to attention.

"You could have just asked," she said. "Two of my marriages were elopements."

Chen smiled. It struck her that that was his only response. Almost any other man she had ever known would have felt obliged to make a clever comeback. He made some signal she didn't quite catch, and the guard left, in a wide, fuel-wasting arc to avoid passing between them.

When the door had slid shut behind him, Chen spoke in Mandarin. "Sun Tzu—privacy!"

"Yes, Highness," his AI replied in the same language.

"There," Chen continued in English. "We now have total privacy. But very little time." A chair came to him and enfolded him, and a globe of water found his hand. "I am sorry you were caught up in this, Eva. I would have had it otherwise."

"Where are Reb and the others? For that matter, where the hell are *we*?"

"*Tenshin* Hawkins and his friends are sleeping presently." He sipped his water delicately, and pursed his lips in approval. "Your second question has many answers. We are in an elongated polar orbit, high above the ecliptic, in a region of space where neither the United Nations nor the Starmind could find us, even if they were looking. This pressure itself is many things. Fortress. Laboratory. School. Flagship. My home away from home."

"Is 'prison' in there somewhere?" she asked. "Or can I go home now?"

He failed to hear the question. "Specifically, we are in my quarters, which I invite you to share."

"Damned rude invitation. I hurt all over. Don't you know any better than to subject spacers to high gees?"

"There was a regrettable need for speed and stealth," he said. "All possible care was taken: military antiacceleration technology was employed. Happily, you all survived."

"But in what condition? The others should have woken before me; they're all younger."

"But they left Terra behind much longer ago. Their journey was actually more arduous than yours. But do not worry: I am told that their health is excellent."

"Then when will they wake up?"

He sighed. "I do not envision that occurring, I'm afraid."

She set her jaw. "Ling, quit dancing and spit it out. What's going on?"

"You will recall the economic summit conference in the Shimizu last month?"

"Let me see . . . the one we almost got killed during, or am I thinking of some other one?"

He ignored the sarcasm. "We five have managed to repair our relationship . . . for the time being, at least . . . and are now about to destroy the Starmind and overthrow the United Nations."

Eva Hoffman had known more than a few power-mad men and women in her lifetime, including some who were quite successful at it. Had any of them made such a statement, she would have laughed, or at least wanted to. From the lips of Chen Ling Ho the words were blood-curdling. No flip response was thinkable. "My God . . . ," she whispered, horror-struck.

"We hope to create the first rational planetary government," Chen went on conversationally. "Rather along lines K'ung Fu-Tzu might have approved of, I think. But it scarcely matters. The point is that once the Starmind is annihilated, any mistakes humanity makes will be its own."

REB! For God's sake, WAKE UP!

Just the barest hint of response, like a man turning restlessly in a deep sleep.

"Ling, for the love of Christ, humanity can't *make it* without the Starmind, not anymore, you know that!"

"Precisely why the Starmind must die. The riches it showers on us are like welfare checks: they demean, and degrade, and diminish us. Stardancer benevolence has already devolved us from wolves to sheep, from roaring killer apes to chattering monkeys, in three generations. This trend *must* be reversed, before the inevitable day comes when the Fireflies return. The transition will be painful—but we will make it by our own efforts, as free human beings, or die trying."

"You really think you can kill every Stardancer in the Solar System? *How?*"

He frowned, and chose his words carefully. "Before I can answer that, Eva, I must ascertain your status. I have stated my intentions. Three options are open to you: you can be friend, foe or neutral."

"Nice of you to offer the third choice," she said.

"Yes, it is. But if you choose it, I cannot answer your question, or any other of a strategic or tactical nature. In that event I will sequester you here, in reasonable comfort but complete ignorance, and release you in your own custody when events have resolved. On the order of three months from now."

She noticed that he did not say, " . . . on the *close* order of . . ." and grimaced. "I assume foes don't get briefed either."

"On the contrary," he said. "If you tell me that you oppose me, I will answer any questions you have. You have been an intimate companion to me, Eva: I would wish your death to be as agreeable as possible."

Reb, wake UP! Rise and shine! Dammit, you're gonna wet the bed!

"I see. And if I claim friendship?"

"You get it," he said simply. "After this is over, you can have the Shimizu for a gift if you like. It lies within my fief."

"And you'll take my word."

"Eva, I know when you are lying."

"How long do I have to think it over?"

"As long as you wish. But in ten minutes I must leave here to begin the attack, and I will be unable to return for at least twenty-four hours. If you wish to witness history as it is happening, at my side, you must choose to be my friend before I leave this room." He swiveled his chair away from her and began scanning a readout of figures in no alphabet she knew, politely giving her space to think it through.

The trouble was, she thought, the canny little son of a bitch probably *would* know if she lied. That was bad, very bad, for she had to oppose him—*had to*—and dared not even hint why. After a hundred and sixteen weary years and countless flirtations, death had come for her at last, was a matter of minutes away. She was shocked by how much that realization hurt—but even a newfound fear of extinction was of less importance than the awful responsibility she *must* now discharge before she died.

Why me? she thought—and smothered the thought savagely. That was exactly the kind of self-indulgence she could no longer afford. Instead she made her limbs relax, took control of her breathing, and forced herself to remember the words Reb had once told her.

"It's state of mind more than anything else, Eva. Telepathic sensitivity is largely a matter of sweeping the trash out of the communications room. Try and remember what it was like when one of your babies cried in the night and woke you. There is no 'you' at such a moment, no ego, no identity, no fear, no viewpoint . . . only the need, and the feeling of it, and the will to serve it, to soothe the pain at all costs."

She kept measuring her breath, felt her anxiety begin to diminish. She had not meditated with any regularity since the 1970s, but it seemed to be one of those riding-a-bicycle things. Perhaps it is true that it becomes easier to surrender the ego at the point of death, when you finally admit that you cannot keep it forever anyway. Eva soon felt herself going further away from the world than usual, or perhaps closer to it—climbing to a higher place or perhaps it was descending to a deeper level, though neither term meant anything in zero gravity—went *beyond,* achieving a selflessness she had only been granted a few times in all her years, for fleeting moments.

With it came a wordless clarity, a focused four-dimensional seeing. Dualities of all kinds became as obsolete as up and down: within/without, self/not-self, good/bad, life/death.

She now knew exactly where Reb and Meiya and Fat Humphrey were: how far away, and in which directions. There was another sleeping adept here in this pressure, too, one she did not know. Their consciousnesses were like fireflies—not the mighty aliens but the feeble terrestrial kind, glowing like embers and dancing mindlessly in the dark. She called out to them. Each resonated to her mental touch, but none responded. They could not "hear" her, and she could not wake them.

There was no help here. She must cope alone.

She let herself return to her body.

She had forgotten how weary and frightened and angry it was. From a purely selfish point of view, dying didn't seem like such a terrible idea. Chen was still scanning what looked like the same screenful of gibberish.

"How long have I got?" she asked.

He checked the time. "Another six minutes before I must leave."

No more time at all. "Chen Ling Ho, I oppose you with all my heart."

He closed his eyes for a moment, and inhaled sharply through his nose. "That is regrettable," he said sadly. "As you wish. I will tell you as much as I can before I must go; any questions you still have can be answered by Sun Tzu."

"How can you possibly kill a quarter of a million indetectable people in free space?"

"Do you remember the terrorist bombing of a shipment of Symbiote from Titan, some forty-five years ago?"

"Sure—your father did it. But that was a traveling ocean, constantly announcing its position. What's that got to—"

"This will go faster if you reserve your objections. My esteemed father Chen Hsi Feng was acting in accordance with a plan devised by his noble father, Chen Ten Li. His intent was not merely to destroy Symbiote, but to discreetly secure a large sample of it for analysis. Fine control of the explosive caused the Symbiote mass to calve in a predictable pattern. While all eyes fixed in horror on the destruction, then turned Earthward in search of its source, a stealthed ship was waiting quietly in the path of one of the largest fragments.

"My father was assassinated by a Stardancer trainee, but the conspiracy he had dedicated his life to lives on. That sample has been studied intensively ever since. We now know how to grow a pale white variant which does everything Symbiote does *except* confer telepathy. It has been further altered so that it requires regular large doses of a chemical which does not occur naturally in space to stay alive. One as astute as yourself will immediately appreciate that it is therefore now possible for the first time to create a Symbiote-equipped army which will stay loyal. Starhunters, we call them. Among other things, this base we're in now is to Starhunters what Top Step is to Stardancers."

In spite of herself, Eva objected. "You can't possibly have raised up an army large enough to threaten the Starmind, not in secret. The head start they've had, the way they breed, the motivations you can't possibly offer a recruit—I just don't believe it."

He was nodding. "And since our troops must use radio or laser, limited to lightspeed, our communications and coordination are inherently inferior to telepathy, a crippling disadvantage. You are quite correct: we could never seriously threaten the

Starmind with infantry, even though Starhunters are heavily armed and Stardancers are not. The Starhunters are not intended to kill the Starmind. They are chiefly intended to conquer the United Nations Space Command, and thus the world. He who rules High Orbit rules Terra."

"And what is the Starmind going to be doing at the time?"

"Running for their lives, the few left alive. If they are intelligent enough to keep running right out of the Solar System, a handful of them may live to circle some other star—and good riddance to them, for they can never return. Do you recall how the Symbiote mass was bombed?"

She thought hard. Forty years ago, she had read an eyewitness account by a Stardancer named Rain M'Cloud, who before entering Symbiosis had killed Ling Ho's father to avenge the bombing. Eva seemed to recall there'd been something uniquely horrid about the method of delivery . . .

She felt a thrill of horror as the memory surfaced. "A nanobomb. Concealed in a kiss."

"It worked well—and close study of Symbiote has suggested many improvements. For the last forty-five years, we have been seeding the entire Solar System with similar bombs, self-replicating at viral speed, self-powered, absolutely undetectable. They ride the solar wind, seek out red Symbiote, home in, burrow in and hide. They've been spreading through space like a fine mist for forty-five years. Stardancers breed like rabbits. Statistical analysis indicates that by now, some ninety to ninety-five percent of the Starmind has come into physical contact with either a bomb-spore, or another infected Stardancer."

For a moment she thought her old heart would literally stop. This was what she had always imagined that would feel like. "Radio trigger?" she managed to say.

"Relays all over the System," he agreed. "About an hour from now I will broadcast a master triggering signal from here. At the moment named in that signal, some six hours later, every relay will begin sending the destruct code at once. Maximum possible warning due to lightspeed lag should not exceed one minute anywhere in the System."

"Trillions of dollars," she murmured dizzily. "To murder angels."

"It could not have been done undetected in anything but the wild-growth economy the Starmind gave us," he admitted. "So in the end they have served a useful purpose."

"Some of them will survive," she said fiercely, and felt something tear in her chest. She ignored the pain. "They'll come for you—they're good at nanotech, they'll find a way."

"Quite possibly," he agreed. "That is why we have kidnapped *Tenshin* Hawkins and his friends, and every other human telepathic adept we could locate. Enslaved by drugs, I believe they will function as excellent Stardancer detectors. Is there anything else you wish to know, Eva?"

She was silent, concentrating on listening to her heart, willing it to keep beating.

"Is there any other last favor I can grant you, in the name of our friendship? I fear time is short."

Was there any chance at all that the truth might change his mind? She had no other cards to play.

No, none. She remembered a fictional god she had read of once, called Crazy Eddie, worshipped with awe because in times of crisis he invariably incarnated in a position of responsibility and did the worst possible thing from the best motives. There were usually just enough survivors to perpetuate his memory. It was proverbially pointless to reason with Crazy Eddie . . .

"I . . . I'd like an hour alone to compose myself," she said.

"Done," he said. "Sun Tzu!"

"Yes, Highness?"

"Ms. Hoffman is not to leave that chair, nor this room." The chair's seatbelt locked with an audible click. "She is not to communicate with any person or persons outside this room. One hour from now I want you to kill her painlessly. She may command you to shorten that deadline, but not extend it. You may answer any questions she has, and serve her in any way that does not conflict with these instructions. Acknowledge."

"Program loaded, Highness."

He pushed his own chair away and bowed, a full formal salute of farewell. "Goodbye, Eva. I'm sorry you will not share my joy."

Then he bowed again, quickly. Her tea-bulb missed his head by an inch, ruptured on the unpadded bulkhead behind him and splattered his back with hot tea. When he straightened, she was giving him the finger.

His expression did not change. He left.

✧ ✧ ✧

Pain nagged at her attention, but she had long ago learned to bypass pain. She could still dimly sense Reb and the others; a ghost of the seventh sense with which she had perceived them earlier was still with her, like a ghostly heads-up display on her mind's eye. There was no point in entering deep meditation and trying to wake them again. She had no assets she had lacked the last time she'd tried, was weaker if anything, and the medical technology keeping them stupified was sure to be foolproof.

She was going to have to think her way out of this. Or fail and die.

God dammit, I have not *endured all these years of bullshit to become the greatest failure of all time!*

And with that, an idea came to her. It was only a possibility, and a long shot at that, but it was infinitely better than nothing.

She thought it through carefully, with the slow, intense deliberation of a freezing man with a single match planning the building of his fire. She built event-trees in her mind, assigned probabilities and risks, prepared contingencies, rechecked every calculation. Finally she felt she was ready.

Assuming that she was right, and did in fact possess a match . . .

She checked her pocket, and found her personal wafer was missing. She hoped that was a good sign.

Well, I'm not getting any younger.

"Jeeves!" she said.

He shimmered into existence. "Yes, Madam?"

Chen Ling Ho had cherished the hope that she would agree he was Alexander the Great and accept the role of emperor's companion; naturally he would have installed her AI on-line in case he won her over. He would remove the wafer again after she was dead and his war was over. That much had made psychological sense. What had worried her was a matter of semantics. Was an AI a "person"—in the opinion of another AI? And if so, since AIs were effectively everywhere, was Jeeves a person "outside this room"?

She was still alive. Step one accomplished. Now to push the envelope . . .

"Jeeves, is Rild on-line?"

If the answer was no, Sun Tzu would not know who Rild was, and might kill her out of caution, just in case this Rild was a "person." And Eva thought it likely the answer would be no.

Chen's holographic gear was excellent; Jeeves became discreetly pained. "Yes, Madam. He has been under constant interrogation since our arrival in this pressure."

Good. Then Sun Tzu was aware of Rild, and classified him as "not-a-person-outside-this-room."

"Rild, can you hear me?"

Reb had long ago given Eva access to all but the most personal levels of Rild; she was privileged to summon him. The question was, did he have bytes to spare? Or did the software interrogating him tie up too much of his capacity?

"Yes, Eva," Rild's soft voice said.

She felt like she was tap-dancing on a high wire in terrestrial gravity. Balanced in her hand were all the eggs there were, or ever would be. She began breathing in slow rhythm, composing herself, reaching again for the wordless timeless Evaless place. "Do you have some way to wake Reb?"

The answer came from far away, down a long tunnel. "Yes. A posthypnotic trigger."

Causing a person to be awakened is not communication. "Do it," she murmured, and her eyes rolled up.

This communication, Sun Tzu was not equipped to monitor . . .

Reb was there waiting for her; awake, untroubled, numinous. His serenity helped calm her, eased her fear, brought them closer together.

She merged with him. She became him, and he her. For the first time in her life she sensed what it must be like to be a Stardancer. She had always wondered why beings who expected to live for centuries did not fear death *more* than a human; now she understood. It was not the brain that mattered, nor the mind which invested it, but the energy that wore both like a series of intricate disguises for a time and then became something else. She had dimly known this for a long time; now she surrendered to it.

She *felt* the entire Starmind, all around her, heard its chorus echo in the Solar System, grasped its quarter-million-member dance in its entirety, from the orbit of Mercury to the farthest fringes of the Oort Cloud where the comets winter.

And when that happened, Reb knew all that she knew, simply and effortlessly. And she in turn knew what he knew, which was all that the Starmind knew. Well over ninety-nine percent of that information she would never get to integrate, but she did have time to perceive certain essentials.

Such as: nanotechnological booby-trapping is a game that two can play. And: some nanobombs can be triggered, not by radio signal, but by biting a simple code on the back of one's tongue. And: her great granddaughter Charlotte in Toronto was going to recover. And: Reb loved her, and everything was going to be okay now. And finally: things are worth what they cost, and death is a small coin.

She even had time, in those final nanoseconds, to grasp the full extent of the cosmic joke the Universe had played on her, and to begin to smile.

Then she and Reb and all the other atoms in and of Chen's flagship were converted to a rapidly expanding perfect sphere of plasma, the color of a Stardancer.

Different conditions obtained on Terra; at the same instant, the corresponding base in North China began turning into a large white mushroom cloud, the color of a Starhunter.

24

Noteworthy Events in March 2065

—Military mop-up of the rebel forces went into high gear, spearheaded in space by Admiral Cox and on the ground by General Chang of a mortified China; after the first week, loss of life was nominal. Doubtless many conspirators were missed . . . but they were not free for long. Some ninety-three percent of the relay trigger stations in the Solar System were located and destroyed, although it was apparent that all those who had known the trigger code had died in the same instant.

—After lengthy consultation with the Starmind, the UN high command elected to delete all mention of a plague of triggerable nanobombs in space from its report to the public. This had the effect of making the Rebellion of the Group of Five appear a desperate, doomed kamikaze affair rather than a narrowly averted coup. Despite—or perhaps because of—its irrationality, the story played.

—The media went into delighted spasm, like sharks dropped into a fish farm. Old-timers for whom the business had lost something when people stopped having wars wept openly. The Sacrifice of the Adepts passed almost instantly into fiction—the cronkites and riveras had it to themselves for nearly a week before the first movie and novelization could be released, and then the floodgates really opened. The job of massaging the legend into a pleasing shape began. The performing arts, oddly, did not seem to take to the new subject: most of them already had funded work under way, with more upbeat themes.

—The Board of Directors of the Shimizu Hotel appointed a new manager and a new PR chief. A special monument was installed in the Grand Foyer, to honor their predecessors, who had bravely sacrificed themselves in a vain effort to ensure the security of guests. In return for keeping their faces straight at the dedication of this monument, and their mouths shut forever after, Co-Artistic Directors Rand Porter and Jay Sasaki received lucrative new contracts terminable only by them. Each contained an ironclad artistic control clause.

—The Board of Directors of the Starseed Foundation announced that Top Step would suspend operations while replacements were sought for its key personnel. The current three classes would graduate, those who made it through, but it would be at least four months before any new Postulants would be lifted to orbit. During the month of downtime, Top Step personnel would be busy dealing with the arrival from Titan of the largest mass of fresh Symbiotc ever shipped, a truly stupendous tonnage intended to meet the next fifty years of anticipated demand.

—Rhea Paixao and the group with which she had been trance-dancing two days a week learned belatedly that Manuel Brava had been one of the Martyred Bodhisattvas, and would not be showing up to join them again. His absence had gone almost unnoted; he had been that sort of man. They all went home and mourned—but the following Saturday night, the group spontaneously reformed on the beach, and Rhea was there. When she got home that morning, she began a novel with a Stardancer as a major character.

—In Yawara, North Queensland, the Yirlandji elders chose another witch woman, and held services for Yarra, who had returned to the Dreamtime after dreaming a mighty dream in a place called China. A song was sung for her by the whole tribe, a song by a dead protegée of hers, called "The Song of High Orbit." And indeed some particles of her may have followed the Songline that far, for all anyone can know.

—All over the Solar System, Starhunters began to die, for lack of a chemical so exotic it was not likely to be found on any ship they could raid. The luckiest of them had nearly a year's supply in their system when the source vanished; some had only weeks. The average ran about three months: the Group of Five had tended to keep its undetectable army on a short leash. As this became clear, some chose to emulate the example of *Tenshin* Reb Hawkins and briefly lit the heavens. Some attempted to surrender to the UN Space Command, and some to Stardancers; the survival rate in the latter category was much higher, but neither agency was really geared up to produce the needed chemical in bulk. Starhunters became the first new addition to the endangered-species list in thirty years.

—People in business suits all over the planet and throughout human space found their adrenal glands flooding as the wills of Chen Ling Ho, Victoria Hathaway, Grijk Krugnk, Imaro Amin and Pandit Chatur Birla came into effect; fortunes were made and smashed as the economic machinery of a species began to shift gears.

—Jay Sasaki took a day off from rehearsals, went EVA in a p-suit, and danced a dance he had choreographed in his mind months ago, but never gotten to perform. It was not taped or seen by any human or Stardancer eye, but when he was done, he felt somehow that it had been appreciated. Its working title, the only one it ever received, was "I Love You, Eva." The next day he asked his half-brother to help him shape a new piece, involving a butterfly with a withered body.

—The Human Genome Project issued its final report to the United Nations; it was formally thanked and ordered to begin dissolving itself. After three quarters of a century, the massive planetwide research effort had at last succeeded in deciphering all the "pages" of the DNA "book" which made any sense, a truly staggering accomplishment. Among other effects, the day seemed now in sight when disease would be spoken of only in the past tense.

Still largely unexamined, of course, were all the "garbage pages," the introns, popularly known as "junk DNA": the quite lengthy segments of genetic material (over ninety percent of the total) which, lacking end-begin codes, never express. The prevailing theory was that they represented several million years of accumulated nonlethal errors in transcription. One of the Directors of the HGP argued passionately before the UN Science Council that there was no such thing as an uninteresting component of DNA, and begged for at least some continued funding. But since introns had no discernible effect on human metabolism, there seemed little urgency— indeed, little point—in studying them, and Council voted to spend the money on more interesting problems.

Noteworthy Events in April 2065

—Minions of the Group of Five continued to be identified and taken into custody, on Terra and in space. Admiral William Cox suffered a transient ischemic attack while overseeing the cleanup in space; lateral paralysis proved reversible, and his cognitive and communicative faculties remained unimpaired; nevertheless he was awarded the Terran Medal of Valor and retired on full pay. He took up residence in the Shimizu, in the restored suite whose last guest, Humphrey Pappadopoulos, had enjoyed it so briefly. He chose it because Terra was not visible from its window. In the weeks that followed, there was always at least one

Stardancer outside that window, available should he wish company.

—The United Nations Executive Council decreed that henceforth June 22, Solstice Day, would be a global holiday in honor of Reb Hawkins and the other slain Adepts, and would be known as Courage Day. On that day no nonessential work was to be performed, and all humans who could possibly do so were requested to take part in a planetwide Hour of Remembrance, scheduled for 3 PM Greenwich (thus 7 AM in Los Angeles, midnight in Tokyo; only residents of the Pacific islands need lose any sleep to participate). There was to be no formal ceremony involved; it was asked only that citizens of Terra go outdoors at that time, contemplate the sky, and remember the Adepts. The idea was a popular one.

—As the media orgasm crescendoed, most of the planet overlooked an offbeat story from New Orleans. It seemed that the area immediately around the French Quarter had fixed itself up, more or less overnight. Centuries of grime vanished; crumbling sidewalks became elegant banquettes again; decayed hulks strengthened themselves and grew ironwork balconies as intricate and lovely as anything in the predominantly white part of town, and the statue of Louis Armstrong in Armstrong Park sparkled as it smiled down on a manmade pond whose water was pure enough for human consumption for the first time in a hundred years. Tourists emptied out of the Quarter to stare enviously—and soon were being charged admission. The Mayor publicly promised that if the rapturists responsible would come forward, he would give them the keys to the city and hire them to finish the job . . . but there was no response.

—Duncan Iowa was asked by ADs Porter and Sasaki to join Nova Dance Company as an apprentice, the company's first spacer. He proved a diligent pupil, and by the third day he was showing the other dancers tricks.

—Hidalgo Rodriguez's wife Amparo finally succeeded in persuading him that the implement in his magic new home obviously designed as the perfect male urinal was in fact intended to be a sink (Ridiculous! Who did dishes while they moved their bowels?), and that he must use this other silly thing instead. And remember to put the seat down afterward. It made no sense at all to him, but nobody had ever said upward mobility was easy.

—Rand Porter, in private conversation with Charles Armstead, finally brought himself to ask the question, "Were all of you in rapport with Reb and the others when they did it? Did the Starmind feel their deaths?" and was told, "We wished to, but they would not permit it. They shielded us." The answer did not help him sleep any better, but he was glad to know.

—Somewhere above the Ring, the Stardancer Rain M'Cloud was finally brought out of catatonia by the combined ministrations of her children Gemma and Lashi and one Olney Dvorak. At once she began dancing her grief. The others, each separated from her and each other by at least a million kilometers, joined her in ensemble and submitted to her choreography. The rest of the Starmind attended, and resonated. The loved ones of all the other dead

Adepts already danced their dances as well. Yet the Starmind as a whole did not grieve, and even among the most grief-struck like Rain there was an acceptance, a resumption of life, a looking forward. There was much to be done.

—Performing arts groups all across the planet began premiering new works. Not a single one was depressing. An inordinate percentage incorporated images or subtexts of space, or of floating, or of flying.

—Pursuant to the last will and testament of Eva Hoffman, a glass quart bottle of Old Bushmill's Black Bush, about half full, was delivered to Jay Sasaki. Later that evening, he and Duncan Iowa lightened its mass by another two ounces, and became lovers.

—The estate of Evelyn Martin formally filed suit against the Shimizu Hotel, its Board of Directors and citizens Duncan Iowa, Rand Porter and Jay Sasaki, alleging wrongful death, loss of consort, slander and assorted other torts and seeking a billion dollars damages from each and every defendant; suit dismissed with prejudice when trial software determined that the estate and the deceased had been married for a total of four days and had not seen one another in the ensuing twenty-seven years.

—Rhea Paixao increased her trance-dancing to three days a week, and began taking her daughter along.

—The Nanotechnology Lab near Top Step announced the commencement of a major new research effort. Its stated purpose was so abstruse that the cronkites gave up and took refuge in repeating the words as if they understood them. No one caught them at it.

—The Right Honorable George Kiku, Undersecretary of Revenue for the United Nations and Assistant Chairman of the Committee on Fiscal Anomalies, took early retirement under his burnout clause, and resumed a long-interrupted study of the guitar. It came back hard, but he took to soaking the fingertips of his left hand in cold tea, and eventually the calluses returned.

—Alert Space Command software noted that an unusually high number of Stardancers were in the close vicinity of Terra, and that many more seemed to be vectoring earthward. But since it did not classify Stardancers as either threat or navigational hazard it did not notify any human beings.

Noteworthy Events in May 2065

—The last Stardancer was successfully disinfected of her submicroscopic bomb, and shielded against reinfection. A misty disk of death still spun about the Sun, but it could now be ignored until it was convenient to clean it up.

—Colly Porter received a vacuum sculpture by courier. It was called "Puffball," and pleased her mightily. Her mother liked it too, and placed it in a prominent place in the living room, beside one by the same sculptor called "Driftglass."

—A dancer named John DeMarco, realizing his dream of a lifetime, was invited to join Toronto Dance Theatre as a principal dancer, largely on the strength of a particularly inspired performance at the Drummond four months earlier. His former Artistic Director never forgave him for accepting, and made a point of telling him (mendaciously) that she had faked every single orgasm.

—LaToya Dai Woo, Assistant Director of the US Internal Revenue Service, resigned under a cloud having to do with inexplicable anomalies in that year's data; while the antiquated computer system was torn apart and rebuilt, she moved to the Shimizu Hotel and took up recreational sex.

—The New Orleans self-renovation phenomenon began occurring in ghettos, slums and eyesores around the planet. One economist calculated that even given the immense cost-effectiveness of nanotechnology, several trillions of dollars had to have been spent by rapturists worldwide. Hardly anyone believed him; he was, after all, an economist.

—Gunter Schmidt finally recovered from the bronchitis which had followed upon his stroll through ice water in Nepal, and succeeded in suing his travel agent into bankruptcy. He then returned to Nepal to catch the May Tiji Festival—and learned on arrival that since the Kali Gandaki had in fact returned, the festival had been declared redundant. The Lo were too busy planting crops.

—Unnoticed by anyone, Admiral Cox slipped out a maintenance airlock and entered Symbiosis. The p-suit he removed in order to do so eventually burned up in the upper atmosphere, flaring as the air tanks went up. Since his bills continued to be paid and his room and AI reported no medical emergency, his absence went unnoted until late June.

—The rising wave of "cheerful art" reached such a crest worldwide that even critics began to notice it. Certain conspiracy theorists among the media began to smell a rat, and whispered along the E-mail byways of "rapturist conspiracy"—ideally some kind of immense digital fraud. To their annoyance, investigation kept indicating that the money funding all this new art was real. And anonymous. So they went public with the old standbys, thinly veiled suspicion and unsubstantiated rumor—and would have gone on to entirely baseless allegations in turn, if they hadn't noticed that nobody seemed to be paying the slightest bit of attention to them. Everyone was too busy attending performances that sent them home feeling good.

—The mammoth new mass of Symbiote reached Earth Orbit, was calved into six chunks, and each was inserted into a stable orbit. The reason for the subdivision was not known, but it aroused little curiosity. Few humans were of a mind to pester the Starmind with nosey questions these days.

—Colly Porter, having been back on Terra for the recommended three months, returned to High Orbit to spend a month with her father in the Shimizu Hotel. Shortly after her arrival she stated the opinion that hugging was more fun when you could use your legs too. This caused her father to blush (humans seldom go pale in free-fall, but they can still blush), and begin rehearsing a speech he had been meaning to deliver for a couple of years now. But in the end he managed to stall just long enough, and was spared the necessity.

—A peculiar glitch began to show up in

automobiles—*all* automobiles, regardless of place or date of manufacture. Changing lanes without signalling at least five seconds in advance appeared to cause total CPU failure. Fortunately, the "crashless crash" safety feature hardwired into the guidance system usually brought the offending vehicle safely to the side of the road. No one claimed credit for the innovation, and public opinion split: some attributed it to rapturists, while others blamed a much older, half forgotten group called "hackers." But the prevailing response of humanity at large was glee, and no one tried too hard to crack the case.

At the end, there, everything seemed to happen at once.

PART NINE

25

The Dunes East of Provincetown
22 June 2065
Courage Day

"This is a good spot, mom."

Rhea thought so too. They were at the ocean shore east of Provincetown, just where the upthrust arm of Cape Cod curls its wrist back toward the mainland. Before them was the sea, next stop Europe; behind them to the west, between them and P-Town, lay kilometers of sand dunes. The weather was perfect, and had been since they had watched the sun rise together over the Atlantic several hours ago. It was now almost time for the Hour of Remembrance, and she and Colly were just finishing the food they had brought with them from home.

There were few others here, even on this global holiday. There were too many beaches a P-Towner could reach without having to walk several kilometers of sand, too many boats available to take them out on the water, especially since the fleet was not fishing today. Nonetheless Rhea had never seen this particular stretch of shore so heavily populated. The idea of Courage Day had caught on.

The spot did not feel crowded; there was no rowdiness; the general mood seemed to be a kind of subdued celebration. People spoke less than usual, and in softer voices; those who listened to music or news did not inflict it on their neighbors; even teenage boys were not horsing around. Rhea suspected things would get more festive later, after the Hour was past, but for the moment there was a kind of solemnity in the air that seemed to call for decorum. It had been a long long time since so many saints had been martyred at once.

"Do you feel like Trancing?" Colly asked.

Rhea looked around. There were a few individuals dancing, but no group had formed as yet. She did not see anyone she knew nearby. "Maybe later, hon. After the Hour."

"Okay." Colly liked trance-dancing well enough, but was not as attached to it as Rhea had become in recent months.

"I'm surprised you have the energy," Rhea added idly. Colly had only been back on Earth for a few days after visiting her father in orbit.

"I know," Colly said. "Me too. Yesterday I was tired as galoonies—but today I feel like Waldo. You know what I mean? Like he must feel. Like, I know I'm weak, but I don't *feel* weak."

It took Rhea a second to get the reference. "Oh, *Waldo*—your new friend in the Shimizu. I forgot all

about him." Come to think of it, Colly hadn't mentioned him once since her return. "How is Waldo?"

Suddenly Colly was a textbook illustration, labeled
Nonchalance. "Okay," she said off-handedly, studying her fingernails. "His frog died, and he likes that
dopey classic rock music now, and his teacher says
he understands calculus." Beat. "And he said he
wants to marry me when we're bigger."

Rhea's heart turned over in her chest. She didn't
know whether she wanted to laugh or cry, only that
she must do neither out loud. *And so it begins,* she
thought. "Oh," she said, with equal casualness.
"I'm . . . sorry to hear about his frog."

"Yeah. Hip was cool."

"So, uh . . . what did you tell him? About the
marriage thing."

"I said I'd think about it."

"I see. Did that satisfy him for now?"

"I guess." Another pause. "He wanted to kiss me."

Rhea chose her words with care. "How was it?"

Colly had run out of fingernails; she segued
smoothly to toenails. "Okay, I guess." Suddenly she
turned and looked her mother in the eye. "But honestly, Mom, I don't get what the big deal is."

Rhea refused herself permission to smile. It cost
her. "You will, baby," she said solemnly. "You will."

"Yeah, but *when?*"

"You won't miss it," she said. The words made her
think of Manuel Brava, and she glanced at her
watchfinger. "Hey, it's almost time."

It was about five minutes before the Hour. All up
and down the beach, conversations were ending,
people were sitting up straighter and facing the sea.

Boats out on the water killed their engines, and their passengers came out on deck. Rhea felt a sudden pang of loneliness, the kind that a child's presence does not assuage. Holidays are always the worst time for those with no significant other.

"Mom? We're rich now, right?"

The non sequitur made her smile. "No, dear. But we're richer."

"Well . . . can we afford to call space for an hour?"

Automatically Rhea started to do mental arithmetic . . . then abandoned the equation unsolved. Her daughter had sideswiped her for the second time in less than a minute. "*Yes*, Colly! That's a *great* idea! Oh, I hope he's not . . . no, they won't be working in orbit, either." She was already autodialing, half-wishing the car was near so they could have visual too. Space images would have been appropriate during the Hour. Ah well . . .

Rand answered almost at once. "Hi, Rhea! Is Colly there? Of course she is—hi, princess!"

"Hi, Daddy!" Colly called back.

Rhea adjusted the volume for privacy. "Hi," she said.

"Where are you guys? No, wait—let me guess. Audio only, so you're out in the boonies somewhere. From the sound of the waves, ocean rather than bay side. The Dunes, right?"

How could someone who knew you that well be hundreds of miles away? "That's right."

"Is Uncle Jay around?" Colly asked.

"Right here, cutie," Jay's voice said.

"Hi, Uncle Jay! Hi, Duncan!"

There was the sound of laughter, then, "Hi, Colly," from Duncan.

Rhea monitored herself to see if Duncan's voice caused any internal fluttering. Nothing. She hoped he and Jay would make a success of it. "Where are you guys, anyway? No wait—let me guess." It couldn't be one of the Solariums: Rand and Jay were celebrities. Somewhere private, with a good view . . . got it! "You're all in Eva's window, aren't you?"

"Right," Rand said. "As a matter of fact, I think I can see you from here. Wave, Colly."

She looked skyward and did so. "Here I am, Daddy!"

"I see you," he assured her. "You've got mayonnaise on your chin."

She checked—and burst into giggles when she found he was right.

"We're planning to do some damage to the legacy Eva left me, as soon as the Hour is over," Jay said. "I wish I could send you down a snort."

"Me too!" Rhea said. "Look, I know the Hour's almost here. We don't have to talk or anything—but can we all stay on-line together until it's over?"

"It's something Terrans and spacers should share," Duncan said.

"It was my idea," Colly said proudly.

"And a good one," Rand told her.

"Are you okay, Uncle Jay?" she asked. "Are you sad about Eva?"

His answer was slow in coming. "Let me put it this way, honey," he said at last. "I'm not exactly okay yet—but I know I'm going to be. You know what I mean?"

"I know exactly what you mean," she said solemnly, and Rhea felt a brief stab of guilt. "Daddy, tell him that thing Captain Kirk said."

"Huh?"

"You know, about leaving."

A chuckle. "Oh. Not Captain Kirk, honey: Rahssan Roland Kirk. An Old Millennium jazzman. He said once, 'Nobody dies. They just leave *here*.'"

There was a pause, and then Jay's voice said, "I think that's true. Thank you, Colly."

"Two minutes," Duncan said.

"It feels like we ought to be *doing* something," Rhea said. "Colly told you we've been Trancing a little, right? Maybe we should all dance or something."

"Well," Jay said, "I figure like this: Reb was Soto Zen. One of his favorite sayings used to be, 'Don't just *do* something—sit there!' Do you guys know how to sit *zazen*? That's what we were thinking of doing."

"Sure," Colly said with just a hint of scorn. "Duncan taught us once. Well, *kukanzen*, not *zazen*, but they're prac'ly the same." She began manipulating sand into an improvised *zafu*, and Rhea followed her lead. She was cautious about exposing her child to organized religion, but Zen did not meet her definition of a religion. It had no deity, for one thing—but more important, it did not require either killing or converting unbelievers.

"It's okay to get up if you get antsy, Colly," Jay said. "Reb wrote a book once called RUNNING JUMPING STANDING STILL. Any of those would be appropriate, I think. And there's a walking meditation called *kinhin*, for groundhogs, anyway. Or you can Trance, if you like. But let's sit a little at first, at least at the start."

"Sure," she agreed.

"I'm the *Doan* today," Jay said. "The timekeeper. I'll ring a bell three times when the Hour strikes, and again when it's over, and we'll all be silent in between, okay?"

"Are you studying Buddhism now, Jay?" Rhea asked.

"Aw, I've been fiddling with it for years. But yeah, I'm getting into it more lately. It's a lot like drinking Black Bush, only cheaper."

Rhea checked her daughter. "No, honey, like this. You don't have to lace your fingers together in a gee field, remember? Left hand on top of right palm, thumbtips just touching."

Colly corrected her *mudra*, and straightened her spine. "Are we supposed to look downward?"

"Technically, yes," Jay said. "But for today I think looking up is okay. There's really no wrong way to do it, if your heart's in the right place. Just follow your breath . . . and remember Eva and Reb and all the Adepts."

"Get ready," Duncan said. "It's almost time."

The beach was hushed, now, save for the omnipresent *whush* of waves. The sky was nearly cloudless, baby blue. Rhea felt an electricity in the air. It was awesome to think that at this moment, all over the world, most of the human race was about to do just what everyone here was doing. Had humanity ever acted with anything like this kind of unanimity before? What a pity it took a tragedy to bring it about. But wasn't that always the way? Nothing brought people together like a good disaster. . . .

"*Ting. Ting. Ting,*" said the phone. Rhea composed herself, drew in a measured breath through her nose—

And the sky turned gold.

Not "gold" in any metaphorical or analogous sense, as one can be said to have "red" hair when it is not really red at all. The whole sky was literally golden, the color of burnished 14-karat gold, the color of the wedding ring Rhea had still not been able to bring herself to remove. It happened all at once, seeming to mushroom outward from several sources like a crystal forming in an instant. It was like a translucent gold roof cast suddenly over the world, shimmering and twinkling, backlit by the sun.

Everyone on the beach—very nearly everyone alive—gasped, and stared upward in wonder. Rhea found that she and Colly were clutching each other's hands, *mudra* be damned. An indescribable sound began to come from the people on the shore. Rhea had once, many years ago, been caught in a riot, and would carry the memory of that indescribable, unmistakable sound to her grave. This was its opposite: a vocal sharing of awe. Perhaps the Israelites had made such a sound when the Red Sea parted.

Some of it seemed to be coming from the phone. "Can you guys *see* this?" she cried. "It's unbelievable!"

"We see—" Rand began, but she did not get to hear what he saw for some time, because his voice was drowned out by another. It seemed to come from

everywhere, yet did not have the echoing quality of
loudspeaker broadcast; it was as though every AI on
the beach had been co-opted at once.

*"This is Shara Drummond, calling the human race.
I need your attention."*

Rhea knew that her heart should be racing. Shara
Drummond—the first Stardancer! Addressing all
mankind directly, for the first time since her original Stardance, sixty-five years ago . . .

Yet somehow Rhea felt herself growing calmer. She
met Colly's eyes . . . and they resumed formal *zazen*
posture, side by side, but continued to hold hands.

*"I have taken over all data channels and AI's in
human space to talk to you, because something
unprecedented is about to happen. A radical change.
It may seem frightening at first, but I promise you
it will be all right if you do as I ask. The Starmind
is here to help you through this . . . but you must do
your part, and no one can do it for you. The first
thing you must do is get everyone on Terra outdoors,
and everyone in Luna onto the surface. I mean
everyone. Essential services personnel, hospital
patients, the dying, the housebound, prisoners in solitary, all human beings. If you know of someone
trapped indoors, get them outside now. And hurry!
There is no time to lose. I will tell you what I can—
but don't stop to listen if you know of some human
who needs help getting outdoors; the information will
be repeated many times.*

*"A turning point has come in the history of the
human race—one set in motion by the Fireflies on
the day they came here for the second time, the day*

of the Stardance. We Stardancers were created in large part to help you through it."

Rhea thought quickly. Thank God Tia Marguerite and Tia Marion were out on Ti Louie's boat—it was an hour's hard walk back to the car. Everyone else she knew in town was mobile too. Suddenly she missed Rand so much her stomach hurt. "Are you guys hearing this too?" she murmured.

The phone's LED said the circuit was still open, but there was no reply. She thrust it absently into her breast pocket.

"I'm afraid your life is about to change forever. Your old life is over; a new one is about to begin. I know that will not be welcome news for many of you. No baby wants to be born; they all come out crying. But they stop. I'm afraid you have no more choice in the matter than a baby does: the contractions are beginning, and no power in the Solar System could stop them now. All we of the Starmind can do is see that the birth takes place as smoothly and painlessly as possible. We have sacrificed much to that end . . . but today is not our Courage Day, but yours. I can only ask you to trust in me—and in the Fireflies, who refused to let me die in orbit so many years ago.

"On that day, my planet was like a womb whose fetus is overdue for delivery. Such a fetus grows too large for its environment, begins to pollute its ecosystem with its own waste products, begins to degrade its surroundings. In the decades that followed, you— and we, the Starmind—have cooperated to help correct most of the damage to our home planet, using nanotechnology to minimize new wastes and recycle

old ones efficiently. The womb is repaired—but it is time for the fetus to leave it behind now."

Rhea did not guess what was coming; it was only a shadowy intuition. But it was enough to make her heart sink. She stared around that perfect beach, that eerie golden sky, as if to memorize it, and clutched Colly's hand. At an answering pressure, she met her daughter's eyes—and found them serene, untroubled.

"It's okay, Mom," she said. "It's Courage Day."

Shara Drummond's voice continued:

"You know that the Fireflies seeded this planet with life. You know that much of what you are is written in your DNA. Some of you may know that large segments of the information encoded there appear to be gibberish, and do not express somatically—the so-called junk DNA. These genetic 'instructions' are never carried out, because they lack the end-begin codes that would activate them.

"In just a few minutes, a kind of telepathic trigger signal will go out from Titan. There is no way to avoid or shield against it: it will be as unstoppable as a neutrino, and faster. Designed by the same beings who designed DNA in the first place, it will insert end-begin codes in certain introns—and switch them on. Everywhere in the Solar System, the nature of human tissue will change, permanently.

"It will become transparent to gravitons. In plain language, it will become immune to gravity."

Rhea moaned.

"Please listen to me and try to be calm. Many of you on Terra may have the idea that what is usually miscalled centrifugal force will send you flying off the planet at high speed. This will not *happen.*

When you go weightless, the net upward force acting on you will not exceed .003 gee. Your clothing should suffice to hold you in place; even shoes will probably be enough. Ask your AI if you don't believe me; I'll be releasing it to your control again soon. Nonetheless you will be in free fall, with the usual physiological symptoms most of you know: dizziness, stuffy nose and so forth.

"This period will last for perhaps five minutes. Then machines will turn themselves on. There are three of them. One is buried deep in the core of Terra, one at the heart of Luna, and the third at the core of Mars, though no one is there to be affected by it now. Each is designed to generate antigravitons . . . a special kind of antigraviton which will only affect altered human tissue."

The next sentence was delivered slowly, deliberately.

"Like it or not, you will find yourself rising into the sky."

A wordless cry went up all around the beach—doubtless around the planet—a discordant amalgam of clashing emotions. Shara Drummond seemed to anticipate that, and waited for it to die down.

"DO NOT FEAR," she said then. *"It is not death that waits for you in the sky, but a new kind of life. You will not freeze or suffocate as you climb, I promise you.*

"For the last sixty-five years, the Starmind has worked at modifying our Symbiote, in preparation for this day. The gold you see in the sky is the variant we have shaped, a variant designed to survive, for a time, at the interface between Terra and space. It

*cannot come down to you . . . but you will find it
waiting for you about five kilometers above the
ground, just as the air is getting too thin to breathe.
Touch it anywhere, drink it, and it will shape itself
to you. It will breathe for you, and bring you higher,
changing from gold to red as you leave the atmosphere behind.*

"This is why the Adepts made their sacrifice. If
the Group of Five had gotten their way, all of you
would have died this day. The Five knew nothing of
this, nor could we tell them. Without a Starmind, you
would have suffocated as you left the stratosphere—
and would not be hearing me now. But thanks to
Tenshin *Reb Hawkins* and the others, you will live
to reach space.

"And we the Starmind will be waiting for you. To
show you your new world. Your new home. You will
be one with us, and we with you, Homo caelestis
forever."

A vast soundless sound filled the world. Rhea
heard it inside her head, as if on headphones. It was
music, and she even recognized it: something Rand
played all the time, something by Brindle whose
name she could not recall. But to her tortured
imagination it seemed like the Trump of Doom that
Christians believed would signal the Rapture. She
found that she was clutching Colly to her fiercely,
keening without words. The words that raced through
her mind were, she knew, probably shared by millions; indeed, they might have been the final thought
of most of the humans who had ever died: *Not yet!
I wasn't done yet!*

It was a protest the universe had never heeded yet. As she drew in a breath to scream it aloud, Colly spoke against her breast.

"Don't worry, Mom," she said. "I didn't want to come out either, remember?"

Rhea remembered. Colly had been born three weeks overdue. She had stayed stubbornly in the womb . . . until a pitocin drip induced labor, and forced her out. And Colly had come to like this world.

"It's okay," Colly insisted. "We're gonna go see Daddy now."

She kept her deathgrip on Colly's shoulders, but pulled back so she could see her face. Colly was smiling. "Can you feel it?" she asked.

With a thrill of something like horror, Rhea felt her weight leaving her. She tried to hang on to it, but could not. Within a minute it was gone completely. Her sinuses began to fill, and she felt her face reddening as blood redistributed itself evenly throughout her body. She felt mild dizziness too. It was just like climbing to orbit in a shuttle—except that the rest of the world around her continued to observe the law of gravity.

Shara Drummond's message began repeating.

Colly picked up an uneaten apple, held it out, and let go. Rhea's body-awareness told her that she was in zero gee, so persuasively that it was jarring to see the apple fall normally. Colly giggled.

Suddenly she squirmed out of Rhea's grasp, a trick she had perfected at age five. Rhea cried out, but it was too late: Colly had already unfolded her legs from beneath her . . . causing her to rise into the air.

Without thinking, Rhea sprang after her and caught her like a tackler, hugging the child to her. They found themselves about six or seven meters in the air, sinking with the gentle slowness of a feather beneath the weight of their clothes. This high in the air, Shara's repeating message was almost inaudible. Others around them were airborne too. *A convention of Nijinskis,* she thought wildly as she drifted down. *Oh, Jay would love this! And Rand . . .*

"I wish Dad and Uncle Jay could see this," she said aloud.

Colly was grinning, exhilarated. "Just pay attention," she said. "We can give them an instant replay later."

They landed gently on sand, a few meters west of their takeoff point. With space-trained instincts and Trancer skill, both let their legs absorb the energy of landing, so they did not bounce away again. For a moment they bobbed there together, poised at the very membrane between earth and sky. They could hear Shara's voice clearly again, now that they were close to the earth—and many competing sounds too. Some people were screaming, some were laughing, some were yelling contradictory advice; some were flailing helplessly in the air, trying vainly to swim back to earth. And some were finding out how high they could jump. Out on the sea she could see people leaping higher than their masts, moving lazily in the air, like drowners in reverse.

"Let's Trance, Mom," Colly said. "We can do it for real, now."

Rhea had a sudden vivid memory of Manuel

Brava, the night she had trance-danced for the first time.

Be ready, he had said. *It's gonna be good.*

And this was the Hour of his Remembrance . . .

Somewhere in Rhea's heart, something gave way. Without regret, she closed the book that was her life . . . and began a new one. "All right, Colly." She released her embrace. "Take my hand, though, okay?"

"Sure," Colly said. "Here we go!"

They leaped together.

A few minutes later, Rhea admitted to herself that she was having fun. More fun than she had had in a long time. It was a little like trampolining or bungee-jumping in ultraslow motion. It was very much like dreams she had been having all her life. It was, in literal reality, what Trancing had always felt like, except that the moments of breathless exhilaration were not fleeting and transient.

Some others around her were also moving in the characteristic flowing movements of trance-dance, now; she and Colly were not the only Trancers here. Out on the sea, some people were walking on water, with exaggerated steps; she could just hear them laughing.

"—you okay?" Rand's voice said suddenly from her breast pocket. "Rhea! Colly! Can you hear me? Dammit, are you okay?"

He sounded half out of his mind with worry. Rhea took the phone out of her pocket. "We're fine, darling. Hang on—I think we're coming for a visit."

"What the hell do you mean? What's going on down there?"

"Didn't you hear Shara up there?"

"Yeah, but it didn't make much sense. She told us to go EVA, find some Symbiote, and take off our p-suits. But what about you? She said something crazy about immunity to gravity, and gold Symbiote."

"That's right. We're about . . . oh, I'd guess twenty meters above the ground right now. It looks like you win: Colly and I are coming to space after all."

"Oh God—you'll freeze, before you can reach the Symbiote."

"I don't think so," she said. "It's warmer than it should be down here. I think that gold Symbiote is having some kind of lens effect. They've had a long time to think this through."

There was silence on the line. The first to fully absorb the news was Jay. He began to laugh with joy. "Oh, Eva!" he cried, "What a glorious joke on you! Oh, how *wonderful*!"

"What do you mean, Jay?" Rhea asked.

"I get it now—I see it—I know why she wanted to die—and why she was dragging her feet—the stubborn old biddy was holding out for *meaning* . . . and she got it, bless her selfish heart—damn, she got the prize—oh, I'll bet she died smiling—"

"I don't understand," Rhea said. "Rewind and start over—slower."

"I'll try. Look, at age one hundred, Eva was done with life. So she went into sixteen years of life review . . . and found no *meaning* in anything she'd done. During a century of living as hard as she knew how, Eva converted X cubic tonnes of food and water into excrement and offspring; she pushed Y megabucks from one imaginary place to another; she experienced Z increments of pleasure or pain; once done, she could find no real significance in any of it. So her last hope for meaning was her death: she spent sixteen years hoping, irrationally, to find a meaningful death, an opportunity to give up her life *for* something. That's why she kept postponing her suicide for so long—why, even after she gave up and made up her mind to die, she stalled long enough to let Reb arrive, and give her a convincing reason to wait just a little longer. The reason was: to live to see this historic day."

"It's a shame she missed it, then," Colly said.

"No, no that's the best part, don't you see?" Jay said. "It is a shame she didn't live to see it with her own eyes, sure. But I'm sure she got to see it through the Starmind's eyes before she died—and more important, she got something even better. She got what she'd wanted in the first place, what she'd already given up on when Reb told her about today: a meaningful death. Think about it: how many humans—how many creatures, in the wide universe—had ever been privileged to sacrifice their lives to save *two* intelligent *species?*"

Colly was the first to see it. "Wow, yeah," she said wonderingly. "If it hadn't been for her and Reb and the Adepts, all the Stardancers would have got killed, and there wouldn't be any of that gold simmy-oat up there waiting for us. All us people would have died today . . ."

"She got the most meaningful death there ever was," Rhea said. She giggled suddenly. "Every damn time humanity goes through some kind of birthing, there seems to be an Eve around."

"Are you *sure* you're okay?" Rand asked. "You sound sort of giddy."

She laughed out loud. "Let's just say a great weight has been lifted from my shoulders. We don't have to be apart anymore, baby. Not ever again. Hang in there—we'll be along directly."

"What should I do?" he cried, his voice agonized.

"What Shara said. And don't be afraid. I'm not. I was, but I'm not anymore. It's gonna be *good.*"

"But—"

"Go ahead. I've got to hang up now, I don't want to miss this. We'll be there soon, love." She let go of the phone, and watched it fall away.

She and Colly were slowly moving away from the ocean, into the dunes. With each leap they came down farther to the west, for the earth went on without them all around them. They were sweating with exertion, now, and the sweat behaved the way it did in free-fall, as content to drip up as down. In her mind's eye Rhea saw the whole human race doing this. Hovering. Tottering on the brink. Trembling on the verge.

The ground was coming up again. You didn't even have to look: when you could hear Shara clearly again, it was time to prepare for your landing.

"Colly!" she cried. "Want to go for the big one?"

"Sure," her daughter said.

Rhea began undoing her clothing. Colly got the idea at once and skinned out of her own clothes. They let go, watched their clothes fall. This time, when they hit the earth and rebounded, they kept on rising.

They kept dancing for a while as they rose, but

the view was simply too distracting to concentrate; after a time they stopped moving in space and just gawked, letting the wind do with them as it would, turning end over end. The earth moved slowly and majestically beneath them. Soon Provincetown was below them. It was weird, inexpressibly weird, to see P-Town with hardly a soul on the streets. The beaches were full of hopping fleas, and the sky was starting to fill with naked people. It reminded Rhea of news footage of hot-air balloon regattas in the desert.

"Look," Colly said, pointing. "There's our old house."

Rhea saw it. For a moment it filled her heart, and called her back. Her beloved widow's walk. Below that, the tower room in which her unfinished novel waited, and below that the bedroom into which she had been born. Kicking and screaming.

"Goodbye," she said to it. "I'll never forget you."

"'Course not," Colly said. "Me either."

Suddenly they were rising faster, as though propelled by a great wind from below. It felt surprisingly like surfing vertically.

"Hang on," Rhea cried.

"Here we come, Daddy!" Colly called.

And they rose up forever, going for the gold.

EPILOGUE

High Earth Orbit
22 July 2065

It did not go totally smoothly, of course. Human beings were involved; at least some chaos and tragedy had to result.

But there never were more than the two choices: evolve or die.

Perhaps it need not have been done as it was, by surprise. Perhaps humanity, forewarned and prepared, might have agreed to leave its ancestral womb forever, peacefully and without panic. The decision not to risk it was irrevocably made on the day the original Six entered Symbiosis and founded the Starmind, back at the turn of the millennium, back when half of the human race was hungry and poor, and pessimism was still the hallmark of intelligence. Once Charlie Armstead elected to leave Courage Day out of the report he sent back to humanity from Saturn in the historic Titan Transmission, it was too late to turn back: the Starmind was committed to secrecy.

If you could somehow establish telepathic contact with a human fetus in its ninth month . . . would it be a kindness for you to tell it everything you know of the birth trauma to come? Would it benefit from the foreknowledge—or panic, jam the birth canal, and kill itself and its mother? After all, less than one percent of the race ever voluntarily chose to go to Top Step and become Stardancers. Being human is a hard habit to break. Shara Drummond, Charlie Armstead and their companions believed—all the Starmind still believes—that humanity might well have died rather than leave Earth, given the choice. So they did not give it the choice until the last possible instant . . . and spent sixty-five years secretly preparing it for that instant.

This cost the Starmind much ethical anguish over those years—and sharp tragedy at the eleventh hour—but right up until the Day of Courage, the overwhelming consensus of the massed brains of the Starmind was that the stakes were just too high to permit any risks. One of the few concrete facts the Fireflies told the Starmind before they left us to work out our own destiny is that *Homo sapiens* is at least the *third* sentient race to be raised up in this solar system.

The first sentient race ("sentient" defined as "capable of art") lived eons ago, on a planet some call Lucifer, whose shattered remains are now known as the Asteroid Belt.

The second such race appears to have been somewhat more advanced: they "merely" blew the atmosphere off the next closest planet to the sun, Mars. But they are just as dead.

We appear to have squeaked through to the finish line.

Had we too failed our most final of exams . . . well, there hangs Venus, within the habitable zone, its reducing atmosphere ready to collapse into a viable biosphere at a chemical nudge. . . .

Perhaps when I was a human fetus, I would have consented to be born. But I am glad, all things considered, that I wasn't consulted.

Volumes larger than this one could be—are being—written about the chaotic events of the hours and days that followed the Hour of Remembrance, the countless millions of varying human reactions to Shara Drummond's call.

No volume however large could describe what happened when over six billion minds entered telepathic symphysis in a single great cascading wave, nor will I try even to hint at it here. Suffice it to say that only the presence of a quarter of a million trained and prepared telepaths made it possible at all. Symbiosis is profoundly disorienting in its first onset, and some find it terrifying—Stardancer Postulants used to spend three months in Top Step preparing themselves for the transition. But human beings are tough, when they have to be, and we had to be.

Even now, a month later, the integration process is still ongoing. It might not be too inaccurate to say that the new HyperStarmind has achieved consciousness, and is working—slowly!—toward awareness.

Despite the very best efforts of a quarter of a million linked minds planning for over half a century, a little more than two percent of humanity perished in the mass transcendence to *Homo caelestis*, most through stubbornness but some from sheer stupidity. No telepathic entity can take lightly the deaths of so many millions of souls—especially needless deaths, on the very verge of immortality. But at least their surviving loved ones *know* with utter certainty that everything possible was done to save them; there is mourning for them in the Starmind today, but no recrimination. Cells die whenever a baby is born; it is no one's fault. Balancing the sorrow to some extent is the joy of all those who love an autistic or retarded or catatonic or mute person—for now they can communicate with their loved one on a level far deeper than words could ever have reached.

Approximately one half of one percent of humanity were unaffected by the telepathic tocsin from Titan or the subsequent flood of antigravitons: genetic defectives whose DNA had sustained too many nonexpressing mutations over the millennia, whose introns were fatally damaged despite massive redundancy in the coding. But nearly ninety percent of those eventually reached space and joined the Starmind too . . . for there were suddenly spacecraft to spare.

And a little over five percent of the human race flatly and stubbornly refused to go—improvising an astonishing variety of desperate methods to remain near the earth's surface, to remain only human. Within a month, however, their number had shrunk from five percent of the former total to about two.

The present population of Terra, then, consists of a little more than one hundred and sixty million people—on a planet with wealth and technology and room enough for six and a half billion. Most of them are wearing weights. You are one of them, or you would not be reading this. And the odds are that despite your new wealth and lebensraum you are lonely and/or hurt and/or angry and/or afraid.

You do not have to be any of those things. If you insist on staying on Earth, your life need not be hard: we will continue to beam down power, and programs for your nanoassemblers, and other things you will need—or you can make your own way as your forebears did, if that pleases you.

But you do not have to stay.

The golden sky of Earth is blue once more—but there is plenty of red Symbiote in orbit. And even now, Terra holds more than enough resources to send you to join us. Even if you are one of the rare genetic unfortunates—and if you are, we have the resources to heal your introns, once you enter Symbiosis.

That is why I am writing this.

All you have to do is find a phone. Shara Drummond is accepting collect calls, and will tell you how to reach the nearest functioning spacecraft. We're waiting for you.

Some of the oldest Chinese legends speak of a mysterious "edible gold," one taste of which confers immortality. It seems unlikely the ancient Chinese could have had any direct knowledge of the Fireflies or of Symbiote—it may simply be that, given enough time, *any* prophecy will eventually come true.

For millions of years, loneliness has cascaded down through the millennia, an ever-expanding wave of loneliness, powered by itself, by its own terrible self-creating hunger. Confined in bone boxes, we sought solace by rubbing our meat-mounts against one another, and so made more prisoners of bone and flesh to replace us and keep loneliness alive and expanding across the ages.

Now loneliness is only an option, rather than a sentence. Your sentence has been commuted: you are released, not on, but *upon,* your own cognizance. The cell door is open at last: you can walk out any time you are ready. You have been ready since you were born.

And it is safe now. You can leave your cell without fear, without shame, without self-doubt. No matter what horrors you flatter yourself lie uniquely in your skull, no matter what unforgivable deficiencies you claim to yourself, you will find understanding and total acceptance in the Starmind. Everyone else did. One of the nicest things about living in zero gravity is that it is no longer possible for one person to look *down on* any other. There is no rank, no class, in the Starmind. There is no obsession, for there is no need for it. Yet paradoxically, somehow I can look *up to* many of my fellow Stardancers— and look *into* any who consent. All of them, sooner or later.

To join us is *not* to "lose your ego." It is to gain nine billion more. Love on that scale has never been imagined, in all the ages of the world. I tell you that it is better than you *can* imagine.

There is a reason why I have been chosen—out of more than nine billion!—to tell you this story of the final days. And the reason is *not* because I used to practice the writer's trade, although that has proved helpful.

This task fell to me because fate placed me in a unique position. I yearned to live out the rest of my days on Terra so badly that I tore my heart in half, and risked the heart of my daughter, to stay there. Yet I live in the Starmind now, and will live out the rest of my days in space—and am deeply joyous. I have lost *nothing* . . . and gained the stars.

And more. Buchi Tenmo was quite right about self-generated reality: I still have Provincetown. I smell it as I write . . .

In fact, I have P-Town now far more than I ever did before . . . for now I can see it through the eyes (through *all* the senses) of Tia Marguerite and Tia Marion and Cousin Tomas and all my relatives and friends, can know it through the perceptions and experiences of every other former resident, nearly everyone living who has ever seen it. If binocular vision creates three-dimensional visual depth, imagine the kind of depth with which I now know my beloved home. Over a hundred years of Provincetown, times millions of people, raised to its own power! I have more of my beloved home than a hundred thousand normal lifetimes could have given me . . . and I no longer need it. I have much deeper roots, now.

And my husband, who needed the attention of strangers, expressed in dollars, so badly that he tore his heart in half and risked his daughter's heart for it, has more raw attention available to him than he could ever have imagined . . . and sacrifices *nothing* for it . . . and needs it not at all.

And his brother, who risked his job and thus his art and thus his life, all to be near him, is now with him always. Just as intimately as I am, for the Starmind understands genetics as no human ever did. I carry their child in my womb now . . . a girl who is already Shaping herself, and will begin dancing soon.

That is the reason why I have chosen to tell my own story through more eyes than my own—right up to the moment when all our viewpoints converged.

Can you see that, if any of those three surviving protagonists in the foregoing comedy had known as much about what was really going on as you did when you read their story, they could not have acted as foolishly and destructively as they did? Can you really want to keep wasting as much time and energy as they all did, blundering through the dark of their lives, squinting through the twin chinks in the bone box and trying to read the hearts of others through theirs?

I/we have also reconstructed Eva's story, and made it part of mine/ours, partly for the additional perspective it adds, and mostly to show that I/we can. Reb knew her, and so the Starmind does, and always will. No one will ever completely die again . . . so long as there is one brain in the Starmind that ever knew him or her. I'm teaching the unborn daughter in my belly about Eva right now—since Rand and Jay are going to give her Eva's name.

"O wad some power the giftie gie us, to see oursels as others see us! It wad frae monie a blunder free us, and foolish notion."

Robert Burns was right. The gift has been given. Take it . . .

What has happened to our species may seem unprecedented. But it is not. We have made other Jumps of comparable magnitude, up the evolutionary scale. From the sea to the mud to the trees to the mountaintops to the skies . . . and now to space itself, free of the womb altogether.

There is less than no future in being a Neo-Neanderthal . . . for the *next* evolutionary Jump is *already in progress*. A Starmind of nine and a half billion brains possesses the necessary complexity and depth to begin to make sense of the Cosmic Background Babble. Deep in the Oort Cloud where the comets play, far from the sun, something is presently nearing completion that will help, a thing that has no analog in human experience. The infant is listening, learning to hear; one day it will learn to talk. There are as many stars in this galaxy as there are neurons in a brain: imagine a mind made up of a galaxy of Starminds!

For millions of years, an endless succession of generations of upright, lonely apes have gazed up in dumb yearning at the stars, at the infinite depth and breadth of the universe, at the teasing promise of the other 99.9999+% of reality. Now, at long last, we have come home.

Join us—as soon as you are ready!

I am Rhea Paixao, and my message to you is: the stars are here.

When it comes to the best
in science fiction and fantasy,
Baen Books has something for *everyone!*

IF YOU LIKE . . .
YOU SHOULD ALSO TRY . . .

Marion Zimmer Bradley . . . . Mercedes Lackey,
Holly Lisle

Anne McCaffrey . . . . Elizabeth Moon,
Mercedes Lackey

Mercedes Lackey . . . . . Holly Lisle, Josepha Sherman,
Ellen Guon, Mark Shepherd

Andre Norton . . . . Mary Brown,
James H. Schmitz

David Drake . . . . David Weber, John Ringo,
Eric Flint

Larry Niven . . . . James P. Hogan,
Charles Sheffield

Robert A. Heinlein . . . . Jerry Pournelle,
Lois McMaster Bujold

Heinlein's "Juveniles" . . . . Larry Segriff,
William R. Forstchen

Horatio Hornblower . . . . David Weber's
"Honor Harrington" series,
David Drake, "RCN" series

The Lord of the Rings . . . . Elizabeth Moon,
The Deed of Paksenarrion

IF YOU LIKE . . .
YOU SHOULD ALSO TRY . . .

Lackey's "SERRAted Edge" series . . . . . . Rick Cook,
Mall Purchase Night

Dungeons & Dragons™ . . . . . . "Bard's Tale"™ Novels

Star Trek . . . . James Doohan & S.M. Stirling,
"Flight Engineer" series

Star Wars . . . . Larry Niven, David Weber
The "Wing Commander"™ series

Jurassic Park . . . . Brett Davis, *Bone Wars*
and *Two Tiny Claws*

Casablanca . . . . Larry Niven, *Man-Kzin Wars II*

Elves . . . . Ball, Lackey, Sherman,
Moon, Cook, Guon

Puns . . . . Rick Cook, Spider Robinson
Harry Turtledove, *The Case of the Toxic Spell Dump*

Alternate History . . . . Gingrich and Forstchen, *1945*
James P. Hogan, *The Proteus Operation*
Harry Turtledove (ed.), *Alternate Generals*
S.M. Stirling, "Draka" series
Eric Flint & David Drake, "Belisarius" series
Eric Flint, *1632*

SF Conventions . . . . Niven, Pournelle & Flynn,
Fallen Angels
Margaret Ball, *Mathemagics*
Jerry & Sharon Ahern, *The Golden Shield of IBF*

Quests . . . . Mary Brown, Elizabeth Moon,
Piers Anthony

Greek Mythology . . . . Roberta Gellis, *Bull God*

IF YOU LIKE . . .
YOU SHOULD ALSO TRY. . .

Norse Mythology. . . . David Drake, *Northworld Trilogy*
Lars Walker, *The Year of the Warrior*
Lars Walker, *Wolf Time*

Arthurian Legend . . . Steve White's "Legacy" series
David Drake, *The Dragon Lord*

Computers . . . . Rick Cook's "Wiz" series
Spider Robinson, *User Friendly*
Tom Cool, *Infectress*
Chris Atack, *Project Maldon*

Science Fact . . . . Robert L. Forward,
Indistinguishable From Magic
James P. Hogan, *Rockets, Redheads, and Revolution*
James P. Hogan, *Minds, Machines, and Evolution*
Charles Sheffield, *Borderlands of Science*

Cats . . . . Larry Niven's "Man-Kzin Wars" series
Esther Friesner, *Wishing Season*

Horses . . . . . Elizabeth Moon's "Heris Serrano" series
Doranna Durgin

Vampires . . . Cox & Weisskopf (eds.), *Tomorrow Sucks*
Wm. Mark Simmons, *One Foot in the Grave*
Nigel Bennett & P.N. Elrod, *Keeper of the King*

Werewolves . . . Cox & Weisskopf (eds.), *Tomorrow Bites*
Wm. Mark Simmons, *One Foot in the Grave*
Brett Davis, *Hair of the Dog*